PRESS GANG

JOHN KIELY

The Publisher's Apprentice

Ballarat

Published in 2014 by The Publisher's Apprentice
(An imprint of Connor Court Publishing Pty Ltd)

Copyright © John Kiely 2014

PO Box 224W
Ballarat VIC 3350
sales@connorcourt.com
www.connorcourt.com

ISBN: 978-1-925138-10-8 (pbk.)

Cover design by M. Giordano.

Photo: Trip through South East Asia on the carrier *Sydney* at Hanoi, 1956 (provided by author)

Printed in Australia

PRESS GANG

CHAPTER 1

David Reed sat with his girlfriend shapely brunette Meg Mann, pensively contemplating his latte, a spoonful of sugar poised to pierce the delicate flower shape on the surface created by the barista. "This voting scam story seems to be getting you down," Meg said. "I thought journalism was about journos making life miserable for everyone else, not the other way around. You say you love the game. How did you get into it anyway?"

They were sitting at the footpath tables of a café in Bridge Road, Ridley, warmed by unseasonable winter sunshine.

"How did I get into it? I was 16. A teacher told my mother the only subject I was remotely competent in was English, so she took me to the offices of the *Gazette* where I became a copy boy, running around the desks answering to bellows of BOY! from sub-editors. One guy was alcoholic. Booze was forbidden in the office so he used to smuggle whisky in and hide it in the library. He would say to me 'January 1905'. I would go up to the library gallery, pull out the big bound file of copies of the *Gazette* from that month, and behind the file would be a bottle of scotch in a paper bag. I would put it under my jacket, then go down and slide it under his desk. Old Alco, as I came to call him, was a bully to the other copy boys, but never to me. So the early lesson I learned was that it paid to have a lever on people – but of course not you, my darling Meg."

"I'm grateful for that!"

"That reminds me, Meg. You've never told me how you got into banking."

"I did economics at university, but found I like dealing with people more interesting than adding up figures, so being already at the bank, applied to be a personnel officer. When the bank wanted me to do more work for the same money, they promoted me to staff liaison officer. Sounds very important. Now, seriously, what's the problem with your voting story?"

"Remember I told you I've had this anonymous tip that federal elections are being corrupted with dead men's votes. But I'm not getting anywhere."

"Well drink your latte and cheer up. Somehow you'll crack it."

Out of the roaring traffic in Bridge Road, a steel-grey Verada veered towards them, clipping the metal barrier protecting their table and sending their coffees flying. "Shit!" Reed yelled and Meg shrieked in fear. The Verada roared on up the road without slowing and disappeared. "Bastard!" Reed cried at the vanishing vehicle.

A waiter ran out of the café. "Sorry, sir. Isn't that shocking. Come on in and have some more coffees."

"I think I actually need a double Drambuie," Reed said, but settled for coffees. It was then the thought struck him: this was possibly no accident. The Verada not only didn't stop; it immediately sped up to get away. Could this be a warning from his "friends" at the Voting Security Bureau? Dammit, he didn't get the car's registration plate details, not even some of the letters or numerals.

"I have to get back to work pronto, Meg," he said abruptly. I'll see you tonight and we'll make glorious, riotous love, all right?"

"If you say so, m'lord."

At the *Gazette* headquarters, now a 35-storey steel and glass tower, he rode the lift to the 21st floor, going straight to the office of News Editor Graham Butler to tell him about the Verada.

"David, I'm really glad you're alive but are you sure it wasn't just an accident? People are getting killed on the roads of Ridley every day. Why would anyone want to try to cripple or kill you?"

"Graham, I told you about that federal voting rort I was investigating. Well, I got a hostile reaction from Voting Security Bureau chief Whiteley when I raised it with him."

"What did he say?"

"He ridiculed me. 'Using the names of dead people to vote? Rubbish', he said. 'What proof have you got? One anonymous tip? An anonymous tip? You've got to be kidding.' That's what he said and hung up in my ear."

"Well, he's right isn't he? You need a lot more than that."

"But Graham, why would Alan Whiteley dismiss the idea out of hand without bothering to investigate? The guy who rang me sounded scared. What if he's telling the truth? It's a hell of a story."

"If it IS a story, it has a long, long way to go. Meanwhile, I have a new job for you that will get you away from this sordid city for a while – a cruise in the Pacific to give us a piece for the Travel pages."

"When do I go, and where?"

"Tomorrow, to the Pacific."

Reed spent the afternoon checking details with Bluewave Pacific Cruises then headed home.

"What would you like for dinner, my darling?" said Meg.

"You, my dear," he said.

"No, dessert comes after main course remember," she said, waving a reproving finger.

So it was pumpkin risotto, a glass of pinot noir, warm showers and then tumbling into bed laughing. His fingers stroked her ebony hair, slid slowly down her superbly sculptured, tanned body and he drew her close to him. As they melded deliciously, the stress of the day vanished.

On the deck of the Bluewave Star next afternoon 35-year-old Reed, 180cm and slender, watched the skyline of Apollo City, including the thin spike of the *Gazette* tower, blurring as it receded. On the deck itself was a sickening sight: groups of grossly fat tourists wolfing salads, sandwiches, cakes and custards as fast as possible, as if at their last meal.

After several days of this, and drunken passengers vomiting over the ship's rail at night, the Bluewave Star reached the idyllic isle of Tuvalu. Small boats took the tourists ashore where native people under palm-thatch huts were grilling large freshly-caught fish, the fish to be washed down with mugs of the local brew, kava. Some of the more athletic passengers stripped to swimming gear and went snorkeling in the azure lagoon.

At twilight the Bluewave Star began to sail away. Reed went to the stern to have a last look at the small slice of paradise. Instead of looking down to deep purple water, there, floating away from the stern of the liner were 10 or 12 large black plastic bags of garbage, hurled out by crew. When Reed returned to Apollo City, his travel article ended with this scene and the sarcastic sign-off: "Thanks, white man." Bluestar Pacific Cruises let the *Gazette* know that there would be no more free cruises for *Gazette* staff. Butler came out of his office to tell Reed: "Sending you on one of those cruises is like sending a Jew to a pork-chop barbecue."

Reed: "Sorry, boss, but it was a pretty gross act. Can I get back to that voting-stack story now?" Butler cocked his head to one side then reluctantly nodded.

How to find out if dead people were voting? Reed went back through library copies of the *Gazette* for about six months, noting the names in dozens of funeral notices. Then he went to the Voting Security Bureau's website where citizens could check whether they were enrolled, but immediately struck a snag. He entered the name of one of the deceased – Kathryn Mary Allramp – but found that to check an enrolment you had to have full given names, address and date of birth. Stymied. He went home for dinner.

In bed he was reading *Memoirs of a Geisha*. "I always thought geishas just danced, dressed beautifully and served tea or sake delicately," he told Meg. "Did you know men paid to deflower the young geishas and they became permanent mistresses?"

"No, I didn't know. But does that surprise you? There's a guy in Britain who has offered 25,000 pounds for taking someone's virginity. I think men should pay for it. Come to think of it, you didn't pay a cent to deflower me."

"Deflower you? Me? It would have been a privilege I would gladly have paid for, my darling, but I do suspect that someone beat me to the prize. Even so, there have been lots of dinners, movies and flowers, if not deflowering, and I've gladly paid for them all."

"You are so sweet. Come to me."

Later: "David, you haven't once mentioned the voting ramp story tonight. Having any luck?" He shook his head and explained the dilemma of needing detailed information on the dead.

"I know how you can get that," she said. "The funeral parlors would have all the details."

"Meg, why didn't I think of that? You are the world's greatest personnel officer!" he cried. "How can I thank you?"

"Just put out your bedlamp and go to sleep."

At the office next day he told Butler he now had a new angle to follow on the voting scam – through the funeral parlors.

Butler: "I've got a new angle for you, David, a new story in fact. A French company has bought out the Avalon aircraft manufacturer as you know and they have told the workers to take a pay cut. I guess they just want to start getting some of their money back in a hurry. Well the workers aren't copping it. They're out on strike and blockading the plant. Get down there pronto because we've heard the company might call in the cops."

Reed grabbed a car and a photographer and headed out. At the plant he found about 200 angry, placard-wielding workers surrounding the gates and sitting in a large, black sedan in a side street he saw United Aero Workers Union boss Charlie Brandsworth.

"Hello, Charlie. David Reed from the *Gazette*. How long do you think your men can hold out without being paid? How long do you think the French can hold out having borrowed a couple of billion to buy the place and not making any aeroplanes?" Brandsworth looked down the street. "Oh, oh. Now the fun starts."

Four police wagons had pulled up in front of the strikers and one officer got out with a megaphone, ordering the workers to disperse. The crowd yelled abuse, but nobody moved. More police got out of the wagons, armed with batons. "Get 'em!" screamed a worker and the whole mob surged forward, whacking police with their placards and fists. Eight of the strikers rocked the leading police wagon until it rolled on its side.

"Are you going to try to stop them?" Reed asked Brandsworth.

"Are you nuts?" Brandsworth replied.

The police ran back to the remaining three wagons, piled in and roared away. Brandsworth ordered his driver to get the sedan nearer the mob, jumped up onto its bonnet then onto the roof, raised his arms and yelled to the men: "Soon the police will be back in big numbers and with tasers, teargas and guns. Go home! Get the hell out of here now! We'll live to take on Avalon another day!" With some muttering the crowd broke up.

Brandsworth to the driver: "We'd better get out of here, too."

Reed: "Charlie, this is not going to go down well in the media – strikers bashing up cops."

"Well, that's up to people like you, my friend. Are they just a wild, vicious mob, or are they ordinary men desperately worried about providing for their families? It all depends on the picture you paint. Apart from the odd scab we have a magnificent union and I'm proud to be head of it."

Reed: "Scabs …?"

Brandsworth: "Here's your photographer. I hope he got a shot of the police taking out their batons before our men retaliated. 'Bye, David. Go well'."

Butler marched down the newsroom towards Reed. "Great story on the Avalon battle, David!" he boomed – pour encourager les autres, Reed thought, or because Butler had some difficult assignment in prospect. But then Butler said quietly: "I don't know which of the idiots around here sent that email about you but it's probably just jealousy."

"What email?"

"Nobody has told you?"

Butler took him to another reporter's desk. "Show David that email," he commanded. The reporter clicked with his mouse and Reed read: 'How can you *Gazette* people work with that creep

Reed? Did you know he's a sex abuser of little kids? Been getting away with it for years. The police will get him eventually. Can't wait.'

Reed suddenly realised why when he had returned to the office nobody had spoken to him. "This has gone right around the office?" he asked Butler.

"Even I got it," Butler said. "Maybe it's jealousy, or just some idiot's idea of a joke. Don't worry about it, but I thought you should know."

Reed decided he wasn't leaving it at that. He asked the reporter to forward a copy to him, told the *Gazette*'s I.T. experts about it, forwarded it to them and asked them to try to trace the origin. Two hours later they came back with the verdict: it was sent from an internet café in the suburb of Ashleigh. Reed printed out a copy of the email and headed for the café. But the owner was in no mood to help trace the sender. "We get dozens of people in here every day sending emails, my friend. How would you expect me to know which one might have sent it? Anyway, I don't even admit that it came from here. You want to ruin the name of my café? No thanks, and goodbye."

Back at work one thing still puzzled Reed. How did the sender get the email addresses of his colleagues. "Easy," said Butler, when Reed asked him. "Email addresses are at the bottom of every opinion piece your colleagues write, aren't they. QED, mate. Now forget about it. As I said, it's just some nutter having a joke." But coming after the Verada bump, Reed had a different view. The 'joke' was deadly serious.

Whoever you are, mate, you've made a mistake, he thought. The next stop was the funeral parlors. Now began several days of going back to the *Gazette* files for funeral notices over about a year. Electronically he could also look up past funeral notices from papers in other states. Eventually he had a mass of information, but decided to concentrate at first on funeral parlors not too far from Apollo City so he could visit them rather than just telephone asking for details. The first was at Hurstlane, a suburb in the wooded hills about 30kms from the city centre.

He got only about two minutes into telling the manager why he was there. "Sorry, Mr Reed. There's no way we would give out such private information. People still grieve a long time after a family death, you know, and they would great resent us if we co-operated in any intrusion. This is a close-knit community out here and if word got out, it would seriously damage our reputation."

Reed: "But there's a great national issue at stake here, the possible corruption of our democracy, I assure you word would not get out ..."

"I doubt you can guarantee that, Mr Reed. I'm sure you will find some other way to save the nation's honour, but not at our expense." This coming after the internet café reaction made Reed realise the hunt could be long and difficult.

The reaction at the second parlor he visited was even more extreme. "What proof have you got there's vote-rigging, eh?" said the manager, rubbing a grey moustache ginger from too many cigarettes. "I'm not interested in helping you knock the Government. I think they're doing a damned good job."

Reed: "I'm not saying it's the Government party. I don't know yet who is doing it."

"Our job is burying people, mate. Come back when you have someone who needs planting."

Reed headed back towards Apollo City, putting on a Mozart tape to lift his spirits. It was then he saw the grey Verada in his rear-vision mirror. "I just wonder ..." he thought and pulled off the main road, threading a circuitous route through side streets, pretending to be looking at various houses. The Verada followed – and stayed behind him as he rejoined the freeway. Reed realised there might be one way to determine whether this Verada was the Bridge Road aggressor. He pulled to the side of the freeway and stopped, forcing the Verada to pass. On a front fender was a dent and a scratch of black paint. The café barrier in Bridge Road was painted black. Yes, this was the Verada that had tried to scare him off. This time he made no mistake, flattening the accelerator to get close enough behind the enemy to get the number plate, WRC4608, then dropping back so not to alert the driver. The prick must have followed him from the office car park, Reed mused.

Back at the office he phoned a police-sergeant friend. "Henry, can you do me a favor? I'd like to know who owns a grey Verada, WRC4608."

"Now David, you know we don't do that sort of thing," Henry said, with a tinge of banter. "That's against regulations, particularly if it's the media."

"Henry, I've written special little pieces at your request and got them into the paper to help you. Editors don't like that sort of thing going on under their eyes, either."

"All right. All right. What's the rego number again?"

In half an hour he was back on the phone with the information. "I don't think this will excite you, David. It's registered to the Voting Security Bureau, not some drug peddler."

"Thank you, Henry. It's quite interesting, nonetheless."

"David!" Butler boomed at his usual decibel level, "I know you're still trying to resurrect the dead , but I want you to go back to the Avalon story. I've had a high-level tip that the Government is thinking of putting troops into the factory and Defence chiefs are really pissed off about it, saying it's not their job to be breaking strikes."

On the phone union chief Brandsworth was phlegmatic. "Put in the troops? Ha. What a giggle. The Government are just bullshitting if they're saying that. How many planes do you think the troops could turn out? Or do they plan to hold rifles at the heads of my men and say 'Work!'? But I don't think the Government's that silly mate. It won't happen. Anyway, here's something you can put in your paper: we've just decided to go back to work – but on go-slow, and I mean r-e-a-l-l-y slow. Get it? But that will stop any talk of troops and still put the squeeze on the French bastards."

Reed was inclined to agree. He didn't think Butler's tip would ever stand up as a story. Instead he tackled Brandsworth on another issue.

"Charlie, remember last time we met you referred to scabs in the union?"

"Did I?"

"Yes, and that prompted me to do a bit of research."
"Oh, did it."

"Yes, I got on the computer and found that union member Alain Renard has three times been reported in the *Gazette* as publicly criticising the union stance on the pay issue. Surely that rates as scab behaviour doesn't it?"

"I don't read every issue of the *Gazette*. And how do I know Renard wasn't misquoted?"

"What? Three times?"

"Not unheard of, my friend."

"Renard is a French name. How long has he been with the company?"

"Wouldn't have a clue."

"And you're not interested in finding out?"

"David, someone with your experience should know that we in the union movement deal with our own problems, and quietly. Capisce?" Reed took the hint. If Brandsworth had any suspicions he would sort out the issue himself. But that wasn't good enough for Reed. Journos needed spicy stories, and often. The more human interest, the better, and human treachery excited a lot of interest. He decided to sit in the car outside the union offices and pump any members turning up. They were easy to identify: many of them wore the union badge on their shirt, Guernsey or coat. Reed settled down with the day's *Gazette* and the Mozart tape and waited. Eventually two members approached and Reed stepped out. "Excuse me, I'm David Reed from the *Gazette* and I've been following the Avalon struggle and I wondered if I could ask you a couple of questions.

"The *Gazette*, that right-wing propaganda mouthpiece of the bosses? No thanks," said the beefy, ruddy-faced older one. His companion said nothing and both strode on. Reed went back to Mozart, but twenty minutes later got lucky. To the young unionist who approached he went into the usual preamble, then said: "Your boss Charlie Brandsworth tells me there's a scab within the union and I've done some research that actually shows he might be right. I wonder if you would help me. Do you by any chance work in Avalon's accounts section or pay office?"

"As a matter of fact I do, in the pay office. But why do you want to know that?"

"Well there's this guy Alain Renard who has been publicly knocking the union's battle to stop pay cuts. I believe he's French and I think he's the scab Brandsworth is talking about, but Brandsworth either doesn't know for sure or won't admit it."

"What's this got to do with me?"

"You could find out, for instance, whether Renard is on a lot more pay than other people doing the same work as he does. Whether he was brought out from France. And whether he is getting any special lump sum payments such as large bonuses. That's what I suspect a scab would get from a company."

"Why would I do that for you? If I got caught I'd be fired on the spot."

"That's true. Yes, I'm asking you to take a risk, and you'd have to be very careful to do it in a way that you couldn't be traced. But think what you'd be doing for all your mates."

"Even if I wanted to help, how can I when we're on strike?"

"I've just talked with your chief Brandsworth and he's announcing a back-to-work, but on a go-slow."

The young man sucked his lips in nervous contemplation, looked around to see nobody else was observing them then said: "I'm probably nuts to agree, but I'll do it if I can. We're just working blokes and these bloody Froggies are trying to screw us. My name's Larry Roberts and if I get anything I'll ring you."

Back at work Reed tapped out a piece announcing that the aircraft workers were going back to work, admittedly on a go-slow, but no doubt averting any contemplated use of troops in the Avalon plant. That should keep Butler happy for a few days, he thought.

That night he took Meg to a movie. She chose a Tom Cruise one. God, Cruise is boring, Reed thought. What Meg could see in the automaton he could not imagine. The standard perfectly-aligned teeth, nose and eyes, yes. But could he *act*? Did that handsome face ever show any emotion? Hell no. Oh well, a Cruise movie. Anything to keep my sexy little beast happy.

Having drinks at a bar after the show, Meg gently touched his cheek.

"How's the great voting expose going? Are you getting anywhere? You seem very preoccupied these days."

"It's at a bit of a dead end at the moment because every time I get back into it Butler comes up with some other project he wants me to tackle."

"Is it worth pursuing? After all, it all began with just a tip from someone you don't even know. Why not do something like … I know … all the illegal brothels that this town tolerates and the pollies who use them?"

"What – and do a Petronius?"

"What is a Petronius?"

"Petronius was a who, not a what. He was a favourite of Nero, advising the Emperor on how to hold great parties, do things in style. He wrote the *Satyricon,* describing parties where slave boys brought snow water for washing the hands of the powerful, then kneeling to pick the gentlemen's toenails, singing all the time. The "gentlemen" meanwhile would fight over who was going to have their way with which boy. Didn't you learn any of this at university, Meg?"

"No, I was too busy studying economics and politics."

"Well, here's what happened to Petronius. Nero got tired of him and ordered him to commit suicide. So much for brothel reporting."

Reed fondled her breasts. "Do you feel in the mood?"

"I'll have to think about that. Mmm … I think so."

The next morning brought soft sunshine, and a budding magnolia tree in the front yard shone purple and white. The world could be black and ugly if you just read the headlines, Reed thought, as he set off for work, but hopefully there would always be magnolia trees in some people's lives.

At work he looked through his list of funeral parlors and chose three more to visit. He went to the office carpark to get his own red Audi which the *Gazette* paid him to use, funding fuel, tyres and depreciation, but stopped, realising he needed a way to avoid being followed by the grey Verada. He went back to the carpark attendant, got the keys for a Mercedes which happened to have dark tinted windows, and set off. At the first parlor, in Bellwood, he struck gold.

Manager Craig Hayes listened to Reed's preamble then surprised him: "If what you say is true, it could destroy people's faith in democracy. It's a dirty trick. I'll give you access to our files on one condition: you must promise me that you won't reveal how you got the info. Some of the relatives may eventually guess, but they won't have proof. I need to know one other thing: are you going to other funeral directors?"

Reed: "Yes, I am. I need to see quite a few of them to discover the extent of the problem."

"Good. If there are quite a few sources that would take any heat off me. I want to keep the staff out of this so if you encounter any of them you are here to check on the prices of coffins and funeral services. Right?"

"Right."

Reed was taken to Hayes' office and spent the next four hours keying into his laptop dozens of identities – full names, addresses, birth dates and the electorates in which they had lived. Hayes even brought him coffee twice.

"You're a good man, Mr Hayes."

"Oh, I don't know. That's not Brazilian coffee." They both laughed.

"You must find journalism pretty demanding," Hayes said. "What's the worst thing that ever happened to you?"

Reed cogitated. "The worst thing that ever happened to me was that a politician once told me about a rival pollie having been caught in bed with another minister's wife. I told my editor about it but said I just didn't believe it. Two days later the story was all over TV and in the rival *Sentinel*, and it was true, and the minister's wife said she had found true love and was leaving him. I'll bet you don't have things like that in the funeral business as it's rather special. What's the worst thing that ever happened to you?"

"It's not hard to think of that," said Hayes. "One day a few years ago a dill in our mortuary mixed up the lids on two coffins and we sent both bodies to the wrong funeral services. Relatives at both churches who went to have a last look at their loved ones found themselves looking at a stranger. We had to apologise – and forget about putting in a bill for either funeral. Could have been worse, I suppose. We could have cremated one of them – the wrong one. The worst thing was all the publicity – thanks to you journos. But we recovered. One thing people don't stop doing is dying."

Reed, back at his office desk, found that he had a total of 482 names. Hayes had let him go through the files stretching back more than four years. Now began the critical part, keying into the Voting

Security Bureau's website names, other details and electorates, to see whether any of them were still "alive" electorally-speaking.

Within an hour he had eliminated about 30, with nobody still "alive", but then, to his elation, he hit paydirt. Kathlyn Rose Kinsbury, of 25 McKinnon St, Wolvery, born 11/04/1934, who died eight months ago, was, according to the Voting Security Bureau, still alive and ready to vote. Wolvery was in the Eredale electorate, a marginal seat for the Government, so Reed decided to concentrate on the deceased who had lived within it. If there was someone at the bureau corrupting the system, they might have concentrated on marginal electorates. Three hours later, at home time, he had 27 more "resurrections" and he slammed a fist on the desk with glee. Twenty-eight mistakes in one electorate looked decidedly dodgy. Historically, seats had been decided on less. *This,* Mr Butler, was going to be an award-winning story. But Reed realised that to nail the VSB, ideally he would have a list of 100 or so phony names. So he would have to go right through the whole 482 names the parlour had given him. It took him another two days, working at home and finally he had a glorious total of 127 "ghosts". Fantastic. Butler would now be ropable about his absence from the office, but what-the-hell. He hunted through the phone directory for other funeral parlors within Eredale electorate, finding four more. Next week he would be on the road again.

His phone rang; it was Butler. "A Larry Roberts rang here asking for you. Switch put him through to me. He wouldn't tell me what it was about, so I gave him your home number as it seems to be your office nowadays. He said he'd ring you there." Reed had been thinking of going to the pub for a few beers but now he sat at home and waited, settling down for Beethoven and a quiet ale until Meg came home. But soon the phone rang.

"Larry Roberts here. Look Mr Reed ..."

"Call me David, Larry."

"Look Mr Reed, I don't know where you got your information, but it appears to be right. Renard is on a whopping salary and it took me a lot of searching to find it. It isn't processed by the normal pay office staff, but done by the chief accountant who, by the way, isn't in our union. I had to spend quite a bit of time on alternate searches to even come up with Renard's name. And you're right about another thing: he has had two sizeable bonuses in the last three months. Odd that, eh? Maybe he is a company stooge as you suspected."

"Larry, thank you for that. Can you do me one last favour? Tomorrow would you go back into the files, print out what you have just told me, and mail it to me at the *Gazette* office." Reed realised that once the Renard story broke, Avalon might be able to track back through their computer files and pin the blame on Roberts, but he figured the union would be well able to look after him if the company tried to sack him. Besides any sacking would make another good story and blacken the company's name.

Meg walked in and flopped on the living room sofa. "God, I'm exhausted."

"What! An exhausting day at the bank? What did it? Reaching up to the top of filing cabinets?"

"Very funny. How droll. Have you mastered long division yet?"

"Sorry, my darling. What went wrong?"

"I need a drink."

"Better than that, instead of you rummaging around in the fridge to make us a dinner, let me take you to the Kingston Tavern."

"Done."

It was a walk of just two blocks to the pub. In the dining room, freed at last of clouds of cigarette smoke thanks to legislation, they sat at the long bar, ordering pinot noir, filet mignon, flounder and peach tart. A 20-something guy garlanded in Crocs footy scarf and jacket plopped down beside Reed with a "G'day". Reed nodded. Crocs ordered a beer then nodded at the Aboriginal barman who was outfitted in white shirt, black bow tie, perfectly creased black trousers. "He's come a long way from his bark humpy, hasn't he?" Crocs said. Reed just raised an eyebrow.

"Should be back there," said Crocs.

Reed: "Why so?"

"Because he's a boong. Probably knows nothing about food or booze. Well … probably a bit about booze," he snickered. "They call themselves the first people, y'know. What bullshit. Do they think all the rest of us are second people?"

"No. It just means their ancestors were here about 50,000 years before ours were." Reed said.

"Oh, crap. I've been here 27 years. The oldest of them has been here, what, 70 or 80 years. I've been here longer than many of their kids and my mum and dad have been here longer than most of them. What they're doing, y'know, is trying to claim the whole country is theirs."

"No, they are not, mate. The whole country was taken from them and now they are slowly being given back small bits of it."

"Wait on, pal. My ancestors in Britain were Angles, I think. The Normans took their land from them. Y'reckon I could go over there and claim a lump of Berkshire or whatever it's called?"

Reed, bored witless now: " Well, actually, if I remember rightly, the Angles were from northern Germany and invaded the ancient

Brits in about 400 AD, so some descendants of the Brits might sue you. Anyway, why don't you get on a plane and give it a go?" The barman returned with the pinot noirs and Reed made a point of sniffing one glass and saying, "Mmm, that's a good pinot, thanks a lot." Crocs picked up his beer and moved to the end of the bar. "God, Meg, what did I do to deserve that?"

"I guess you look like a racist. Must be those Aryan blue eyes and sharp nose. Jawohl, that's it."

"Why did I bother to bring you out to dinner?"

"Because you haven't anyone better-looking to invite." With Crocs out of range, dinner went swimmingly. They always enjoyed a good bout of ribbing.

"What's doing about Avalon?" Butler queried peremptorily the next day.

"I'm waiting on some documents an insider is mailing to me," Reed said.

"When I get them I should have a decent story."

"I hope whatever you're getting rattles the bloody union. The Government shelled out millions to get the French to take over sick dog Avalon. We need to keep the damn company alive."

"The union won't like this story, I can tell you," Reed said smiling.

"Actually, Charles, after I get this angle up, can you pass the Avalon thing to someone else? I want to push on with the vote-rig story. It'll be a ripper in the end."

Butler's face creased with a scowl. "I run things here, remember. You're spending days and days on the vote story and where are you getting? Yeah, it'll be a big story – one day – and perhaps." He walked off. Reed decided that next day he would head off to visit more funeral parlors. "Christ," he thought, "here's a story that will rock the nation if I crack it, and dickhead Butler doesn't seem to get it."

Next morning he took the office car with shaded windows and drove into Eredale electorate. The manager of the first parlor he approached was diffident, but when Reed explained the issue and exaggerated a bit, saying that other parlors had co-operated, he relented and gave him access to files going back five years. Three more parlors to go. This would take the rest of the week. At the next parlor the following day, his pleas were rejected – and he was ejected. But the last two obliged and by the Friday night he was thrilled. He had a total of 1126 names to check against Eredale voting rolls. He rang Butler. "This is going to be sensational, Charles. I've already got 127 fake enrolments and I've got another thousand or so names to check so I'll need ..."

"You'll need another bloody week in your home office, is that it?"

"Yes, that's it. And when the paper wins Scoop of the Year at the annual Media Awards night, I'm sure you'll be happy to step up on stage to take the crystal statue, eh, Charles?"

"Don't get smart-arse with me, mate. I've been very tolerant of your antics lately."

"Yes, sir. I promise to behave – but it will be a great night at the awards." Butler snorted and rang off. How did that guy ever get to be News Editor, Reed wondered.

Three days later he had a total of 441 "ghosts". Eredale had been won by the Government with a razor-thin majority. Reed went to the website for the electorate and checked the figures. The Government candidate had won by just 214 votes – after a recount.

So unless the fake votes had all been cast for the Opposition and the Government still outpolled it, it was all a cheat. Anyway, a great story either way. Cop that, Mr Butler. Reed realised that if the fixer in the Voting Security Bureau decided his fakes were in danger of being exposed, he could eliminate all the "ghosts" from the electoral register, so Reed needed a witness to verify that some people long listed as dead were still on the rolls. At the office he co-opted the finance editor's secretary Jill to be a witness. On his laptop computer he called up 40 "ghosts" one after the other, getting Jill to verify that the names were still on the roll. Then he typed out a note for her to sign, listing the names, and attesting to what she had seen.

Reed now had weeks of work sitting in one huge file on his laptop, the names and addresses of all those voting "ghosts". At home that night, he copied the file and emailed it to his work computer, but then reflected that the Bureau might just try to hack into the office computer system, search for any such file and kill it. So he called up his laptop copy again, burned it onto a CD which he put in his concealed wall safe, and went to bed.

The crash of glass, roar of an explosion, and crackle of flames in the bedroom jerked both he and Meg awake about 3am. Christ! They leapt out of bed, felt the searing heat on bare bodies, and grabbed dressing gowns from the wardrobe. Reed seized her arm and pulled her into the hallway, heading towards the back door. He pushed her outside then grabbed the red fire extinguisher bolted to the kitchen wall near the refrigerator and rushed back to the bedroom. The curtains, the small bedroom table and the sheets and blankets at the end of the bed were all alight, and he began spraying them.

"I've got a hose!" his pyjama-clad neighbour Bernie shouted through the broken front window." The blast had awakened him.

"Great!" Reed yelled. "Let 'er rip!" And Bernie did. Between them, in three or four minutes they had the flames out. On the bedroom floor, Reed found the remains of a glass bottle. The bedroom faced the street, and from there someone had thrown a petrol-filled bottle through the window.

"Jeez, Peter. What happened? I heard a bang, looked out the window and saw the flames. Did a heater blow up?"

"No, Bernie. When you looked out the window, did you see a car on the street?"

"No, I didn't. Jeez, do you think it was an attack? Who would want to do that to you? They could have killed you. We'd better call the cops."

Reed decided that Bernie was right. This time he had better call the cops. He had all the evidence he needed about the racket so it wouldn't matter if the Voting Bureau got some tip-off about him. It was obvious now that someone in the Bureau somehow already knew about his investigation.

Meg's blue eyes were filled with fear. "They tried to kill us. They must be mad. I don't want to live a life of fear. Are you going to go on with this story after this?"

"This is no time to stop, Meg. I have the goods on them and once we publish there's no way the cops won't have to go in there and clean up the Bureau. But look, I can't risk you being injured in this. Someone must have been following me from the office to find this place. We'll have to find somewhere else to live and, in fact, for a few weeks we might have to split up."

"Oh, no. I don't want to do that."

"Meg, this is very serious." He tried to lighten up: "I'll still make love to you over the phone."

She couldn't help laughing. "I do love you, David. I'm not just thinking of myself. I don't want you to get hurt either."

"OK. I have an idea. We go and stay at the Ritz Hotel in Riverlands until I've wrapped up the story, then we head off for a holiday. Once the story has broken tomorrow morning – along with the juicy detail of this attack, there'll be no point in anyone going after me. OK?"

"First I have to ring the cops." But as he spoke the wail of a police siren in the street split the night air.

"OK. Now give me a big kiss, and let's pack and get out of here."

"What's going on here?" said the square-jawed sergeant at the door. "We've had a report of a blast and fire."

"That's right, Sergeant," Reed said. "Some clown has hurled a bottle of fuel in through our front window."

"Some clown? You think it was a joke? Doesn't look like a joke to me. Can you think why someone would want to do this to you?"

Reed just shrugged. He had realised that if he told the whole story now, police media liaison would hand it to all the media in the morning and the *Gazette* would have no scoop. It would be all over TV and radio during the day and in the other papers next day at the same time as the *Gazette*. He had to stall.

"All I know is a bottle came through the window and set fire to the room. Fortunately I had an extinguisher and a neighbour helped, too."

The police searched the room and the garden and took the bottle shards for analysis. Not much chance of fingerprints on that, Reed thought. Fortunately, in taking down details, the sergeant had not thought to ask him his occupation, so that would not be in the police brief. The bombing, for the moment, would just be another bit of hooliganism in Apollo's suburbia.

Meg was slumped on the sofa in the living room. "David, I'm not going to start living in fear every day of my life. We have to move from here permanently not just to the Ritz hotel for a while. There's no point being a dead hero."

"Couldn't agree more. We'll book into the pub tonight and stay there until this place is cleaned up and the bedroom renovated, then I'll sell it."

"Yes, but what do we do then? Buy another house in Apollo? There'll be other stories like this won't there?"

"What are you asking me to do? Give up journalism? Become a bank clerk?"

"As a bank employee, I don't think that's very nice. As far as I know, journalists are just about at the bottom of the ratings when it comes to being respected by the public."

"OK. Sorry. Let's just pack now and get out of this mess and talk about the future when we've both calmed down. First I have a zinger of a story to write. I'm about to spoil Wednesday's breakfast for Alan Whiteley and his Bureau creeps."

At 6am he rang Graham Butler at home. "Butler here."

"Graham, it's David Reed."

"At this time of day? What the …?"

"I've got a great story ready to roll."

"I know. The Voting Bureau."

"Yes, the bloody Voting Security Bureau. I've got proof of 441 votes by dead people in just one electorate. And the seat was won by the Government by just 214 votes."

"You've got proof?"

"Yep. All the names. And a witness apart from me to the fact some of the deadies are still on the rolls."

"Right. Get into the office. I'll meet you there. We'll need graphics, comment from the Bureau, even if it's "no comment" and comment from the Government and the Opposition. It sounds a cracker."

"Thanks Graham. By the way, my house got bombed three hours ago."

"You're kidding me."

"Nope. Molotov cocktail through the front bedroom window."

"Christ. Did you get hurt?"

"No. But we're moving house."

"Is Meg OK?"

"Sort of. It's thrown her a bit. We're going to move to a pub for a while."

"Have you told the cops?"

"Of course, Graham. But I doubt they'll find much evidence."

"The company will pay for the house damage, David. See you soon."

"FAKE VOTES SCANDAL" was the headline that hit the streets the next morning. And beside the splash was a short piece also by Reed detailing the bombing of his house. On the phone not long afterwards came an irate police inspector wanting to know why Reed had not given to the police who attended his home the morning before, the background on the Voting Security Bureau. "I had no proof it was someone from the Bureau," Reed said.

"It just might have been an idea to let us in on your suspicions though," the inspector said, his voice heavy with sarcasm. "No doubt someone in the Bureau has been trying since early today to clean up all their computer files and discs, but, no thanks to you, we have smarter guys who have now gone in and will probably be able to retrieve anything recently deleted."

God, Reed thought, you don't get much gratitude for exposing a national scam corrupting democracy. He said thanks and hung up. He and Meg moved into the Ritz and had three delightful days of sailing on the bay, dinner and movies at night and scrumptious lovemaking. When Meg gave a yelp of delight on climaxing on the second night, Reed kissed her, looked into those blue, blue eyes and said: "You can thank Graham Butler for all this. He's paying!"

A week later two Voting Security Bureau employees were charged with corruption, police alleging it had been their responsibility to delete deceased from the rolls and that there was evidence in a group of cases where they had been notified of deaths and had not acted. The critical issue, Reed thought, would be whether, to get lighter sentences, they confessed which side they had been acting for – the Government or the Opposition. Out there, somewhere, certain smarties were sweating. Interestingly, Bureau chief Whiteley stayed in his job. If the Government had nothing to hide, Reed mused, surely Whiteley would have been pushed aside. But that was a story that, legally, would have to wait until the two decided to squeal at their trials.

CHAPTER 2

"Great job!" Butler told Reed. "You've really scored. And I've got a reward for you."

"Yes?" Reed said cautiously, thinking back to that Pacific islands cruise. Some of Butler's other "rewards" in the past had also been less than rewarding, such as being sent to cover the Royal Agricultural Show, trudging around cattle and sheep pavilions, looking at the latest tractors and combine harvesters, and reporting on who won the crocheting competition.

"The Army has invited us to send someone to look at how our troops are making out in Keralia. It's a big assignment, to look at six provinces over the next three months or so. The Army will give you intensive two-week preparatory training before you go to keep you out of strife. It should make a fine feature series apart from any stories you break. So how do you feel about all that?"

Reed wasn't sure whether to be thrilled or appalled. What the hell would Meg say to him disappearing for three months or more? She might decide after the Bureau business that she just didn't need him. And he might get his head blown off anyway.

"Should be pretty interesting," he cautiously replied to Butler. "When would the Army want me to start?"

"Almost immediately, actually. I have to let them know at the end of this week whom we will send."

"I need to talk to my partner, Graham."

"Sure. But I will need a fairly prompt answer, given the Army's deadline."

Christ Almighty, Reed thought. Here's Meg having to find somewhere else to live; she couldn't stay in the Ritz forever. And she would have only Liam Neeson movies on TV to comfort her at night wherever she wound up. That wouldn't satisfy her for long. Love and loyalty had their limits. He might get the flick long-distance.

That night he took her to the finest bayside restaurant in Apollo. "You're very quiet tonight," she said over dinner. "Not your usual bubbly self. Don't worry. We'll soon find somewhere decent to live."

"It's not that, Meg. I've got to tell you ... something else has come up." He paused and poked a fork at the oysters Kilpatrick entrée. "The paper wants me to go to Keralia for three months to report on how our troops are making out."

"Keralia? For three months? God! The world's craziest war. Muslims not only killing any infidels, but killing each other, depending on the tribe or sect? And stupid us risking our troops' lives trying to stop them. Are you going to do it?"

"Butler hasn't ordered me. He's asked me. But I know if I knock it back it will be the end of any real future at the *Gazette*. Actually, Meg, this is something I've never done, extensive reporting on a war. Great for my career. The thing is; would you stick by me? Would you wait until I got back?"

"What if you come back with a leg blown off?"

"Well, I wouldn't expect you to stick with me then."

"Now I know why you bought us this $90 bottle of pinot noir. Twenty dollars is more your usual style."

"Don't be unkind."

"Unkind? Here you are asking me to find us a new place to live while you waltz off to a war. Typical Boys Own Adventure stuff. Well, the answer, David is: I might. I might agree to you going. I might try to find a house for us. And I might still be here when you get back – if you get back."

"You're a darling, Meg. The greatest thing in my life."

"Are you deaf? I said I might."

"Yes, darling. Have another pinot. Here comes the duck l'orange."

That night he rolled over to her side of the bed to draw her to him but her body was stiff and resistant. He knew when to retreat, stroking her stomach then planting a kiss on her back, without uttering a word.

Next day he arranged the transfer of his house into her name and also $55,000 in term deposits from his bank account into hers and told her to sell the house and use all the proceeds on an apartment or house that suited her, but not in the suburb where they were fire-bombed.

"I know with your financial and fashion expertise you will find a perfect place for us, darling," he said. "Oh, and don't forget to put it in both our names."

"I might – if I remember," she said smiling, then hugged and kissed him.

Three days later, with sleeting rain drenching city streets, a khaki Army sedan pulled up at the *Gazette* office to take him to Kenna base for training for the Keralia assignment. At the base, a major introduced him to the seven troops already in the hut where he would bunk, then showed him the mess hut and the latrines.

"This afternoon," he said, "I'll start giving you a briefing on what to expect in Keralia and how to stay alive. It's not very pretty there at the moment. Have you ever used any modern weapons, like the Steyr?"

Reed shook his head.

"Well, I think you'd better at least familiarise yourself with it while you're here. If you happen to get into a tight spot in Keralia, you just might need to know how to use it."

"Would I be allowed to use it in an emergency?"

"Son, when a shitfight starts, nobody worries about the rules. There's only one rule: get out alive."

Within four days, Reed had learned how to drive an armoured vehicle, how to load and fire a Steyr, throw a hand grenade safely and how to radio for help. And he had a set of protective gear which might save his life if he were fired on or were close to an exploding roadside mine – but not too close.

"Won't I get a chance to fire a mortar?" he joked to the major on the last day.

"If a rocket hits a mortar crew while you are near by, you just might," the major replied, "but I think we'll take a chance on that and skip a demonstration."

On his last day at the base, the major briefed Reed on safety precautions – not for Reed – but for the troops he would be reporting on.

"You must *never* report the exact position of a base or unit. It could bring down a cluster of rockets on us. Likewise, don't try to report exactly where a patrol is going or has been. We have to see your copy before it goes home and we'll just delete anything like that. But you'll be free to talk to the troops. We don't try to censor any grumbles about the Army, the food, lost mail, or the second-rate movies. Any questions?"

"I want to see plenty of action if possible. Will there be any limit on my mobility?"

"No, David. The only restrictions on movement will be to ensure we get you home alive."

That night, Reed took Meg to the Charcuterie restaurant at the top of the Apollo Tower. Two meals there would cost him half a week's salary, but you were 32 storeys up with a view right down the bay of liners at piers and container ships all lit up, steaming in and out of the port.

"So, my darling, this is our last night together," she said, curling a wistful lip.

"Hey, ease up, my love. Not our last night, I hope. Our last night for two or three months at the most."

"Did they teach you at Kenna how to kill people?"

"Not quite. But I did get to fire a Steyr automatic rifle. Blazing away took me right back to my days of National Service. The guns are much better nowadays. As a Nasho I had to learn on old Thompson sub-machine guns and Bren guns. The old Thompsons had a kick like hell and used to climb to the right when you fired. You could easily kill a mate instead of the enemy. National Service did me a great favour though."

"How's that?"

"Well, we were six to a hut and, having been working in a newspaper office since I was a kid, I smoked nearly a packet a day – like everyone else in the office. In the hut, I lit up a cigarette on the first night. Kanga, a big kid from a farm in the outback was one of the other five. We nicknamed him Kanga because of the way he bounded around like a kangaroo, instead of just walking. Kanga said, 'Don't smoke in here.' I said, 'Mind your own bloody business.' He came over to my bunk, lifted me up off it by the throat and said, 'Don't smoke in here, all right? I croaked 'All right', decided to give up the fags while doing Nasho, and never smoked again. I reckon I'll live to 100 because of Kanga, God bless him."

"Did you see any action while in National Service?"

"Sure did. I was based with a signals unit in a mansion in Mont Robert, as you know one the the ritziest suburbs of this town. I learned to touch-type, how to use a teleprinter, even a bit of Morse Code. It was very stressful. We used to sneak over the back fence of the base at night, jumping into a resident's garden, then off to Malvern Town Hall for a night of square dancing, then back through the garden, over the fence and into the base. I got decorated – a prize for being in the best square dancing troupe. We got rumbled though. The neighbouring resident complained to the base captain about his lettuces being trampled and we got threatened with no leave. It was a tough war."

After crisp roast duck and crème caramels, Reed said, "Coffee?"

"No, take me home to bed, David."

"Is that an invitation?"

"Do you need an invitation?"

"Garcon! L'addition, s'il vous plait!"

In the four-poster bed with two gargoyles at the apex of the headrest, Reed slowly kissed her breasts. "Will you be happy until I get back? It's only two or three months," he said again.

"Mmm … I'm certainly going to miss that."

"We'll have the rest of our lives together."

"Is that a proposal?"

"I guess it is."

"Make love to me."

"With pleasure."

"Well, of course."

"Have you noticed you always have the last word?"

"I do."

They slept an hour beyond dawn.

The Skylifter dropping down towards the main drome at Keralia's capital Chelucha had four armoured vehicles, two motorbikes, five crates of ammunition, 20 troops and Reed aboard.

"Welcome to Keralia. You were pretty lucky," a sergeant told him, shaking hands at the bottom of the steps.

"Why's that, Sergeant?"

"Well things have got pretty hot around here. The terrors have somehow got hold of some anti-aircraft rockets and they've had a go at a couple of planes coming in. Fortunately, they're lousy shots or lousy rockets. And we have got missile-deflecting gear on some. You would have been a fat, juicy target, but you didn't attract one shot."

"Glad to hear it."

"We'll overnight here then go by chopper tomorrow to one of our bases in the southern mountains." Reed was taken to a run-down hotel on Chelucha's main street. "It's not much chop," the sergeant said apologetically, "but, believe it or not, it's one of the best the town has."

Reed looked around the room that had been reserved for him: dreary furniture, with the wardrobe door hanging forlornly by one hinge, the mirror in the bathroom stained and cracked in one corner, grubby curtains either side of dusty windows looking onto the cart, bicycle and people-crowded street.

"We'll call for you about 8am," the sergeant said; he waved and left.

Reed went to the lobby counter. "Is there somewhere near here where I can get a good coffee?" he asked.

"Second corner down on the right, sir," said the 186cm, ebony-skinned clerk, his smile baring a set of teeth to rival the ivories on a Steinway. "Could I suggest that Sir leaves his wallet, watch and any mobile phone here in the hotel safe and take just enough dollars to buy cake and coffee. We are living in dangerous times here in Keralia. Even walking the streets can be dangerous." Hearing this, Reed weighed whether it was worth going for a coffee, but decided if he was going to write about the nation, he had to get out and experience life in it. He handed over the valuables, kept a few dollars, and left.

Walking to the right, he came upon the coffee shop but, seeing on the other side of the street a large, open marketplace, he decided to wander through it. Soon he came upon a stall stacked with sunglasses. The stallholder held out to him two pairs of sunglasses in each hand. "You buy!" he said emphatically. Reed pointed up with a finger of his left hand to his sunglasses already perched in his hair. "Why you do this?" bellowed the well-muscled stallholder, dropping the sunglasses from his left hand, and pointing a finger skywards. "This very insulting! Why you do this to me?" Reed spread his arms in capitulation, said "Sorry, I did not know," and retreated. Bloody hell, he thought, I've got a lot to learn about this place in a hurry." He decided to skip the coffee and headed back to the hotel for an indifferent meal of goat meat, curried beans and canjero flat bread. In the lumpy single bed he took ages to get to sleep, dreamed he was making love to Meg and woke at 5am with an aching erection. The lukewarm shower water soon dealt with that and he sat reading a paperback he had brought with him: *A Short History of Keralia.*

After a breakfast of porridge and more canjero, the sergeant turned up on time and they headed for the airport, there boarding a helicopter already loaded with 12 troops and their gear. A two-hour flight took them over rolling arid plains, then threading through narrow ravines, finally to land at a small, sandbagged Army outpost, consisting mostly of dug-outs, a couple of rudimentary huts, two mortars set up near by and one artillery piece. Reed, being near the 'copter door, jumped down to earth and began to walk away. In a second, the sergeant knocked him flat to the ground.

"What the …?" Reed gasped.

"I saved your bloody life, David. You never walk away from a chopper at right angles. When the blades have slowed to idling, they dip quite a bit at the 90-degree point you were walking towards. Another metre of so and a blade would have sliced your head off."

"Hell. I owe you a lot. I should have realised that, you know. Back home a few years ago, a journo went out to report on an offshore oil strike. When the chopper landed on the oil rig, he got out the wrong way and had an arm sliced off. I should have remembered that."

"Maybe that's why they're called choppers," the sergeant said with a grin. "Anyway, you're just in time for some action. We're sending out a patrol and you might as well find out right away what it's like. In the hut on the left you'll get a helmet, goggles and protective gear, not that the jacket will mean much if you get sprayed by an AK-47. So keep your head down."

"Where will we be going, Sergeant?"

"Oh, a village about 30k from here. The terrs have been giving the villagers hell there – demanding money, kidnapping young women to rape then kill. The same fuckers want to impose strict religious law on Keralia, or at least they say they do. They're so phoney – dealing in dope in a big way yet threatening to kill anyone they catch drinking alcohol. Raping women, but wanting all women to wear stifling clothing. It's weird, mate."

"So what's the plan? Just catch and kill?"

"What else? No use trying to talk to terrorists. We have a handful of villagers who are prepared to help us with info. We talk to them, and make sure we talk to about 20 others so the terrs can't easily identify who is helping us. We can't start to bring in aid workers, or build schools and hospitals until we know they won't be blown up or burnt down."

"Do we chopper to the village?"

"Nope. The terrs have some shoulder-fired rockets and plenty of rifles. We can't afford to have choppers going down. Armoured vehicles are a lot cheaper and besides, we've now fitted them with such heavy armourplate that even the roadside bombs don't kill unless someone is unlucky enough to have their head sticking out up top. We've had a couple of cases where the blast has tipped the vehicle over, crushing the gunner. Not nice."

An hour later in two armoured personnel carriers they rolled down a mountain pass into the village. On the outskirts, women were working in the fields, chopping at furrows with crude wooden hoes. In the main street – the village's only street – men sat at tables in the sunshine, smoking and talking.

"It's a man's world all right," Reed said.

"Yeah," said the sergeant. "Not long after I first came here, I asked a Keralian through my translator, why it seemed that women did the hard work while men mostly sat about. The translator talked to the man, then told me: "His answer is that the men are smarter.""

Reed: "Hmm."

Reed noticed that several of the men in the street had AK-47s. Before leaving Apollo City he had been told by a foreign affairs editor at the *Gazette* that in Keralia, having an AK-47 in the house was like having a broom. Everyone regarded it as a necessity.

"How do you tell who are the friendlies?" he asked the sergeant.

"You don't," he replied. "If you see someone lift their rifle towards you, you lift yours towards them."

"Sergeant, you haven't told me your name. I might want to use it in one of my reports if that's OK."

"You already know it. It's James Sargent. Yep, really."

"So it's Sergeant Sargent. You're kidding."

"No kidding. Look." Sargent reached over for a jacket in the vehicle and put it on, showing the name label. "The Army tried to get me to change my name by deed poll when I first enlisted, but I refused. Imagine the shit I got from my mates and even more when I became Corporal Sargent. But they won't rubbish me once I'm Major Sargent."

Sargent climbed out and with his translator approached the locals at one of the tables. Two of his men held rifles at the ready, but pointed to the ground. After a few minutes, Sargent motioned to one of the men to come over to his APC. There a short conversation took place and the man returned to his tablemates.

"I sensed that guy was friendly towards us," Sargent told Reed, "so I brought him over here to find out what's been going on. That way his mates couldn't listen in and perhaps blab to the wrong people."

"Was he any use?"

"I think we're in for some action. He says four terrs were in the village yesterday, demanding food and money. They offered in return some hash. He says they headed on up the valley so that's where we're going. By the way, I think you'd better take one of these, just in case," handing Reed a Steyr. "I take it you've used rifles before?"

Reed nodded. "Yes, I did six months Nasho."

"Good. Just make sure if things open up that you don't hit one of us."

"I promise."

"And don't tell anyone back at base that I let you have it."

The APCs roared out of the village, leaving a curtain of dust. The hills either side of the road were clad with pine trees, perfect cover for the al-Shamar rebels. The gunners atop the APCs kept sweeping their weapons from side the side.

About three kilometres out, a high cliff bordered one side of the road. As the front APC approached, a large boulder came hurtling down in front of it, forcing the carrier to swerve to the right. At that moment a huge blast rocked the APC as the road erupted about 40 metres in front of it. The driver, unable to see ahead for a curtain of dust, slammed on the brakes as his gunner bobbed up and opened fire, spraying the pine forest to the right.

"Keep going! Keep going!" Sargent roared into his radio in the APC behind. "It was an IED!" Then aside to Reed: "Improvised Explosive Device the boffins have called the bloody things, though what's improvised about them I fail to see. They are very carefully

planned. Fortunately for us, though, the bastard with his finger on
the button fired too soon."

Rifle fire opened up on the APCs from a rocky outcrop far up
the slope to the right and the front gunner ducked down while still
firing his weapon. Sargent's APC carried an 81mm mortar and two
of the crew swung into action, lining up the outcrop. Blam! It was
a miss, but a near-miss.

Three armed men jumped up and begin firing at the APCs, then
Blam! the second mortar landed right near them, shrapnel slicing
into their bodies and the fight was over. Whoever had pushed the
boulder down from the cliff was in no mood to carry on the fight
single-handed.

Reed had stayed huddled down in the second APC.

"You can come out now, soldier," Sargent said laughing. "We've
won. All we have to do is go and pick up any bodies. We'll drop
them in the street on the way back through the village."

"Do you think that's a good idea?" Reed asked. "Some of the
villagers might not like to see Keralians treated that way, even if
they are al-Shamar."

"I think, David, a more important message is that if you join al-
Shamar you are likely to end up dead in the street. Ask his opinion,"
Sargent added, pointing to his translator, a young bearded Keralian.

Reed shrugged and let the subject drop.

Four troopers crept up to the rock outcrop, dodging from tree to
tree until they could see three bodies, then walked up to them. Reed
heard a gunshot, but the troopers did not run for cover but instead
began to drag two of the bodies down to the road, along with three
extra rifles. Reed wondered if one of the troopers had fired the shot,
and if so, why.

"Did someone else fire on you up there?" he asked. None of the troopers answered and he was left with an ugly surmise: the third terr was still breathing when the troopers got there. This was a nasty war.

Perhaps in deference to Reed's comment, they left the two insurgents' bodies at one end of the village rather than in the centre. Reed took photos of the bodies. Sargent shook his head at that, but said nothing. Back at the outpost, with the sun sliding behind a mountain peak, eight men were given early rations and deployed to the perimeter on watch. "Dinner" in one of the huts was canned fish, canned fruit and billy tea or coffee.

"How long do you think this war will last?" Reed asked Sargent.

"How long is a fishing reel?" came the answer. "You'd know as much as I would. I'm not even sure how we came to get into it."

"Well, al-Shamar is out to topple the Government, arguing that it is corrupt, which, given the background of al-Shamar is quite a joke."

"Yeah, well the UN Security Council fell for it and sent us, Yanks, Chinese (can you believe that!) Russians and Brits to get rid of the terrs. But the force numbers are just token, as usual with the UN. I still don't know why we got into it, though. We just go where we're sent."

"Sarge, I think the Security Council actually united for once because of all the goodies to be had in Keralia – oil, gold, iron ore, uranium, coal – you name it, it's here."

"I don't believe we're killing people just for that."

"Fair enough – up to a point. Al-Shamar claim to be religious, but they're not exactly saints, I agree."

"Precisely! For that reason, David, you'd better think twice before writing about what you've just seen at the village." Reed remained silent.

Sargent slurped some coffee, dribbling a little down the pronounced cleft in his chin, so deep that it made Reed think of a vagina, and then of Meg. He wondered how she was coping. He wondered if she were thinking of him right then. No, it was near midnight in Apollo City, he remembered. She would be asleep. Or would she? Maybe she was out with someone. There was no way he would get any mail out here in the boondocks, so no way was there an answer to any of these questions.

"This your first war assignment?" Sargent asked.

"No, I had a few days in Afghanistan when your guys first went there."

"You journos haven't exactly got a great reputation, have you? I read about a year ago that, in the public's estimation the only people lower than you lot are real estate salesmen. You've seen us in action today. I could tell you didn't like some of it. So what's the worst thing you've ever done in your game?"

Reed looked around the hut. Nobody else was listening. "I was writing on politics for a Sunday paper when a pollie was very sick in hospital and moves were being made to chop him as leader. He wasn't having any visitors apart from family, so I turned up as a brother-in-law. When I told him I was a journo, he cried out to the whole ward that I was a fraud. I slunk out. He died the next day. The scene stays with me."

"That's the worst thing? You've had a sheltered life. What's the best thing you've ever done?"

Reed thought for a while. "When I was quite young, a paper I was working on in Apollo City was bought out by a rival and closed down. Because I was on a contract, the takeover company either had to pay out my contract or give me a job. They put me on a monthly magazine they owned. The small staff there gave me the big freeze when I turned up and at the end of the first day I asked them what the beef was, that I hadn't ask to go there, I had been put there. They told me a father with five kids had been given the bullet to make room for me so my contract would not have to be paid out. I went straight to the managing editor, called him a prick, sold my new car at an auction house and got on a boat for Britain. I found out later they even reinstated that father of five. Actually it was great for me, too. I worked in Fleet Street for four years, getting great experience on different papers. But, of course, that's also when I did the worst thing I remember. So, full circle."

"Neat, eh? Fell on your arse, then on your feet."

Reed waved a hand at the mountain peaks visible through the hut windows. "What about you, soldier? How long do you plan to do this dangerous work?"

"As long as they let me, I guess. I don't really know how to do anything else. Then I'll use my pension to buy a small farm block, put 40 cows on it, plant some fruit trees and a veggie garden and drive into the village pub every night to drive the locals nuts with war stories." He took a drag on his cigarette. "That's if I don't get cut to shreds by an IED or RPG in the meantime."

"RPG? Have the terrs got rocket grenades here, too?"

"We got a tip-off two months ago and raided an underground store only 4kms from here. It had grenades, rifles and some ammo, but no rocket launchers. So they are out there somewhere."

"One question, Sarge. I want to get out a story on the action today. How can I get it back from here to the paper?"

"Over behind that desk is a radio link back to our HQ in Chelucha. Talk to them. Write out your piece then they'll get someone to record what you say as you read it out. Then they'll play that recording over a radio link to our people in Apollo City and they will forward it to the *Gazette*. Simple."

"Simple? I hope so. Any censorship along the way?"

"Not if you give us a fair go. Better get the story away tonight, too. Tomorrow we are going on a rather tricky job."

Reed sent the recording off, detailing how the troopers had gone up the hill and then had come a lone shot, leaving the readers to wonder, as he had done. On the end, he added a message to the Chief of Staff to pass on to Meg: "Still alive. Missing you badly."

Next day at 5am he was roused by a rough shake of the shoulder. "Come on, soldier," said Sargent, standing over him, "we're hitting the track in half an hour. You've just got time for some corn flakes."

Again it was into the mountains, this time to a sawtooth line of peaks so jagged they reminded Reed of a holiday he had had at Val d'Isere in France where he missed a sharp turn on a ski-run, went over the edge of a ridge and tumbled about 400 metres, coming to rest in a bowl at the bottom stripped of helmet and skis. When he came to and looked back up, he could see two sets of exposed jagged rocks which he had somehow missed. He even went into a small bluestone chapel in the village to give thanks.

Reed was surprised to see not two, but six APCs lined up and manned when he left the breakfast hut. He remembered Sargent's reference to a tricky job. "What's the operation today?" he asked him.

"There's a series of caves we believe the terrs are using up there," Sargent replied, pointing to the long range. "It's time we took the bastards out. They've been dominating the valley villages for ages."

As they neared the peaks, two men got out of the leading APC with bomb detecting gear and dogs and began to walk one on either side of the dirt road.

"It's a pain in the arse having to go this slow," Sargent said, "as it also gives the terrs plenty of time to get ready for us. But at least we'll get there in one piece."

"How many rebels do you think there are in the caves?" Reed asked.

"Our best guess is up to 80," Sargent replied. Reed looked back at the small line of APCs. Sixty troops, he estimated. With the rebels dug in and knowing the area, this wasn't beginning to look like a fairly balanced operation. They did have a couple of mortars, but what use would they be against caves? Reed wondered. A few of the troops had grenade launchers but they would be exposed while getting near the caves. And sending riflemen into the lairs could be suicidal.

Leaving their APCs, the first men got within half a kilometre of the first large cave and fired a volley into the mouth, hoping to provoke a response. There was none. Two men went off to one side of the slope, well away from the cave, crept up until higher than it, then down to the mouth. One stretched out his rifle until part of it intruded into the entrance, hoping to provoke any impetuous rebel inside. There was no response. Gingerly the two crept into the cave and vanished. Sargent waited. Three minutes later the pair emerged, one spreading his arms and shrugging in a gesture of puzzlement. The cave was empty.

Twenty minutes later they approached the second cave, but did not even get near it before about a dozen rebels poured out, taking up positions behind the odd tree and rocks and opening fire. Sargent had his response all organised. Within three minutes of his radio call, two American fighter bombers came roaring into the valley, Sargent ordered smoke grenades fired in among the rebels and the jets dropped a spread of bombs, obliterating them. Then came the coup de grace: missiles fired straight into the mouth of the tunnel. They collapsed the entrance, burying any rebels inside. Reed used his mobile camera to take brief videos of the blasts. The rebels might have food and water, but eventually they would run out of oxygen. The troops waved to the jets and cheered. The pilots went up the valley, turned, and roared down again, waggling their wings in salute then jetted away.

"The day has only begun, David," Sargent said, "but don't worry. We can call those boys back again if need be."

The APCs moved on up the valley towards the next caves. The first three showed no signs of life, but at the next, a large one, armed men could be seen running out into trees and scrub. They had seen what happened to their comrades lower down and had no intention of being buried alive.

But again Sargent was on the radio, calling for another air strike. "We'll just sit back here and wait," he told Reed. "I've told them to spray the mountainside when they get here and we don't want to get in the way of that."

It was three-quarters of an hour before the jets returned. Sargent ordered two mortars lobbed into the area to which the insurgents had fled to signal the jets where to strike. The two swooped in, fired a barrage of rockets, made another pass dropping bombs, then came back a third time with napalm. The mountainside lit up in a vast wall of flame and smoke.

"God, I'd hate to be there!" Reed told one of the troops near him.

"Yes, their goose is truly cooked," the trooper said seriously, apparently unaware of his pun. Sargent sent a group of 10 men to search the charred scrub.

"Got to put any poor bastard still alive out of their misery," he told Reed, "but this is turning into a good day. That's now anything up to 100 terrs who won't be bothering us any more. We'll have a few beers tonight."

"One thing puzzles me, Serge," Reed said "Why are these guys up here in caves? Where are their families? What sort of a life is it?"

"They're mostly young guys, David. They've been brainwashed that they are going to be glorious martyrs.

Remember that cartoon about Allah at the pearly gates saying to a group of suicide bombers 'No, no, no. We've run out of virgins'? Well these poor dupes haven't seen it and never will. They are brought to the caves for training and brainwashing then use motorbikes when they want to attack something. If they need food, they just put the hard word on any locals."

As it was now getting on to late afternoon, Sargent decided to head back to their outpost. About an hour after starting down from the peaks, the road erupted in a huge blast, hurling the lead APC onto its side, the tyres bursting into flames. Troops jumped out of the other carriers, some fanning out either side of the road looking for gunmen, others rushing to the APC to drag out the stunned and injured.

"Thank God for the new armour plating we had fitted underneath," Sargent told Reed as he climbed out to help. There were no rebels near by; the IED must have been set off by remote control. Three troopers in the overturned APC were injured, one badly. Others were just stunned. There were no beers in the mess hut that night; instead Sargent was busy organising the ferrying of the wounded back to the main base. Reed, radioing off another report for the *Gazette*, wondered how long his luck might last on this assignment. Maybe Graham Butler wasn't thinking of a "reward" in sending him here so much as a removal.

Sargent called a rest day the next morning, saying his squad had done enough to earn a break. That night they were playing cards and having the promised beers when two explosions rocked the small outpost.

"They're grenades!" yelled Sargent as men scrambled for their weapons. Sentries on the perimeter opened fire into the blackness, aiming where flashes came from, hoping to hit the grenade launchers. Three troops groaned and squirmed in the dirt, hit by shrapnel from the shoulder-launched grenades. Another lay still, huddled against sandbags.

"Spray the bastards!" Sargent roared, leaning against the sandbag wall and firing his Steyr into the night. Reed, finding it irresistible to see what was happening, stood in the doorway of the hut to watch and WHOMPF, was struck down by a bullet to his right thigh, sending him crashing headfirst against a doorpost. The pain was agonising and he blacked out.

He came to and realised the throbbing was not his head, but the blades of a chopper. "What's going on?" he asked an airman looking down at him.

"You're on the way back to Cheluca to hospital to repair the damage."

Reed felt a stab of pain in his thigh then saw the bandages and the night came back to him.

"The guys at the outpost knocked you out with a drug so you wouldn't feel the pain," the airman said. "You've been out to it for about two hours."

"How many of our men got hit?" Reed asked.

"Seven apart from you. Three have flesh wounds, as you have. Two others are on stretchers there behind you and two others, sad to say, didn't make it."

"How about James Sargent?"

"He's OK. He used a grenade launcher and got the terr who fired grenades. We ended up getting five terrs."

An hour later his hospital bed was surrounded by nurses and a Keralian doctor.

"I want to send off a report to my paper," he said, thinking that apart from the drama of the night, he wanted to reassure Meg that he was not seriously injured.

"We need to repair your leg wound immediately and you've had a nasty knock to the head," the doctor said. "The story had better wait. Besides, we don't have staff to spare to be organising it for you."

"I'll just write it out and surely someone can get it to the Army radio unit."

"All in good time, Mr Reed. First, we clean up your leg. So it's off to the operating theatre. Nurse: wheel him in."

Two hours later he came to again, back in the ward. The same doctor came by. "Ah, Mr Reed. Feeling better? I have arranged that if you write out that article you were referring to, I'll get it across to Army radio. A nurse will bring you some paper and a pen. I suppose you are writing about last night's shindig."

"Yes, I will be."

"I hear you fellows had quite a battle up in the mountains, bringing in jets."

"Yes, we did."

"Must have been a lot of insurgents to need that."

"No. It was just that the rebels were hiding out in some of the big caves up there and it was the only way to smoke them out – or bury them in, actually."

"Bury them in?"

"Yes, the missiles closed the entrance of the biggest cave, sealing it."

"Good lord. Did you know that families live in all those caves?"

"Families?"

"Yes, families. This part of Keralia is a bit like Turkey's Cappadocia. Hundreds of families live in the caves and work the fields in the valleys below."

"Are you sure all the caves have families?"

"Certainly any cave of reasonable size. It's much cheaper than building houses. People have lived in them for centuries, millennia maybe."

God, thought Reed. Now I do have a story. But I need more proof than this doc's word. There must be Keralian officials here in Chelucha who would have proof. Then there's the problem of how to get it out to the *Gazette*? Army radio would never pass it. I'll have to find someone to take it out. And if I do, that'll be the end of this assignment. So what. This is a story that has to be told.

"Doctor, how long will it be before I can walk easily again?"

"Well, we'll stitch you up thoroughly, so you could leave in couple of days' time. But walking won't be painless."

"Will you give me some painkillers?"

"If you insist. But don't overdo it. I don't want you back here. We're too busy."

"I promise."

He wrote out a bland report of the attack on the caves, with a cheerful note for Meg tacked on the end, telling her he had a light wound but was recovering, and gave it to a nurse to be delivered to Army radio.

Two days later at Keralia's Housing Development Ministry, after identifying himself as a reporter, he learned the horrible truth. Not only did families live in those caves, but 42 men, women and children were known to have been living in the big cave collapsed by the jets' missiles. Men in the valley were still trying to dig them out, an official told him, but so far they had found only two bodies – a woman and a child – and the rescuers expected to find no survivors because their oxygen would have run out.

"Is there a telegraph office near here where I can send an article?" he asked the official.

"Type it out here, give us the email address of the *Gazette*, and we'll send it direct for you," the official said. Reed spent another day trying to find Keralian Government figures who would comment on the horror, but none would oblige. Then he fired off the story through the Housing office.

Christ, Sergeant Sargent is going to hate my guts for this, Reed thought. But I had to do it.

Actually, he was wrong about Sargent. He had to return to

Sargent's unit because he had gear to collect and to get papers allowing him to leave Keralia and to his astonishment, Sargent showed no animosity.

"I can understand you felt you had to write that, David, once you knew about it. It's terrible to think of women and children buried alive, but shit happens in war and it's often the innocent who suffer. What craps me off is the gutless so-called heroic martyrs who use their homes as part of the war machine then cry foul when families get hurt. I'll get used to being thought a monster," he added, raising both arms in a gesture of resignation.

"Maybe in a future article you could spare a few lines to kick the heroic martyrs I just mentioned. Anyway, here's a surprise. I thought the Army would want to boot you out of here once the PR flak-catchers saw your report, but no. They've decided that the public will accept some mistakes being made as long as they are being told the truth. An amazing new tack, eh? I wonder how long it will last. But never mind ... welcome back, Mr Reed!"

Reed spent four days just sitting around the outpost allowing the leg wound to continue healing, then Sargent asked him if he were well enough for another assignment. "The opium poppy fields not only leave half the population here zonked, but yield the money that finances guns, ammo and bombs for the terrs. So at this time of year we go looking for the crops then call in choppers to spray them. The poppies curl up and die. It's one of the operations I really enjoy because I feel in the long run the country will benefit. Aid workers have told me they see zonked-out parents give opium pipes to their young kids and, of course, a lot of the crap is turned into heroin to bugger up our kids at home as well."

The patrol left early next morning, this time headed not for the mountains, but for intensely-farmed flats to the south-west. At each farmhouse, four armed troops would approach warily with a translator and explain to the family that they were just checking the area. Then troops would walk into the fields to identify the crops. When they found a poppy crop, they would quietly drop a small radio beacon among the plants, come back to the APCs, wave to the watching farmer and drive off. Two or three hours later, after a radio call from Sargent, a chopper would fly in and spray the crop with herbicide. "It's tough on the family," Sargent admitted to Reed. "The poppy is their main source of income. But what we hope is that eventually they will get the message and switch to maize and vegetables."

Reed noticed that at one farmhouse two of the troops were quite a while emerging after having gone in just to thank the farmer for his co-operation. And as they came out, one quickly stuffed a plastic packet of white powder into his battle jacket which carried the name Walker. Reed quietly moved over to walk behind the pair.

"You shocker. You deserve a smack," the second trooper told Walker. They both guffawed. Walker looked embarrassed when he realised that Reed was looking at them.

"A gift?" Reed asked him.

"Er ... aah ... yep."

"I'm surprised they have anything to give, out here."

"It's aah ... just a bit of cocoa."

"That'll go down well. Not as good as a beer, though," Reed said lightly to put the pair off guard. He decided to keep an eye on the two for the rest of the day. He had never seen white cocoa and now he suspected that the "gift" was more likely white rock opium. And were these guys smoking it or selling it? One way to find out was to offer to buy some. That would have to wait until they were back at the outpost. The battle unit went to six more farms that day and four of them had poppy crops. Two of them also had grain crops.

"Shit, this makes it a tough decision," Sargent told his corporal at the first one with a grain crop. Do we wipe out their food crop as well?"

"Why don't we just warn them that next time we find poppies it's zappo?" the corporal suggested.

"Done," said Sargent – within Reed's hearing. Reed was tempted to tell Sargent immediately about the white packet in the trooper's jacket, but decided to wait to try to get evidence on how wide any racket might be. It wasn't long coming. As the men filed back to their huts at the outpost he stayed close to the trooper he suspected.

"Didja land any O?" an artilleryman asked the trooper. The trooper looked around him, saw Reed, and responded, "Piss off."

"Just jokin'," the artilleryman said, having now also noticed Reed.

Reed decided to just keep an eye on whom Walker sat with and talked with over the next couple of days – who were his friends.

After one rest day spent playing cards, cleaning weapons and writing letters home, Sargent had the men up again at 4am for another mission. They were going to a riverside village, he said, to carry out house-to-house searches for weapons, always a tricky operation. It was almost customary for the farmers and tradesmen to keep an AK47 or similar rifle in the house. As there were no police for kilometres, it was the standard form of security for families against robbers and rapists. What the troops would look for were stashes of more than one rifle, significant stacks of ammunition, and heavier-calibre stuff such as grenade and rocket launchers. These would be confiscated.

The house raids went well for about three hours, but as troops reached the far end of the village a man carrying a rifle opened the door of one hut and lifted the weapon.

The machinegunner on the nearest APC opened up, spraying the hut, the rounds slicing through the bark walls turning them to chaff. From within came rending cries and screams. The man with the rifle threw the weapon in the dirt, ran in to the hut, ran out again moments later, threw his hands to his head in grief and cried "Nao! Nao! Nao!" Sargent and two men went cautiously to the curtain that acted as a door and one, using the tip of his rifle, pulled the curtain aside. On the floor in a heap lay a woman, a teenage girl and two little children, in a welter of blood. None of them stirred. The mother was clutching the smallest child.

"Christ Almighty!" Sargent exclaimed and looked back at the machinegunner.

At that moment a rifle shot rang out. The Keralian from the hut had picked up his weapon, put it under his chin, reached down, and pulled the trigger, blowing out his brains.

"Oh. No. Jesus! Jesus! Jesus! What a mess!" Sargent cried. His men stood around, silent. Villagers straggled out of other dwellings and stood in groups, saying not a word. But the hate in their eyes was manifest. This, thought Reed, sure is no way to win hearts and minds. He said as much to a trooper next to him in the APC.

"You may be right," said the trooper. "On the other hand, the policy of 'touch us and we'll incinerate you' seems to work in some countries, so why not here?"

"Which countries would they be?" Reed asked. The trooper shrugged.

Sargent went back into the hut with a paramedic to be certain that the four were dead and came out shaking his head. "Let's get the hell out of here. The village will have special mourning and burial ceremonies to carry out and they won't want us anywhere near." The APCs rolled out, back the way they had come.

"I take it you are going to want to file on that," Sargent told Reed when they were back at the outpost.

"It's war, Sarge, and my duty to report the tragedies as well as the triumphs."

"Hmm. It's my duty to protect my men and if the media undermine support for our war on terrorists and we back out, there will be a lot more tragedies, thousands and thousands of them."

"I agree, Sarge. But the public are entitled to know what is happening if they are to support the action. It's not easy to balance the two, I know."

Sargent, Reed and four troopers sat down to dinner of canned chicken and rice.

"What do you do when you're not reporting on wars?" Sargent asked Reed.

"Oh, a bit of everything. Business scandals, political scandals, bureaucracy scandals, even scandals involving vicars and priests."

"Sounds like you're just a scandal-monger, David."

Reed, ruefully: "I suppose you could say that, Sarge."

Just then a shot rang out from close by. Sargent leapt up from the table and ran out. A couple of troopers ran into the hut next door, then Reed heard cries of "Oh, no! Christ! Oh, no!"

Reed followed Sargent to the hut. There on the floor, with his head a bloodied mess, was machinegunner Bernard King. Like the Keralian father whose family King had accidentally wiped out, the trooper had put a pistol under his chin and pulled the trigger.

"Get the medic!" Sargent yelled. But it was obvious to Reed that no medic could save the man.

"I should had had someone stay with him all the time," Sargent said, shaking his head in remorse. "He's a devout Catholic and the wipeout up there in the village would be agony for him. This bloody war is hell, hell, hell. God, I hope *something* good comes of it before much longer."

Reed sent off a report to the *Gazette*, but it had to be couched in legal terms. No autopsy had been done on gunner King, so Reed could not report the death as suicide, but he enveloped in one paragraph the fact that King had accidentally wiped out a family and soon afterwards had been found dead in his hut. "Military police have yet to determine if it was an accident," he wrote, but knew the public would draw the obvious conclusion.

Two almost uneventful weeks went by with patrols checking on farms and hamlets. Then once again Reed saw trooper Walker emerge from a small farmhouse carrying a plastic package. Back at the outpost he decided to watch the trooper's every move.

At dusk two nights later, a battered black sedan pulled up near the outpost. Walker, carrying a grey satchel, spoke to one of the sentries then got into the sedan, heading off on the road to Chelucha. Reed went to Sargent, said he needed to go to Chelucha and asked to borrow a Jeep.

"I'll give you a Jeep – but with one of our drivers," Sargent said.

On the way to the capital, the driver asked Reed jokingly if he had suddenly decided he needed a woman.

"Not quite," Reed replied. "Something else that gives me a kick." He was thinking of cracking a big story, but the driver misunderstood.

"If you want a hit, you should have asked Walks," he said.

"Walks."

"You know, Walker. You've seen him around haven't you? Everybody knows he's dealing in the stuff and he's got four or five mates in it with him. I think they're crazy and one day they'll get lumbered. But nobody's going to dob them in while we're out here in this shithole risking our lives."

"Where do they flog the stuff, or do they use it all themselves?" Reed asked.

"They use some, but they're making heaps selling it to the brothels in Chelucha – making heaps, because it costs them almost nothing when they force the farmers to cough up."

The jeep had been making good time and on the outskirts of the capital Reed and the driver caught up with the black sedan.

"Walker's in that sedan," Reed told the driver. "Can we follow it at a discreet distance and I'll know which brothel to go to."

The driver roared laughing. "So you're going to have smack *and* a bang," he said. "You're catching on to Keralia pretty quick."

The black sedan turned into a side street off the central avenue of Chelucha and pulled up at a double-storey shop.

Reed's jeep was back at the central avenue corner. "Quick. Pull up here," Reed asked the driver.

In the doorway of the "shop" stood a dark-haired, full-lipped, full-hipped woman in a surprisingly tight pair of jeans, given the restrictive rules governing the lives of most women in Keralia. Reed asked his driver to pull back into the central avenue. "Look, I'll find my own way back to the outpost," he said. "Even if I have to get a cab. Because I think I'll be quite a while."

The driver smiled. "Have a good night out," he said and left.

Reed walked up to the jeans-clad doorwoman, nodded, and walked in.

Down a hallway and a turn to the right brought him into a room with rich vivid drapes and four large mirrors. Lolling on couches lining two walls were several young women. In one corner was a desk with phones and a computer, and behind it a scrawny Keralian in the act of handling a thick bundle of banknotes to trooper Walker. On the desk was the grey satchel.

"Doing good business, eh Walker?" Reed said over the trooper's shoulder. Walker spun around. "What the hell …?" Reed reached over to the grey satchel and pulled it open. Inside were half a dozen plastic packets of white powder.

"Hey! Mind your bloody business!" Walker cried. "Whaddya think you're doing?"

The Keralian desk jockey grabbed the satchel and put it under the desk, came around and began to shove Reed towards the hallway exit.

"Blow the gaff on this and you're dead meat!" Walker cried after him. "Dead meat!"

Reed realised he was on the verge of getting a big story, but needed one more piece of evidence. Thinking quickly, he pulled four banknotes from his pocket, held them in the face of the Keralian manager and said, "I want girl. I want girl." In a universal sign language, he made a circle of the thumb and index finger of his left hand and made a thrusting motion into it with the index finger of his right hand. The manager hesitated, let go of Reed, and beckoned to him to choose a girl. Reed walked across the room and pointed to a young woman who smiled at him. The manager nodded, snatched the banknotes and pulled aside one of the large drapes, revealing an open door to a small room with a bed and more mirrors. As soon as Reed and the girl went in, she began mechanically to strip, revealing a slender body, but with fine brown, bulbous breasts. She began to stroke Reed's groin with one hand while loosening his tie with the other, slowly removing his shirt, then undoing his trouser belt. Reed felt a genital surge but then the thought struck him: what if she has AIDS? The urge did not die away, but he gently guided her down onto the bed and began to massage her clitoris, thinking to bring her to a climax. I must make sure I wash my hands thoroughly after this, he thought. But the young woman did not want to be masturbated, and gently pushed his hand away. Reed realised he needed to stay for some time to give the appearance to the manager of having enjoyed himself to the full, so enveloped the young woman in his arms, kissed her breasts then lay back just holding her.

They lay there for half an hour, but then she became restless, broke free of his grasp and got up to get dressed. Reed did likewise then went out to the manager who was still at his desk. Reed put another five banknotes on the desk, pointed down to where the satchel had been secreted, then held a thumb and two fingers to his nose and sniffed. He pointed to the money then repeated the sniffing action. The manager looked uncertain, eyed Reed up and down, then reached under the desk and pulled out the satchel. He pulled a packet of white powder from it, poured half the powder from it into a smaller plastic bag taken from a drawer, and handed it to Reed. Great, thought Reed. I get this analysed and I've got me a scoop. He nodded to the manager, waved goodbye to the young woman who just curled a lip and quickly looked away.

Back on the central avenue, the dilemma struck him: where in hell would he get the powder analysed to have proof it was a drug? That doctor, he thought. The hospital might have a lab and he just might do it for me. He was right; the doctor was happy. "Opium is ruining our country, Mr Reed," he said, and ordered a lab technician to carry out the tests. Reed had to stay in Chelucha for the night to await the test results. He booked into a hotel.

"Mr Reed, you were right," the doctor told him next morning. "It is white rock opium. But, frankly, it's not much use going to the police here if that's what you were thinking of doing. They just ignore the trade."

"No, I wasn't thinking of that, doctor," Reed said. "I'm more interested in exposing what some of our army friends are up to."

"Be careful my friend. There are dangerous people everywhere in this country."

Reed now had to get the story out to the *Gazette* and he had left his laptop back at the outpost. Another problem: he could hardly take it to Army radio for transmission. Then he remembered: the Housing Development Ministry. "So! Back again, Mr Reed!" said the official who had helped him previously. When Reed explained the problem, the official went to a computer, brought up an email page, smiled and waved a hand to tell Reed to take a seat. In the next hour Reed knocked out a 1000-word report to the *Gazette* that he knew meant big trouble for not just for Walker and Sargent, but for the officers above them and for the Government officials above them back home. Even so, he hit the Send button with a satisfied thump.

CHAPTER 3

Reed took a taxi back to the outpost, having to pay a stack of Keralian dollars to persuade the driver to make the trip. Soon he ran into Sargent,

"I hear from our jeep driver you've had a high old time in Chelucha," Sargent said. "A high old time."

"I thought I'd sample the local fare," Reed replied.

"So not the tabouli, but something meatier," Sargent said, smirking. Reed wondered whether Sargent would be in such a good humour when word was relayed from Apollo City Army HQ about his latest reporting effort. Two uneventful days passed in which the group went out on patrols, checking farms and villages. But Reed did take one precaution: he went up and confronted Walker.

"I know about your drug racket, mate, and I've emailed both my office and the Apollo City police HQ and named you. If anything happens to me, you'll spend the rest of your life in the slammer." Walker said nothing and turned away. On the third day, Reed noticed a coolness towards him from some of the other men and that evening came a brutal message. After the evening meal he had walked up to a nearby ridge to watch the sunlight fading on the snow peaks. A rifle shot crashed the quiet stillness of the valley and splattered a dark grey chunk of rock about three metres to Reed's right, at waist height. He spun about and ran his eyes over the outpost below, checking for any movement. But there was none. A second or two later, two armed sentries emerged from a tent and began checking the surrounding slopes through binoculars, obviously looking for any insurgents. Reed waved to them energetically, so not to be shot, and walked quickly down from the ridge.

"That shot hit a rock right next to me. It had to have come from down here at the outpost," he told them. They looked sceptical.

"Why would anyone here take a shot at you?" one asked.

Reed thought he knew why, but said nothing. Confirmation came when he returned to the huts and was met by Sargent. There was no friendly "David" when he spoke.

"I've had a communication from HQ that the *Gazette* splashed a report by you, Reed, that my men are running a drug cartel here in Keralia. These guys are risking their lives to make the world a bit safer for you, Reed. I'm stunned that you would do the dirty on them. So what if they use a bit of dope? Tens of thousands of young people are doing it back home, along with lawyers, doctors and directors."

"I'm stunned that you apparently sanction your men being involved in criminal activity, Sarge," Reed replied. "By the way, is there any chance that you'll be investigating why I was shot at? Perhaps even checking Walker's rifle?"

"There's no proof where the shot even came from. And it could have been just an accident. Anyway, the Army has withdrawn your embedding status. You're out of Keralia on the next plane. And consider yourself lucky we're even giving you a ride to Chelucha."

"Thank you, Sarge," Reed said drily.

Reed packed his clothes and equipment and encountered icy silence from the jeep driver who took him to a hotel in Chelucha.

"Thank you, mate," Reed said as he alighted half an hour later. The trooper said nothing but gave him a two-fingered salute. Reed shook his head and walked into the hotel, relieved to be leaving the Army behind, but somehow also sad. At the hotel desk he was able to book a flight out to Apollo City the next day. After dinner he decided against taking a stroll down the central avenue, instead went to his room and before climbing into bed jammed a chair under the knob of the door to the corridor. In cities like Chelucha, at night you could never be sure.

Next day, though, the plane out wasn't leaving until 4pm and he soon found sitting in a hotel room unbearably boring so decided to stroll through the large market in the centre of the town. Again he passed the tall, burly Keralian selling sunglasses, who again held up a left index finger, pointed it at Reed and shouted, "This still insulting! Why you did it?"

"Because of this!" retorted Reed, now holding up his right index finger which was a stump with the top half missing. This was the result of an accident when he was a 10-year-old, oiling the rusty chain of his upside-down bicycle. His kid brother had come along and idly spun the back wheel, trapping Reed's finger between the chain and the sprocket. Reed instinctively wrenched back, ripping off the top half of the finger. The Keralian again screamed abuse – in Keralian – and Reed fled into the centre of the market, vanishing among the stalls. After all he had been through with the Voting Security Bureau and now the Army, it would be a shame to be murdered over a pointed finger, he thought. He circled the edge of the large market threading his way through stalls of clothing, clocks, shoes, chicken, fish, tabouli and dead turkey and found his way back to the hotel. He resolved on a long lunch there with no further exploration of Chelucha. He sat in the dining room and texted to Meg: "Darling. On way home. Flight Q7435. B there Tues yr time. Thought of u evry day. Love R." I wonder if she'll meet the plane, he thought.

The jet's engines thundered, pushing him back in his seat, the rumbling of the wheels on the tarmac gave way to a smooth climb into the blue and Reed finally relaxed. He had escaped. Dear Old Apollo City, here I come.

She wasn't at the airport and as the jet taxied into its bay and mobile phones were allowed to be switched on, there was no message from her either. Not like Meg. He clicked on her mobile, but it was switched off. He tried their home number but it went to message. He rang her number at the bank but another woman answered the phone. He clicked off. He hoped Meg had a day off and was out shopping. And he wondered whether in all the time he had been away, she had been able to buy a new house or apartment for them. He tried to put anxiety on hold until he reached her, but first he had to make contact with the office. The journey from the airport to the city, down the clogged freeway, seemed to take an age and the taxi driver thumped the steering wheel in frustration. One thump hit the horn button and the car in front responded with a two-finger salute. That took Reed straight back to the sunglasses stall in Chelucha market and he had to laugh.

He walked into the newsroom at the *Gazette* and to his astonishment, pleasure and then embarrassment, some of the staff stood and applauded as he walked down the room to news editor Butler's office. He waved a jocular but admonishing hand at those clapping, but also shook hands with several. Despite nearly 20 years in the news business he had never seen anyone get such a reception and felt there was something absurd about being regarded as some sort of hero. Anyway the illusion fell away abruptly when he knocked on Butler's glass door and the voice within barked "Come in!" Butler shook his hand and said "Well done, Reed. Great story at the finish. TV, radio and the bloggers all came in on it after we broke it. Have a couple of days off, then we'll talk about what's next." That was it. No offer to go out to lunch or that he was getting a raise. Oh, and shut the door as you go out, Reed thought.

He turned and left, to be greeted again by back-slapping colleagues, but his mind was again on Meg. He took a lift down to the car park, got his office car and decided to go to his former home to check whether Meg had been able to sell it.

He knocked at the front door but there was not response. He had a key, so risked going in. The house was empty. The window curtains were drawn and the fruit bowl on the kitchen table was empty. He could not remember ever having seen it that way before. Now apprehensive he went to their bedroom and looked in Meg's clothes cupboard. It was bare. In the computer room he used as a home office he found a note on the work desk. He could hardly bear to pick it up.

"David, I am sorry to leave you like this. I just have to get away for a while. I can't stand the tension of constantly wondering if you are ever going to come back from the next dangerous assignment. I do love you and I am going to miss you, but I have to decide whether I can bear to stay with someone and wonder almost every week whether I am truly going to spend the rest of my life with them – or just one day soon have to bury them. If you cannot wait for me to make up my mind about this, I will understand. XXX Meg."

Reed slumped on a couch, stunned. Four years of riotous love, of sympathy, laughter, teasing, shared triumphs and disappointments, spats and reconciliations, all suddenly at an end with a note on his desk. He put his head in his hands and for the first time since his schooldays, he wept.

What had he done to deserve this, he thought. Yes, he took on some tough assignments but that was what journalism was about. If society was going to stay reasonably honest and fair, someone had to tackle the dirty jobs. He looked again at her note, at the last sentence: "If you cannot wait for me to make up my mind about, this, I will understand." Was there a subliminal message there? Was she not too upset at the possible prospect of a permanent split? Had she, in fact, found someone else to be with? The thought scarified him. He had to discover the truth. One person would know: Meg's mother Caroline. He opened his mobile and pressed her number.

"Caroline? David here."

"David. You're back safe."

"Yes, I am. But I've just had quite a shock."

"Yes, David. About Meg."

"She told you."

"Yes, she did, David. She told us she needs a break."

"Did she say where she was going?"

"I'm sorry, David. She asked me to keep that confidential while she sorted things out."

"You mean, between her and me?"

"Yes."

"Caroline, I have to ask you this. Is there someone else in her life?"

"I'm sorry, David. I just can't answer that. She hasn't said."

"I tried to ring her mobile, but couldn't get through. Do you know if she has changed it?"

"I'm sorry, David. I can't answer that."

Reed couldn't decide whether that last reply meant the mother did not know or whether it meant she did not want to say. He did not dare ask, because Caroline might remain the only possible link to reuniting contact with Meg.

"Caroline, I do love your daughter very much. Can I call you again to see if there is any message for me?

"Of course you can. But Meg would still have your number wouldn't she?"

"Yes, I suppose so. If she rings would you tell her I send my love and want her back. I will keep the house going and the bed warm. 'Bye, Caroline."

The house. Ironic, he thought. He wondered whether Meg had put the title in both their names. Obviously she had not sold it. Well, now it could wait to see how life turned out. He looked in the refrigerator to see if there was anything appetising that would make a dinner. His eyes ran over frozen sausages and steaks, mouldy pumpkin, limp broccoli and blackened carrots. The Grenadier's Arms hotel down the corner seemed much more inviting and he slammed the fridge door shut.

Over the next fortnight Butler left him alone to unwind. He wrote two feature articles about life in Keralia, the troops' aims there and the seemingly over-optimistic chances of bringing Western-style democracy to the country. Some of his colleagues, noticing that he seemed withdrawn and distracted, attributed it to his war experiences, but the one thing on his mind was his absent woman. Each day after work the thought of returning to that cold, silent house repelled him and he would park in the driveway, then walk down to the Grenadier's Arms with its inviting bright lights and open fire. He was sitting staring into the flames and sipping scotch and soda one evening when the blonde sat down in the sofa opposite.

"Fire-gazing has a certain magic, doesn't it? she said.

He looked up at her. Thirty-ish. Enamel white skin, full red lips, large azure eyes, breasts threatening to burst out of a tight black top, well-rounded hips. She had the lot.

"Magic? I guess so," he said.

"I look into the flames and sometimes I see the past, at other times the future," she said.

"It must be disconcerting to see into the future, I would think."

"Oh, no. It hasn't worried me. What you imagine is going to happen rarely does." Then came the classic line. "Do you come here often?"

"I do. But do you? I haven't seen you here before."

"I've just moved into the area – and excuse me for intruding on your privacy but I don't know anyone in the area and it's nice to have somebody to talk to."

Reed looked at the woman and found himself wondering just what Meg was doing at that moment? Was she at a pub drinking with some guy? Or holding hands in the dark of a cinema? Or in bed clinging to the guy and writhing in ecstasy? He broke the train of thought.

"Your glass is nearly empty. Would you like another drink?"

"That's nice of you."

"What can I get you."

"Another pinot noir, thanks."

Within an hour they had had two more drinks each and exchanged names. She was a sales person in the local department store. No, she wasn't married. She had had a partner, but he worked in a stockbroking firm and two months ago had been transferred to London. He didn't transfer her with him, she said drily. She asked Reed if he were married. He hesitated, then shook his head. She noticed the pause and asked: "Partner?"

"Not any longer," he replied.

Reed mulled it over: she would probably come home to dinner and bed with him if he asked her. But should he do it? Was it a betrayal of Meg? Would he never feel the same about Meg again, having for so long seen her as prospective wife and life partner? To hell with it. He had slept with several women before he met Meg and that had not affected their relationship. Why not have a good night in bed with Ms Pinot Noir?

"Dinner? I'd be delighted," she said and they walked to his house in the moonlight. Thinking of the barren refrigerator, he stopped at a supermarket on the way to load up with bread, meat, vegetables and packaged dessert.

"All good chefs I've seen on TV drink a good wine while creating," he said as they entered the kitchen. "How about it?"

"Well, if it leads to a better meal ...", she said, smiling.

"Red or white?"

"Whatever you're having."

"Red it is. Goes well with sirloin."

"You haven't told me much about yourself, apart from being a journalist."

"That's all there is to tell, really. I've been doing that ever since I left school."

"I've been told all journalists drink a lot, womanise and tell lies easily, even in print."

"Correct on the first and the last. Not sure about the second. I think most of them are too busy drinking and fibbing to sleep about much. What about you? What about salesgirls? I imagine they sleep with the floor manager, or the sales manager, or, top of the tree, the finance manager. That's quite likely, isn't it?"

"Oh, rubbish. If only it were true!"

"Oops, I'm burning the steak!"

"Perhaps I should take over the cooking, Monsieur Chef."

"Monsieur Chef? I think it's about time we exchanged names, M'amselle Pinot Noir. Je m'appelle David."

"Hello, David. I'm Jennifer. Jenny to my friends."

"All right, Jenny. Come and help me with the vegetables, and can you make up a delectable sauce out of something you'll find in that cupboard over there."

"Do you often pick up girls at the pub, David?"

"Do you often pick up guys?"

"Come on. Be a gentleman and answer the question. I asked first."

"No, Pinot Noir, I mean, Jenny. You are the first in … well, in about four or five years. And do you often pick up guys?"

"Only when I see an attractive one. You are the first in what may be a long or short queue. Who knows?"

"Ah, Jenny. I can tell we are going to get along famously."

"Well, for tonight anyway, I suppose."

"Oh, don't be unkind."

"Reality bites, David. Reality bites."

He found himself liking her, her sense of humour, but she's right, he thought. This strictly ought to be a one-night stand. Life was too complicated to launch straight into another serious relationship. Even this house probably was no longer his. Having been in a relationship with Meg for so long, probably half of it was hers. He would be moving on – literally.

Two more pinots each with dinner, 10 minutes of boring television, then he asked her if she would like to go to bed.

"Your wish is my desire," she said, kissing him fully on the mouth.

In the bedroom he put on a disc of Mozart then they slowly undressed each other, she stroking his arms and chest after shedding his shirt. He unbuttoned her blouse and reaching around her, unclipped her bra, exposing firm, porcelain-white breasts highlighted by dark brown nipples. He kissed each one gently, then drew her down to the bed. Stripping her, he gently massaged her clitoris, provoking murmurs of pleasure.

"I take it you are on the pill," he said quietly.

"Of course," she said, "but I'd like you to slip on a condom if you don't mind."

"I assure you I don't have any diseases."

"That's not really the point."

"Oh, all right, Ms Pinot Noir. Just a moment."

Then he slid slowly into her, resolving to go softly, slowly, so the delight lasted as long as possible. He woke about midnight, remembered where he was and what he had been doing and oddly, felt a stab of regret. Yes, it had been pleasurable, but perhaps he should have waited longer until he determined the state of his relationship with Meg. Where the hell was Meg? Even if she were worried that he was going to get himself killed in the job, fancy going off somewhere without even talking to him about it. Weird. He tried to go back to sleep. When sunshine stabbed into the room through the window shutters, Ms Pinot Noir stirred and woke, staring at him then smiled when she registered who he was.

"I have to get ready to go to work," he said, "but I can run you home on the way."

"I'll be fine," she said. "I live not far from here. I'll just let myself out."

"What about breakfast?"

"I don't eat breakfast. Just a cup of coffee. Keeps me slim. Didn't you notice?"

"Well I did. But you must have hearty lunches and dinners, because ..." He reached over and cupped her left breast in his hand. They both laughed.

"I'll make you a coffee."

"Thank you, David."

Having done that, he got his coat and laptop and came back to her to say goodbye. "See you around," he said.

"Don't you even want my phone number? Will I have to haunt the Grenadier's Arms to have a change of seeing you again?"

"Sorry," he said, tearing a page from a notepad on the kitchen table. "Just leave the number there."

She wrinkled her nose in disapproval of the mechanical response. When he got home that evening, he found the piece of paper blank. He shrugged.

At the office, news editor Butler was almost cordial. "We've got a promotion for you, David. Ferguson is retiring as our national political correspondent and you are now one of our big names, so we want you to take on that role. It will mean a bigger salary, of course. OK with you?"

"Can I have some time to think it over?"

"Well, Ferguson finishes up tomorrow so we have to appoint a replacement pronto."

Typical Butler, Reed thought. A bloody bulldozer on two legs. I must Google his history and see if he ever did any real journalism himself. "How long would the appointment be for, Charles?"

"Who knows? How long is a piece of string? You might love it, become famous, be there for the rest of your life."

Reed realised there was one possible advantage. Apart from international trips with political leaders, he would spend his time in Apollo City and if there were to be any reconciliation with Meg, that would make her happier.

"OK, Charles. I'll take it, thanks."

"You start tomorrow," Butler grunted.

That evening he rang Meg's mother again. "Caroline, next time Meg gets in touch could you pass on some good news – that I have taken on the job of national political correspondent on the *Gazette* so I won't be running around the world getting shot at. Tell her I do miss her and want to be with her again. Tell her I'll have my mobile on day and night."

"That's good news about the job, David. Of course I'll tell her if she rings."

The next morning as he walked up the great block of stone steps and through the gothic pillars leading into the national parliament, a wave of nostalgia swept over him. Years before he had been there as a cadet journalist, working in the *Gazette*'s parliament office as assistant to political columnist Ron Morley. He remembered Morley without affection. The columnist would send Reed to interview a member of parliament; Reed would come back and write a story; Morley would criticise the introduction to the report, then put his name on the piece and send it through to the *Gazette* with a Ron Morley byline on it. "Droit de seigneur," he told the young Reed, who later had to ask a friend what that meant and when told was at least glad that the theft amounted to metaphorical rape rather than actual.

Other memories came flooding back of those young days: the time he was sitting up in the press gallery, looking down on all the assembled MPs far below when an apple he put down on his sloping desk rolled over the edge and plummeted down to thump onto the bald head of MP Eddie Daly, a Workers Party firebrand who was regularly being suspended from the House for raging against whichever Conservative was holding the floor. Young Reed was aghast as Firebrand Eddie looked up at the press gallery, and he waited for the explosion. Oddly, it did not come. The MP signalled to an attendant to take the offending apple back up to the press gallery. Perhaps Eddie reasoned that he needed to keep at least some of the media on-side, but young Reed was certainly astonished that he was not ejected from the House.

Reed spent a week going around shaking hands with the "flaks", the dozens of media secretaries, spokespersons and advisers among whom all MPs now cosseted themselves, explaining his new role. The whole parliament had been refurbished since he was last there and the *Gazette* office now had fine teak desks and lavish chairs, floor-to-ceiling filing cabinets, even digital TV sets. He hardly recognised it. Another comfort: this time there would be no

Ron Morley. His first month was fairly routine, describing battles over a contentious finance bill with one provision benefiting trade unions, the Labour Government's main supporter politically and financially. Then, late one afternoon, came the call from Caroline.

"David? It's Meg's mother here."

"Yes, Caroline."

"I have some news for you. I kept telling Meg that you wanted to see her and today she rang and said she was coming to see me tomorrow. She also asked about you and said she would be happy to see you. So would you like to come to dinner?"

"Are you sure she wants to see me? It's been weeks since she left and I haven't had a word from her."

"That's what she said, David. I didn't imagine it."

"Great, Caroline. What time for dinner?"

"Seven. See you then. 'Bye and all the best."

The thoughts tumbled one on top of another. Was she perhaps just bored and reprising a part of her life? Or had she realised where her future lay and wanted him back? What if they started all over and then she dumped him again? She had hinted she wanted marriage, children and a settled life. Was that what he now also wanted? There was one way to find out – take her on holiday if she were willing, sleep with her, then see if he wanted to be with her for the rest of his life. Butler would bellyache about him wanting to take a holiday so soon into the new role, but bugger Butler. Life was too short to let any Butlers dominate it.

"Hello, Meg. Long time no see." He smiled as he said it so there clearly was no sting in the cliché. He took her by her alabaster shoulders, held her in front of him and gave a searching look, drinking in her azure eyes, the raven hair, the full, rich red lips. "God, I have missed you."

"Well, you will go off fighting wars," she said, cocking her head imperiously. Then softly: "I missed you too, David." She kissed him lightly on the lips, then they fell together.

"Come on you two; the dinner's getting cold. You can have more of that later," Caroline harrumphed. After dinner he sat on a sofa with Meg.

"Where are you staying at the moment, Meg?"

"Well, I have been staying down the bay at Edenvale, but I'm still working at the bank, but with a different branch. Tonight I've booked into a hotel here in the city centre."

"Meg, I know this is a bit rushed, but what about coming home – yes, to *our* – (he emphasised the word) home with me for the night, and let's see how we go from there?"

She paused and chewed her bottom lip. "What about this, David … What about we go back to my hotel and talk it all over?"

"On neutral ground?" he said smiling.

"Yes, on neutral ground."

"Great idea."

David gave Caroline a strong hug when they were leaving. "Thank you for bringing her back to me, Caro."

"It's early days, my boy. Don't start thanking me yet. But, anyway, good luck."

At the hotel, instead of going up to her room, Meg suggested a drink in the lounge. They sat and for a few seconds just looked at each other.

"When I heard you'd been shot I thought I would never see you again," she said.

"I had some interesting moments there. Wouldn't want to spend my life in Keralia, Meg, I must say. But look … I have some good news. I have taken a new role at the paper … national political correspondent. In future, maybe just the odd junket flight to the opening of some international conference, but no more wars, I promise. Also, if you will be in it, I want to take you straight away on a tropical holiday … white sand, green surf, blue skies, golden sun, waving palms and orange cocktails. What do you say?"

"Ah … can I have time to think about it?"

"Of course. How about we go up to your room and relax while you do that?"

"David, you are incorrigible."

"I like to think so."

Up in her room he telephoned room service for champagne. After half an hour of chat about Keralia, her work, his parents and hers, he kissed her on one bare shoulder, then gently trailed his lips across her partly-exposed breasts to plant another kiss on her right shoulder.

"Meg, I want us to start all over. Can I take you to bed now?"

She tilted her head and smiled, letting him wait. "Just this once, Lothario."

"I do love you, Meg. It's not just the fantastic sex we had, but your lively mind, your generosity, your interest in everything around us and your firm ideas of how the world should be."

"I notice the sex was first on your list," she said archly. "So take me to bed this instant."

"Yes, Your Majesty. At once, Ma'am." He swept her into his arms, dropped her onto the bed and switched off the lights. Later he lay staring up into the dark. He could not help wondering how many other guys had been to the well while he was away in Keralia. But then he thought of that young woman in the brothel in Keralia. Had it not been for fear of HIV… And then there was that fireside blonde Jenny. C'est la vie, he thought.

"What about that holiday, Meg?" he whispered as she lay enclosed in his arms.

"Mmm. Sounds a good idea. Especially that bit about lying back on white sand with orange cocktails."

"Can you get time off, say two weeks?"

"The bank owes me holidays, so that will be no problem."

"Goodnight, my darling. I'd better scram before I fall asleep and get us both into trouble with the front desk. Oh, and can I have the number of your new mobile, so we can get organised?" She wrote it into his diary, kissed him, hauled the doona over her head and rolled over to sleep.

"Did I hear you right? Just into a new role and you want to take a fortnight's holiday?" Butler said bitingly. "What's going on?"

"What's going on, Charles, is that I'm just back from a bloody war and I've finally been able to make it up with my partner who ditched me because of it, and we badly need a break. Two weeks off won't break the company bank."

"Oh, well, piss off, then. But I'll put Matthewson in your place and if he makes a go of it while you're away, tough titty."

"Thank you, boss."

"Get outta here." Butler gave a dismissive wave of the hand.

I wonder what management manual this guy once read, Reed thought. One day the prick is bound to get his deserts. And we'll all throw a party.

The first few days at Surf City were bliss. Each morning, sun-creamed-up Meg lay topless on the sand as a dozen other young women did, turning her milk-white breasts a light tan. Then she and Reed retreated into their canvas beach tent to read and doze, lulled by the steady roar of the surf. Once he reached over to caress her breasts then inched down over her stomach, but she gently took his hand away.

"Not here, darling. It's not a nudist beach. I think we should wait until tonight."

"Yes, Your Majesty."

He picked up his hired surfboard and headed for the breakers, paddling out about 300 metres. After about half an hour, just as he was thinking of returning to the sand, he felt a mighty thump on the board.

He turned and there was a grey nurse shark, sinking the greatest row of teeth Reed had ever seen into one side of the board near the rear. How those teeth had missed his right leg he would never deduce. He froze in terror. What the hell to do now? If he got off the board, the damn thing would take him. Instinctively he went on the attack, turning and punching the beast on the nose. Still it retained its grip and now, because he had turned, his legs were trailing in the sea. He punched again. Still the shark clung to the board. In desperation, he jabbed his right thumb into its wicked left eye. It jerked back and released the board.

"Shark! Shark!" Reed screamed to other surfers near by. But someone on the beach had already noticed his fearful struggle and now a shark siren wailed across the beaches, sending swimmers flailing frantically to get out of the water. Reed rode a wave into the shallows and Meg rushed out to meet him.

"Stay out of the water!" he screamed. "Who knows where the damn thing is." She ran in anyway, clasping him to her. "Are you all right? Are you all right?" They ran onto dry sand, Reed dragging the board behind him. Two lifesavers rushed up to check he was not injured.

"It looked like a grey nurse," he told them. "Why are they called grey nurse? There's nothing bloody caring about them."

"Well, mate, they don't lay eggs. They nurse through pregnancy until they give birth to fully-grown young sharks which can straight away see and smell and can take off to hunt fish, maybe never seeing mum again."

The second lifesaver chimed in. "Don't think it was a grey nurse, mate. They rarely go after humans. Their diet is other fish. You're probably a very lucky man, mate. I'd say by the look of the teeth marks on your board, you might have been entertaining a great white."

That night Reed made love as passionately as Meg had ever known. "Mmm, that was delicious. Were you worried it might be your last?" she joked as he sank back on his pillows.

"What do you mean?"

"Well, if you go surfing again tomorrow and that shark's still out there waiting for you, it could well be your last, couldn't it."

"Good point, my darling. So I won't go surfing tomorrow. We'll try the casino."

And they did. Meg had not been in a casino before and gasped when next evening they walked into the vast, glittering cavern of Diamond City with its 3000 chattering poker machines, baccarat and blackjack tables, and bars. Reed churned the handle of a poker machine for about 20 minutes without a win, then waved Meg into the seat, saying "You might get lucky." She didn't. After another 20 minutes she said: "This is boring. Why don't we go and have a drink?"

"You're right," he said. "This is a stupid way to spend money."

The nearest bar was crowded, with all sofas taken and drinkers standing two and three deep at the bar. One group of young men formed a noisy circle, skolling drinks, boasting of conquests and erupting in laughter. A football or cricket team, Reed thought as he sipped his tequila sunrise.

"I asked her what she wanted to do," a redhead in the group retailed, "and she whipped up her skirt like this!" he shouted, bellowing laughter and flinging his arms in the air. The beer in the glass in his right hand sailed over his shoulder and splashed all over a portly woman at the bar behind him.

"What the fuck do you think you are doing, you moron?" cried the woman's partner, a man in his fifties, and he swung a round-arm punch that landed on the redhead's cheek with a resounding thwack. Redhead looked stunned, then struck the man in the face with the empty glass which fortunately did not shatter. "Cunt!" shouted the husband and tried to throw another punch, but Redhead got in first with a straight right that knocked the man to the floor. As some of the circle of mates cheered, Redhead raised a leg to kick the felled opponent.

"No!" shouted Reed, shoving Redhead so hard on one shoulder that he fell over.

"David! Stop it! Come on! Let's go!" cried Meg, grabbing him by the arm and dragging him away. As she did, three bouncers ran up, one yelling, "What's going on here?"

"Just a little disagreement, mate," said Redhead, picking himself off the floor.

"All out! All out, the lot of you!" commanded the head bouncer, pointing to the nearest door. Those in Redhead's circle looked at each other then started to walk.

"Thanks a million, Meg. You probably saved me from a real going-over."

"This holiday is turning into a drama-a-day, David. Sharks. Fights. Can we just have a nice, restful, peaceful, relaxed, uneventful holiday for the remaining days?"

"Yes, darling. I promise."

"Well, believe it or not, I think I need another drink, but let's go somewhere to a yobbo-free bar and relax."

"Yes, darling."

At a bar two blocks from the casino they settled into a luxurious leather couch with cocktails.

"I should have realised by now that life with you will never be boring," she said. "Tell me, when did you first start getting into trouble?"

Reed looked at the ceiling, searching his memory. "I was four, I think. Two things happened at the same time. We lived in a humble street of a working-class suburb, surrounded by grimy factories and with a quarry at one end of the street. My sister Pattie had been given a tricycle for her sixth birthday and I took it one rainy day and went up to the quarry with it. The rain had been heavy and the trike got bogged in heavy mud, so I left it there, came home and said nothing. Pattie later came running to Mum and said, 'Someone's stolen my bike.' Still I said nothing. Later Dad came home, found the trike in the quarry and I got a whack on the bum with a wooden spoon, the favourite form of discipline in those days."

"So you should have. What was the second thing?" Meg asked.

"Opposite us lived the aunt of Freddie Mitten who, as you know, later became the state's most famous footballer. Little Freddie's mum often used to leave him with the aunt. One day Freddie, who was about my age was at the front gate looking across the road to our place. I unlatched our gate, went over and, for the hell of it, started to feed Freddie little handfuls of the fine, dark gravel lining their driveway.

And Freddie dutifully swallowed it as I gave it to him. But his aunt came out, saw what I was doing and screamed at me. I knew it wasn't a good thing to do as I wouldn't eat gravel myself, even at that age, so I ran home. But the aunt followed me and shouted abuse at my Mum. So once again it was the wooden spoon! After that I started to grow up."

"Are you sure?" Meg said, playfully punching him in the chest, then giving him a long, warm kiss. "Tomorrow morning I'd like to go shopping and I know you detest window shopping, a woman's favourite pursuit, so maybe you could take in a movie," she added.

"I'll think of something to do, " he said. She brushed back from his forehead a drooping forelock. "That Hitler look is really unnerving," she said. "While I'm shopping, why don't you go to a hairdresser and get a proper cut."

"Jawohl!" he said, snapping his right arm up in salute and clicking his heels together.

"Stop it!"

"Jawohl!"

The next morning he strolled into the main shopping centre,

found a hairdresser, walked in and said, "A buzz cut, please." And came out with head shaven, leaving a black stubble only. After half an hour of wandering from shop to shop at the centre he spotted her in a handbag shop.

"Good morning, madam," he said. "What a lovely bag you are holding. Could I buy it as a present for you?"

She looked at what was left of his hair and slowly shook her head in disbelief.

"Do I know you? I don't think we've met." He laughed, picked her up by the waist and swung her around.

"Yes, you have! You met me in another life. Remember? I was Herr Hitler."

"So you were. Well, what have you done, Herr Hitler? Joined the paratroopers? Why on earth did you do that? I used to love running my hands through your hair, despite that forelock. Now it feels like sandpaper. Oh, never mind. Yes, David, I like the bag and you can buy it for me, thanks very much. By the way, will they know who you are when you return to the office?"

"You might not have noticed, darling, but half the male world now wears buzz cuts. Why I've even seen them on bank tellers."

"Yes, and they are the colleagues I try to avoid. They tend to be so dull. All they talk about is partying and sport."

"Nothing wrong with partying, I hope."

"Please just grow some shiny, black hair again – just for me. To change the subject slightly, have you set a date for our marriage?"

"Eh."

"You heard me. When are we getting married?"

"As soon as you like my darling. What brought this on?"

"Well, sand, sun and gin squashes are great for a while, but I think we should start to plan our future lives."

"Spoken like a bank manager! All right. Let's see. The weather's great in April, so … Paris, London or Venice?"

"Try to be sensible for a couple of minutes, David. April's fine, but in Apollo City."

"I'll have to invite all my boring journo mates."

"I can tolerate that. It's only one day, and you will have to tolerate all my boring relatives. Next: how many children are we going to have?"

"Well, it's great fun making them, so how many would you like?"

"I think three. That gives us a good chance of having both sexes. I've always thought I'd really like to have a boy and a girl."

"Three it is, my darling. I need a boy to wrestle and play cricket with."

"One other thing, David …" He arched an eyebrow. "Can you promise me you will stop going to wars and things like that. We've had a couple of bad scares and if we are going to raise a family and have a happy life, I don't want to end up a young widow on a pension."

"Ok, darling, I promise. No more wars. Sounds good that, doesn't it. No more wars. Hmmn. On reflection it sounds like an echo of Neville Chamberlain. Oh well … no more wars it is."

"And we need to sell that house and get a better one."

"Yes, darling. Well I handed that job to you months and months ago. You'd better get on with it."

"All right, David. I will. Now, about the wedding. We need to decide where to have it, what sort of party to have and trickiest of all, whom to invite. My parents can be quite fussy about who they sit with and what they eat."

"Yes, and my Dad hasn't seen Mum since she cleared out and left the farm. We'd better go up and see him tomorrow and break the news. He's always been asking me, 'When are you going to settle down and get married, son?'

Jim Reed still farmed Hereford cattle on his 300-hectare farm at Oakdale near the Victoria freeway about 150kms north of Apollo City. When his wife walked out of his life, he stayed on alone, living largely on a diet of porridge, baked beans on toast, canned fruit salad and icecream. His only companion apart from the herd was his cattle dog Rusty. Reed didn't play bridge, didn't drink at the Oakdale pub each night, didn't go to the Saturday football matches.

Jim had become used to the solitude of the bush, punctuated only occasionally by some minor drama. Such as the day a large gum tree crashed down over a barbed-wire fence lining one edge of the property. Reed took a chainsaw to the tree so he could repair the fence, but after slicing up all the branches, the roots of the huge base of the trunk lay still embedded in the soil so he brought in his tractor, tied a chain from it to the tree base and started to drag it free of the fence. As he did, a large tiger snake sprang out from among the roots where it had been living and stopped directly under the tractor.

Reed faced this dilemma: he could get off the tractor to unchain the tree trunk and risk getting a fatal bite or try dragging the trunk from the site. When he did that, the engine stalled. He then opened the tractor toolbox and threw a spanner at the snake directly under him. It twitched, but did not move away. Then he tried a screwdriver. Same result. Eventually he ran out of tools.

The dirt track called Oakdale Road ran beside the fence and Reed just sat and waited hoping for a neighbour to drive past. Finally one did. Reed waved frantically to him, hoping for some help. The neighbour gave a friendly wave back – and kept on driving. About two hours later, getting on to dusk, the snake decided to slide away to find a new home. Reed wondered if he should buy one of those new-fangled mobile phones so he could call in the Country Rescue Authority in such an emergency, but decided not to bother, got down to unchain the tree base, and drove home.

When David and Meg drove up to see him, they found him sitting at the piano playing a song from the sixties. "Hi, Dad, taking a break from the cattle?" David said.

"I see you've brought a nice young heifer with you," Jim responded.

"Yes, and we've come with some special news, Dad."

"You're pregnant?"

"Oh Dad, try to be nice. You know Meg is a real lady."

"Just joking, David. So what IS the news?"

"Well, you were pretty close. We are going to get married."

"About time, too, young man. You've been dilly-dallying for what … four years now?"

"Yes, Dad. Well, we've come to ask your permission."

Reed roared laughter. "Permission? Don't bullshit me, David. Nobody has asked permission for 60 years now. However … (here he adopted a lordly manner, arching his head back and pursing his lips) my son … (pause) you have my permission." Another roar of laughter then he turned and swept Meg into his arms, giving her a great hug.

"I don't have much in the fridge here, David, except beer, so I think we'd better go to the pub for dinner."

At the hotel, David returned to a theme he had broached many times before: "Dad why don't you give up this hermit life on the farm and come to live near us?"

"What the hell would I do down there, David? Buy a dismal cottage and sit and watch Days of Our Lives or The Bold and the Bloody Beautiful? I've told you before: I just hope that when my time is up, I just have a good heart attack here at the farm, die here and be buried here."

"What if you have a heart attack but take days to die of thirst?"

"Can we change the subject? Shouldn't you be regaling me with happy info about where you are going to honeymoon, how many kids you are planning to have, how soon you'll make it as editor of the *Gazette*? Things like that?"

"Sorry, Dad. Honeymoon in Venice, three kids, and 2030."

After another hour of small talk, David and Meg said goodbye and were on the road back to Apollo City.

CHAPTER 4

After the Voting Bureau battle, the car union fight and Keralian gunfights, Reed's first two months at Parliament House were almost restful. Much of his time was spent writing soft opinion articles, lunching with politicians from all three sides – the Conservatives, the Democracy Party members (they were overwhelmingly male) and the minority group out to save the planet – and listening politely, but with eyes drifting to the clock, to media "advisers" from all three outfits, wanting to convince him that their MPs alone had the answers to the nation's troubles.

One day, in the Parliament House dining room to which media people were permitted, he was sitting at a table near where TV commentator Laurie Barder was sitting slicing into a steak and reading a paper. Gross-bellied, florid Prime Minister Rolf Whitaker swept into view, trailing two obsequious "minders", and, passing Barder's table, bellowed: "Ha, Laurence. Dining with your friends, I see." Barder glared and said nothing. "You stupid bastard Rolf," Reed thought. "You'll live to regret that." And Whitaker did. Within three days Barder was on TV, excoriating Whitaker over the cost blow-out of a multi-million building project in Whitaker's own electorate. And in the months that followed, all of Barder's reports on the Workers Party were only ever neutral or negative.

At the *Gazette*, editor-in-chief Darryl Sheridan had a soft-left attitude to politics, which suited Whitaker's Democracy Party. Reed had long been aware of this, just from reading the paper's editorial comment. But now he decided as chief political correspondent that he would depict issues just as he saw them and the chips could fall left, right or centre. He felt that, after Keralia, he now had such prestige at the paper that he could be his own man. Even that blunderbuss news editor Butler would have to stow his ammunition.

Despite the introduction of the internet, with email, laptops and iPods, at Parliament House there were still "boxes" in a hallway into which Government and Opposition operatives dropped releases announcing details of new programs or attacks on the opposite side. (The staffers were dubbed "flunkies" by the journalists, who in return earned the derisive title "hacks".)

As Reed rifled thought a handful of leaflets in the *Gazette*'s hallway box one afternoon he came upon this typed but unsigned note: "Good story for you, David, in the minister bonking an under-aged girl. It's true. Go for it. Here's a clue:

Silently, invisibly;
He took her with a sigh."

To Reed that looked like a quote from poetry. But what?

He mulled over it for some time. Why would the note's author not just name the minister instead of fiddling about with a "clue"? Was it just a time-wasting tease from one of the flunkies perhaps displeased with the *Gazette*? But the note intrigued him. Those two lines were hardly likely to be significant to a literary peasant. Reed decided to Google the lines to see what came up. To his surprise it did yield something. William Blake's poem *Love Secret,* from *The Rossetti Manuscript,* and the first two lines of the poem fascinated him:

Never seek to tell thy Love
Love than never told can be:

Various assessments in Google entries suggested Blake was

writing of nothing dark, but merely referring to a young man deeply in love but rejected by his love object. Blake himself apparently had such a situation early in life and even later told wife Catherine about it. Even so, Reed thought, the author of the note left in his box might have concluded that the lines carried a more sinister meaning. He weighed it all up. Could he afford to go chasing this hare and still keep his job if it turned out to be all a silly fiction? Parliament would be prolonged within a few weeks for the winter break; he would wait until then and meanwhile try to devise the best way to tackle the issue. The weeks went by: MPs shouted across the chamber at each other and were expelled by the Speaker for an hour, others held up banners ridiculing the Opposition and were expelled for the rest of the day, flunkies came to Reed with promises of exclusives and sometimes he saw the promised story turn up on the TV news instead. All routine, really. In the great public gardens near Parliament House, planted 150 years before by men of splendid vision, the huge elms began shedding their now purple and yellow leaves. Soon it would be winter and the possums there would be looking for warmer shelter in the roofs of nearby suburban homes.

"If we are going to have children, David, it's time we got serious," Meg said while stirring the cabbage and bean soup on the stove at home.

"Yes, my darling. Whenever you say the word Go."

"Go."

"Oh, I see. It's a matter of relative urgency then."

"Relative?"

"Oh well. You know. Two things: you will have to go off the pill and we'd better organise our wedding. What do you say to that?"

"Go."

He laughed. "Right. Church or registry office?"

"Church, darling. Registry offices are so barren."

"Barren. Well, we wouldn't want to start a marriage that way, would we?"

"You draw up a list of those you wish to invite, I'll do the same and I'll organise sending out the invitations. I'll also organise the church and you can organise the reception. How about that?"

"It's a deal. You *are* a darling."

"Yes, David. I know. There's something else isn't there."

"What's that?"

"Guess."

"Ah … yes. The honeymoon!"

"Got it in one! Shall we say Venice?"

"We shall."

"You are a darling too, David."

For Reed, three routine months passed, reporting on the economy, infrastructure projects, defence allocations and minor expenses scandal involving an Opposition MP. Then one day in the *Gazette* mailbox in the corridor he found, along with routine political party leaflets, another typed but unsigned sheet – lines of poetry followed by a cryptic sign-off.

What dire offence from amorous causes springs

What mighty contests rise from trivial things

I sing – This verse to Caryll, Muse! Is due.

And the sign-off comment: "But this, of course, is no trivial thing."

Reed, using the Internet again, soon found that these were the opening lines of Alexander Pope's *The Rape of the Lock.* But what was the significance of Caryll, Reed wondered. Further research quickly told him that in the 17th century a John Caryll had asked Pope to write a poem jocularly outlining a feud between two families after Baron Petrie cut a lock of hair from a young woman, a joke which her family did not appreciate. *The Rape of the Lock* was the result.

One thing Reed now figured: all this was unlikely to be just a silly jape. For one thing, the person behind the notes was obviously well-educated to know of the poetry of Blake and Pope. And it took a sharp if mischievous mind to cull two sets of intriguing clues.

There were 18 members of Whitaker's National Cabinet: Whitaker, Williamson, McArthur, Palich, Nixon, Gallagher, Isaac, Garcia, Alexander, Fitzgerald, Dennison, Findlay, Carlyon, Blakely, Agius, Collins, Peterson and Kilroy. Reid wrote down the names and studied them. Agius, Palich and Garcia were women, so they, presumably, could be ruled out, though these days, he thought, one could never be sure. The first note quoted William Blake. Did that point directly to Williamson, or perhaps indirectly to Blakely? The second note quoted Pope, so did that point directly to Alexander? Or did John Caryll point to Carlyon, and Baron Petrie perhaps to Peterson? Prime Minister Whitaker was under direct public scrutiny for about 16 hours a day and guarded by security men for much of the other eight. Reed figured he could be ruled out.

That left Blakely, Alexander, Carlyon, Williamson and Peterson. Alexander was in his mid-sixties. Would he be seducing a teenager? Possible, but unlikely. That would leave Blakely, Carlyon, Williamson and Peterson.

Reed now weighed again what to do. This anonymous allegation would, if proved true, eventually bring down the Government. Was it perhaps a trap? Was some government flunky trying to set him up in retaliation for his exposure of the dead-people-voting rort? But was it also possible that some staffer had a troubled conscience – a woman perhaps? Whatever, if the allegation were true, it was one hell of a story. He decided to move carefully – and mostly in his own time, so not to annoy the ever-irritable Butler. Weeks of diligent work followed, chasing stories and writing opinion columns on the economy, defence, crime, housing and foreign relations.

But, having won Meg's consent after briefing her on the allegation of a minister seducing a girl aged under 16, he decided to spend two evenings a week on the search. "If there is a mongrel, shoot him down," she said. One avenue to explore then occurred to him: for years parliament had accepted the practice of allowing Year 12 secondary students to work briefly in parliamentarians' offices, to give them a glimpse of democracy at work. Most of these students were 17 or 18, but perhaps it was possible a 15-year-old had been accepted into the scheme.

On the other hand, the victim – if there were one – could be anyone anywhere that the minister had met. Reid went to visit the clerk of parliament, James Munnel.

"James I was thinking of writing a light piece on the students who come here to get a taste of parliament. Would you happen to have a list of those now here and those who have been here over the past year? I'd like to get an idea of how many take it on, where they come from and whether any of them would like one day to be MPs."

"Mmm … don't know, David. The list is supposed to be confidential. Look, I'll let you have a browse, but no taking of names and addresses. OK?"

"Of course."

Munnel disappeared into an adjoining office and returned with a folder. Reed thanked him, took it to a nearby table and began to peruse. There were about eight pages, but he ran his eyes down each, just looking for the ages. Most were 17, but to his surprise, he found two girls whose ages were given and 15 and 14. And interestingly, both were recorded as still spending some time at parliament. He memorised their names, schools and home suburbs, murmuring them to himself over and over to imprint them on his mind, then closed the folder and returned it to Munnel.

"That was quick," the Clerk said. "Did you get what you wanted?"

"Oh, I think so, thanks James," Reed said.

Barbara Allent, 15, St Mary's Convent School, Broadfield

Eloise Collanby, 14, Hawksley Secondary School, Yanfort.

Out of sight of the Clerk's office, Reed pulled out a notebook and wrote them down. He saw one immediate advantage – no Smith or Jones. It should be relatively easy to find those two surnames in the phone directory. And it was. There was only one Allent there, which indicated that Barbara did live in Broadfield and near St Mary's School.

There were three Collanby entries, but only one remotely near Hawksley Secondary School in Yanfort. Broadfield was the nearest suburb to the home Reed and Meg now leased, so he decided to first track Barbara.

"You need to be careful," Meg said when he told her of the development. "If you are detected trying to track this kid *you* could end up being suspected of being a paedophile."

"You are absolutely right, my darling. I'll be very careful. If you don't mind, some of the time I'll use your car for watching her house."

"David, if a pollie was sleeping with her, don't you think her parents would be a wake-up?"

"Not if he is doing it in his office or somewhere close by before having her sent home."

"David, don't you think this is all rather a wild goose chase."

"And me the goose?"

Meg drily: "Very funny. I must say it all looks a bit unlikely to me."

"I tended to think that at first, but then you have to ask yourself why this anonymous staffer would go to the trouble of quoting ancient literature."

"Have you considered it might be another journalist having you on?"

"Yes, I have actually. And I don't think there are many who would have an interest in William Blake and Alexander Pope."

Reed decided his first target would be Barbara Allent. On evenings when not tied up with some story or interview he would park some distance from the Allent house and wait to see whether Barbara left alone or, more unlikely, a government car pulled up nearby to pick her up. The Allents lived in a stylish Federation house with mullioned windows, roses and violets in the front garden and a generous driveway leading to a double garage. He spent seven nights in the street before even seeing Barbara and then all she did was walk to a nearby shop, buy a carton of milk and return with it. In all, he spent two months of street-watching, sometimes with

Meg in the car to keep him company. After the first week of his watching, she had asked to come too.

"I just want to be sure you aren't making out with some fat-lipped blonde," she said.

"I swear you are the only woman in my life apart from my dear mother," he said."Besides, I don't like fat lips."

"Perhaps. Perhaps. Anyway, I'll come just to keep you company."

"You're a darling."

"I know."

Together they sat and listened to tapes, first a reading of *Anna Karenina*, then of Joyce's *Portrait of a Young Man*.

"Do you think Anna is a bit of a fake?" Meg asked.

"Well, she'd dead now, Reed joked.

Meg punched his shoulder playfully. "She's alive for me – a silly woman who after a couple of meetings with Vronsky falls madly in love."

Reed: "I don't blame her. She had a bore of a husband. And after all, the count was a lot younger. A better performer in bed, no doubt. That's why you fell in love with me, isn't it?"

"You really are kidding yourself."

"OK, OK. Perhaps we had better put on the tape of *Middlemarch*."

"How long are we going to watch this one house, David?"

"No longer, my darling. Barbara probably goes to school during the day when I'm at work and the only time I've seen her out at night was to go to the shop. So let's go home."

Reed decided to switch attention to Eloise Collanby, but knew he was not giving enough time to Meg, so decided to put the detective work on ice for a month. He didn't want to wreck his own marriage trying to detect a pollie who might or might not be dicing with his marriage, his career and his freedom. Over the next hectic month Reed wrestled with articles about district economics, a bungled federal rail project, a minor rort of one parliamentarian's travel expenses and uproar over a $500 million government building project assigned to an Apollo City company known to be a major financial supporter of PM Whitaker's party. Then one night in bed Meg delivered her bombshell.

"Darling, I have some news for you. We are going to have a family."

"What?"

"You heard me. A family. I read that women on the pill for several years should take a break from it, and I thought a short break wouldn't matter, But then I missed my period a couple of weeks ago, thought I'd better check, so went to the doctor and, yes, we're in the family way."

He paused, then, "Darling, that's great." Another pause, then: "I wasn't expecting it because you've been on the pill. But it's fantastic."

"Are you sure? Remember you did say I could – and I quote – go for it once we were married."

"Of course I'm sure. Brilliant people like us should pass on their genes! While we're at it, we'd better start thinking about that marriage – and buying a better house of our own." They laughed together and he hugged her.

"Can I still make love to you for a while?"

"Of course, my darling. Right now if you like."

"I like."

The next day his mind switched back to Eloise Collanby but a doubt crept in. If he did pursue that investigation it might be quite dangerous. As a father-to-be, should he take any risks? Against that, any threats here in Apollo City couldn't be more dangerous than Keralia, and he had survived that. And again, as he was now soon to be a father of a child, he should hardly step back from trying to expose a paedophilic creep if one existed in the Government. But first he sounded out Meg to get her agreement to continue.

She agreed. "Be careful. But by all means go for it."

For three evenings, surveying the Collanby house in Yanfort yielded nothing, but on the fourth, a girl who certainly looked only 14 left the house clutching a mobile phone. Eloise, no doubt, thought Reed. He followed her in his car. After walking two blocks, she went to the door of a bluestone mansion, knocked and was welcomed in by a girl about her own age. That looked innocent enough, Reed thought, and after waiting a while, gunned the car to go home. He wanted to spend more evenings with Meg so dropped the hunt for the rest of the week. On the following Wednesday he was back at Yanfort, waiting … waiting. Again Eloise emerged from the house, again with mobile in hand, but this time wearing an overcoat. And this time she did not go to the bluestone mansion, but sat in a bus shelter to make a call. Reed sat and waited, listening to a radio jazz station. About 10 minutes later a bus pulled up at the shelter and Reed started his engine, preparing to follow it. To his surprise, when the bus pulled away, Eloise was still sitting in the shelter, now looking anxiously down the road. Reed killed the engine and waited. This looked interesting.

Five minutes later a taxi pulled up at the shelter and Eloise got in. Reed followed as the taxi headed to the city's southeast and swung onto a major road packed with traffic. Reed tried to keep a couple of cars behind it, but at a big intersection the lights turned yellow, the taxi drove on through, but the car immediately in front of Reed began to stop for the red. Reed blasted his horn, swung out past the car and charged through the red, narrowly missing a huge truck thundering through the green on his right.

"Christ," he thought. "I could get myself killed on this bloody story. Just as well I didn't have Meg with me. She'd go ape."

He caught up with the taxi and eight or so kilometres farther on it stopped at a hotel, the Regent. Eloise got out and went into the hotel.

"Now this IS getting interesting," he thought. He rang Meg on his mobile and related what was happening. "I'll probably be here for a fair while, darling, so don't wait up for me."

He went into the hotel, tried the front bar, the side saloon bar and then the dining room. No sign of Eloise. He waited for five minutes then toured the three points again in case she had just decided to go to the toilet. Again no sign. That meant one thing: she had gone straight to someone's room. He sat in the front bar where he could also see anyone entering the saloon bar or the door to the dining room, but two hours passed as he slowly drank three beers then just nursed a fourth to the puzzlement of the barman.

"You waiting for someone?" the barman finally queried.

"No, mate. Just passing the time," Reed said. The barman nodded.

Finally Eloise came down a flight of stairs and out to the street. Reed waited until the street door closed behind her then followed – just in time to see her step into another taxi which U-turned to head back in the direction of Yanfort. Reed decided to wait and see if any politician he knew also came down to leave, but at 11pm none had.

He wondered at first why her parents would not be puzzled at the late home-coming, but then surmised that she would tell them she had been visiting the nearby girlfriend.

Meg rang: "Ah, so you're still alive. Any chance of you coming home to warm this bed? Or are you warming someone else's?"

"Darling, you know I would never do that. Sorry it's late. I'll come home now and tell you all about it."

"I'll probably be asleep. Tell me over breakfast."

On the way home it occurred to Reed that if Eloise had a seducer, which now seemed likely, the guy might be single or divorced – as it looked as if whomever she met was staying at the pub for the night, unlikely if he had a wife or partner. That fact narrowed the field quite a bit. Next day in parliament he got on the computer to search the CVs of the 18 government ministers. Two made no mention of family – Eric Williamson, Minister for Infrastructure and Ronald Findlay, Minister for Housing. Because of his slender hunch about the connection of Williamson and William Blake, he decided to check out the Infrastructure Minister first. Two days later he called into the *Gazette*'s newsroom to check for any mail coming there. News Editor Butler called him over.

"Hello David."

"Hi Graham."

"Renton over there," Butler said, jerking a thumb at a reporter across the room, "tells me you are trying to track down a pollie who raped someone. That right?"

"Sort of, Graham." Reed then outlined to Butler the allegation in the mysterious notes and what he had been doing to try to check it out.

"Jesus, David, that's pretty hot. Bloody dangerous in fact. You should have told me about it first up. Look, we all admire what you went through in Keralia but you've done enough risky work over the past year. We don't want you ending up on a slab. What precautions are you taking?"

"Well, apart from letting a bit slip to bloody Renton I have been very careful. I've been watching some houses and keeping well back from them while doing it. I assure you I am not taking any risks. My wife's expecting a child, I've just learned, so I now have extra responsibilities. And by the way, Graham, I'm doing this checking all in my own spare time."

"In this business, David, there's no such thing as your own time. You know that. Anyway, are you getting anywhere with the story?"

"I think I might have it narrowed down to two ministers – Williamson and Findlay."

"But have you got any real evidence?"

"Not yet. That's what I'm working on."

"Well, you mean a lot to this paper now. So be bloody careful. And if you need any backup, just ask. OK?"

"I will, don't worry," said Reed, slightly baffled at this new, tender concern coming from Butler. He decided that he would keep watch on Eloise to see if she revisited the hotel. If she did, he would get a snap of her coming out. Using a camera flash would alert her, but he could get an identifiable shot, he thought, if he snapped her while she was still in the bright light of the hotel entrance. And if events followed the same pattern, he would go back to the Regent early the next morning to see if anyone he knew came out. He explained his plan to Meg that night.

"So you'll be setting off the alarm here at what, 3am?"

"No, darling. 4am."

"Oh, is that all."

"I'll make it up to you."

"I'll say you will. I will expect to be taken to dinner at Giseldos."

"There goes three days' wages, but Giseldos it is. Now, darling, can we get some sleep?"

"Cuddle me first."

Three more nights of watching the Collanby house followed, with no sign of Eloise emerging and on the fourth night she did come out, but only to go again to the bluestone mansion of her girlfriend. Reed began to wonder if his suspicion was all a mistake, but on the fifth night Eloise again went to the bus shelter, again waited for a taxi, and Reed followed it – to the Regent hotel. Eloise got out and went in. Reed repeated the pattern of checking out the front bar, saloon bar and the dining room, then waited in his car for her to emerge, which she did about 11pm. He got an image of her with his mobile phone then waited another hour, but nobody he recognised emerged from the hotel. When he got home, Meg was sound asleep so he set the alarm for 3.30am, took it to his side of the bed so he could turn it off after the first buzz, then slid gently between the sheets so not to wake her. He tried to sleep but kept staring up into the darkness, thinking of the day to come. If he did snap a minister coming out of the Regent in the early morning, did it prove the man had slept with Eloise Collanby? That was the dilemma. Reed would have to get him to admit it. Then a possible solution came to him and he went into a sound sleep.

With that first buzz he snapped off the alarm, slipped out of bed, dressed and was on his way to the hotel. He sat in his car, driver-side window down, watching the front entrance, camera ready. He shivered in the cold. At 4.35am a milk lorry drove up and the driver took three crates inside. From 5am staff dribbled in, five of them all told. A silver-haired, well-dressed male came out, Reed raised the camera, then realised it was not any of the politicians he knew. A few minutes more and now a couple came out, laughing at something the male said. They went to the car park next to the hotel and drove off. It was nearing 6am when another male came out. Reed's eyes widened as he recognised 38-year-old Eric Williamson, the Infrastructure Minister. Reed snapped a shot, slumped down in this seat and waited until Williamson left in a taxi. At home for breakfast he looked at the camera shots. Eloise was quite clear. Williamson's shot was shadowy. He decided he would have to take another week or two and next time use the flash to have definite proof.

And that is what he did. Eloise again left, this time about 10pm. Reed now settled for another dawn exit of Williamson. Being mid-winter he began to shiver, so this time ran the engine every half hour or so to warm the cabin. As the morning light slowly grew he would down the driver's side window and get ready with the camera, now setting the flash. Again individual men and two couples came out the, finally, yes, Williamson. "Eric!" he called and fired, catching a full-face shot of a stunned Williamson, then gunned the engine and roared away.

"Got him! Got him! Got the bastard!," he yelled to himself, slapping the steering wheel with delight, setting off a horn blast which puzzled a driver stopped at intersection lights just ahead. Reed broke the speed limits almost all the way home to wake up Meg and have a triumphant breakfast.

"That sounds great, David. But why didn't you bail him up and ask him what he was doing sleeping with a teenager?"

"Hmm, maybe, Meg. But he's pretty tall and athletic and if he knocked me down and snatched the mobile I'd have no evidence. The paper will take him down, don't you worry."

He could hardly wait to get to the office to get the images safely onto computer and to see Butler.

"You're a regular little crime buster, David," Butler said, grinning. "This will be a lulu of a story, but we have to go carefully. If we don't want to get hit with a massive defamation writ, somehow we have to get Williamson to admit he is the figure we are targeting. He can just say it was a coincidence that he was staying at the same pub as the girl was visiting. So how do we get him to confess to the dirty work?"

Reed held his chin in his hand and stared out the newsroom windows at the far wall of skyscrapers.

"What say, Graham, that we just run a story describing those mysterious notes and some one left for us, tipping us off that a Government minister is sleeping with an underage girl, that the girl lives in a south-eastern suburb, that the two have meeting at a hotel. We describe her as wearing a khaki plastic raincoat, him a dark suit, that she leaves the hotel late at night and he leaves early the following morning. But we don't identify them beyond that. That will trigger uproar from the Opposition and do-good feminist groups and Whitaker will be having kittens. Something or someone is bound to break. Whitaker will grill the cabinet members. Williamson might even hand himself in to the cops or flee the country. Who knows?"

"Sounds OK to me, David. You might make news editor one day."

"Don't think so, Graham. I'm not a big enough bastard for that."

Butler scowled, then quickly changed to jokingly punch Reed on the shoulder.

"You'll grow into it mate. Don't worry."

Editor-in-chief Sheridan agreed with the plan and the *Gazette* hit the streets next morning with the headline MINISTER IN SEX SCANDAL – but without the photos and without identifying Eloise Collanby. By 7am the television stations were all over the story, calling on Prime Minister Whitaker to make a statement and cynically calling on the *Gazette* to name the minister, well knowing there probably good reasons why it had not.

"This is a load of garbage from our notorious pink rag," Whitaker fumed on one TV channel mid-afternoon. "It comes out and makes the accusation without a shred of evidence."

"But prime minister," the interviewer interjected, "the *Gazette* has offered some detail. You're not really saying they've made it all up are you?"

"Well, what are you suggesting? That I call my ministers in one by one and ask them 'Are you a paedophile?' Look, I have serious work to do. Thanks for your interest."

Editor-in-chief Sheridan called Butler and Reed into his office.

"Well, gentlemen, what's the next move on the great scandal? We can hardly leave it all hanging in the air."

Reed: "I've been thinking … we can't yet publish the photos of Williamson because of the defamation risk, but what about we find someone to drop the rumour to one of Whitaker's flunkies that we have photos of Williamson at the pub and photos of the girl. That should put Whitaker in a panic. I'll bet he is already sounding out some of his closest colleagues on who our target might be.

Eventually he *will* have to get around to grilling his cabinet one by one."

Sheridan: "How would we drop the rumour?"

Reed: "Cadet Anderson has been working in parliament with me sometimes. We could get him to have a few drinks with Whitaker's media adviser … you know, accidentally meet him in the Members' Bar. The flunky would be bound to sound Anderson out for anything he knows about the ministerial scandal and Anderson could let drop what we have."

Sheridan: "OK, David. I guess it's worth a go. Let's try that."

Butler: "We still have the problem that Williamson could say it was just a coincidence that he stayed at the same hotel the girl occasionally visited."

Reed: "I think he'd have trouble convincing Whitaker of that if we get Anderson to let drop to the flunky that we have two sets of photos showing him at the pub on two nights when the girl just happened to be there. And don't forget those mystery notes that tipped us off."

Sheridan: "OK, let's go with that – but brief Anderson thoroughly. Get him to run through it with you, David. He'll need a preamble bit of waffle about the day's political news, then casually mention that the paper has another big story coming about the girl and the minister – with photos. That should have Whitaker pissing in his pants."

Butler: "You realise, David, that this is going to take some time. The Anderson approach is going to have to appear quite accidental. It might involve sitting in the parliamentary bar for days, before he happens to be near one of Whitaker's media staff."

"Don't worry, Graham. This is a story worth waiting for."

And thus it transpired. Anderson spent so long waiting for the appropriate opportunity that one barman eventually joked: "Haven't you got a home to go to young feller?" But finally came the moment Anderson had waited for: a Whitaker staffer came and sat at the same mahogany table where Anderson was reading a copy of the *Gazette*.

"You work on the rag, don't you?" the staffer said, nodding at the paper but also smiling.

"That's right. I do."

"What happened to that beat-up about a minster supposedly sleeping with some young girl? It has sort of died, hasn't it?"

"Oh, no. I hear it has some way to go."

"Really? Straight for the dustbin, I would have thought."

"Not quite. I heard that we are just deciding whether or not to publish the photos."

"What photos?"

"Photos of the minister and the girl."

"You're kidding."

"No. that's what I've heard. The issue is with the lawyers for final decision."

The next evening Reed found another of the unsigned, typed notes in his inbox in the corridor outside his parliamentary office. "Well, done, David. The panic is on.Whitaker is interviewing his ministers one by one. My minister was interviewed this afternoon, but he's in the clear." Reed phoned Butler with the news.

"The show's on the road, Graham. I'll be filing a piece that Whitaker is grilling his ministers to find the culprit."

Butler: "Put that note in a plastic bag and keep it. We might need DNA or fingerprints off it."

Early next morning Reed placed himself in Democracy Hall, a vast open space with soaring marble pillars topped by a ceiling of coloured glass segments. But he was there because at the eastern end was the corridor leading to Whitaker's office and he wanted to see which ministers went to see the prime minister, including Williamson – and importantly, how long they were there. Three ministers came and went individually within half an hour. So Reed knew that the writer of the unsigned notes was probably telling the truth. He took care that the ministers did not see him, burying his face in a copy of the *Gazette* as the came and went. It was almost lunchtime before finally Williamson came, head down, face glum. Unlike the other ministers, he was in the PM's office for almost three-quarters of an hour and emerged white-faced.

"You're one dead duck," Reed thought and waited for the prime ministerial execution. It did not come. That night the *Gazette* had to content itself with a short item that Whitaker appeared to be interviewing ministers with a view to discovering which of them was the star at the Regent. To Reed's amazement, he got a call next morning at his parliamentary office from a male who said his name was James Darley and that he was one of Whitaker's media advisers. Reed had not heard of him, but said, "How can I help you?"

"It's how you can help yourself, David."

"How's that?"

"Would you be prepared to let this so-called sex scandal die if $50,000 dropped into your bank account?"

"Are you kidding?"

"No. I'm deadly serious."

"Did you say you were a media adviser?"

"Yes. Why?"

"Well any media adviser worth a cracker would know that no media company would kill the story we have for a piddling 50 grand. Not for a million either. You know, I'd write a piece about this phone call for the front page tomorrow but for one thing ... our readers would never believe it. Piss off, James, or whatever your real name is."

"You'll be sorry, Reed."

Reed hung up. He quickly checked a government directory and confirmed that no government staffer named Darley was listed in it. Two hours later came the bombshell he had been waiting for: PM Whitaker announced that Infrastructure Minister Eric Williamson was leaving parliament "for family reasons".

Family reasons? Reed shook his head in disbelief. Whitaker sure had a sick sense of humour, using the oldest cliché of an excuse for someone bailing out before they were axed. That afternoon, Reed experienced another delicious moment when the phone rang in his Parliament House office.

"David Reed? Asked a quavering female voice.

"Yes, Reed here."

"Mr Reed, this is Caralyn Williamson, Eric Williamson's wife."

"Yes, Ms Williamson," Reed said cautiously, expecting a tirade. But there was just a long pause.

"At first I hated what you published, because the media often attack politicians just for the hell of it. But this morning, after being dumped from the ministry, my husband admitted to me that the nights when he was away supposedly on interstate political business were actually spent in a hotel with that poor girl."

Reed reached over quickly and switched on a recorder on his desk, then continued.

"Are you saying, Ms Williamson, that Eric admitted that he was sleeping with Eloise Collanby?"

"Yes, I am. And I don't mind admitting it to you because I have told him I am applying immediately for a divorce. I don't want to be married to a creep. Some men you just can't understand. And I don't mind if you put it in your paper that I am dumping him, because I want all my friends to know."

"Very well, Ms Williamson. I'll do that. I do feel very sorry for you."

"Eric is the one who is going to feel sorry – sorry for himself." Reed looked up Williamson's home number in his work diary and rang the wife back to confirm his call. He then played back what he had recorded to make sure he had the conversation then rang Butler.

"Graham, we can go full bore with the story, photos and all. I have his wife taped saying he admitted the affair to her. If he tried to pull a defamation case we could blow him out of the water. Anyway, he's likely to be fairly preoccupied for a while as I imagine the cops will be looking to charge him with penetration of a minor."

The *Gazette* headline next morning read: WIFE DUMPS SEX POLLIE and underneath it were large photos of Williamson and of Eloise, but with her face blurred so she could not be identified. To add a little mischief, Reed added three paragraphs at the end about the anonymous offer of $50,000 made to him if the paper dropped the story, but was careful to add that there was nothing to link that call to Eric Williamson. By late morning, newsagents were ringing the *Gazette*'s circulation department saying they had sold out and were there any more copies to be had.

When Reed showed up at the *Gazette* office that morning one colleague greeted him with the cry "Giant Killer" and others clapped. He wrote an opinion piece speculating on what impact the Williamson scandal would have on the Whitaker regime and at the end of the day surrendered to urgings from his workmates to celebrate at the pub across the street, first ringing Meg to alert her that he would be late home. At 10.30pm he looked ostentatiously at his watch and said he had to get home to Meg or he'd be in the bad books for a week. Having had quite a few drinks he decided to take a taxi home, not his office car.

Sub-editor Mick Blackman offered to drive him home, but Blackman slurred as he spoke and Reed decided firmly on a taxi and within 20 minutes was home, had showered and slid into bed beside the delicious, ivory-skinned Meg who greeted him with "It was a great scoop, but God, you smell of beer."

"See you at breakfast my darling," he said, wrapping himself around her.

"Don't snore," she said and wriggled out of his embrace.

A radio news bulletin at breakfast brought stunning news. A *Gazette* journalist had been arrested late at night and charged with drunken driving causing critical injury after slamming into a steel telegraph pole wrecking his car and maiming his front-seat passenger. Reed guessed instantly that the driver was Michael Blackman and a call to a friend on early shift at the *Gazette* newsroom confirmed it. It hit home how close Reed had been to being in that death seat. He looked at Meg sipping her coffee and decided not to spoil her breakfast with any story of a lucky escape.

One way and another she had already been through enough because of his lifestyle, he decided.

Reed found one final typed but unsigned note in his postbox at Parliament House: "Well done." He never did discover the author. The Whitaker Government's standing plummeted in opinion polls and not only Whitaker's spin doctors, but also all the Government MPs refused to talk to Reed. He reported that fact, too, in an opinion piece and relationships became even frostier, with epithets such as "stooge" flung at him in the corridors. He began to think he might need to quit the parliamentary round if he wanted to continue a career in journalism.

Because of the long hours he worked, he was entitled to six weeks holiday every year so decided to take another spell away with Meg.

"Can you persuade the bank to let you have another break?" he asked her over dinner.

"If they refuse, I'll leave and go to a rival bank. Just one thing, though, David. When we get back, could we settle down to a half-normal life where you come home at least once or twice a week in time for us to talk, watch TV and sit down to dinner together?"

"Yes, darling. We will."

To Reed's surprise, Butler readily agreed to the holiday and within two days, thanks to a tourist agency and an A380 Airbus, he and Meg were lying under a brolly on the sun-drenched white sand of a mid-Pacific island. While she read a novel, he applied sun-tan cream to her, gently stroking her skin. Then he lay his head down with one ear to her stomach.

"Can't hear anything," he said.

"Of course not, you idiot. Do you know anything about obstetrics?"

"No. Only how to make a baby."

"For your information, Mr Smug, it takes two to do that."

A couple at a table under another umbrella close by overheard the exchange and burst out laughing. The four exchanged names and got talking.

"Isn't this just paradise," said Meg, looking out at green rollers crashing onto the reef in front of them.

"Yes," said Ted, the other male. "But you'd better make the most of it."

"How's that? Asked Reed.

"Well, I guess from what we heard, that you might be thinking of having a baby, so don't take offence, but the world already has far too many humans. We are becoming the scourge of the planet … seven billion already and on the way to nine billion."

"I think we'll manage," said Reed. "After all, old Malthus ages ago predicted ruin of the planet and we're all here and managing all right with a few billion more than he imagined."

Ted: "Do you really think we are managing? The world's forests are disappearing. Do you know that much of Russia's Kalmykia republic has turned from forest and grassland to desert in our lifetime?"

Reed: "God, cheer up mate. We're here on holiday."

Ted: "Well make the most if it. The human race hasn't got long left, you know."

"Really?" Reed exclaimed.

"Yes. There are already nine nations that have nuclear weapons and some of them hate each other. Within our lifetime there will be 30 or 40 nations with them, and one day one of them will go crazy and fry one of the others. Then it will be on. Armageddon ten times over, mate. The globe will be covered with radiation that will kill everything not at the bottom of the oceans. When the radiation dies down, evolution will have to begin all over again."

Reed: "Well, thanks, mate. I think I'd better get to the bar and have a last double-scotch before it happens. Come on, Meg. Let's get out of here."

As the headed up the sand to the bar, leaving Mr Doomsday under his umbrella, Reed whispered to her: "Of all the islands in the Pacific, I had to pick this one!"

"Darling, you must have plenty of nutters in journalism, some of them your colleagues. In the banking industry counter staff can meet one every day. I thought he was hilarious."

They managed to steer clear of Mr Doomsday over the remaining days of their stay.

CHAPTER 5

B ack in the whirl of Apollo City, with the roar of bus engines, clatter of trams running through junctions and blasting horns of impatient motorists, Reed for a moment wished he were back listening to the murmur of surf and gloom-mongering of Mr Doomsday. Over dinner, he began expatiating on his plan to take up investigative reporting to get away from the late nights of parliamentary work.

"Before we go into that," said Meg, "now that we seem to be a serious couple, I think it's time we went and saw my father. I know he and Mum split ages ago and are no-speaks, and I know that you haven't even met him. Even so, I think I owe it to him to let him know what's going on. OK?"

Reed hesitated. "I guess so. But from what you've told me, he's pretty grumpy. He won't get out his rifle, will he?"

"Oh, don't be silly. Yes, he takes on the world around him. But I actually suspect he'd even be glad to be a grandpa."

"Well, OK. But only on condition you ring him first and sound him out."

Her father, Bruce Mann, lived alone (apart from his two companions, an old white cockatoo with whom he conversed frequently and a black Labrador) in a large house in an outer suburb of Apollo City. A retired mechanic, he spent most of his time at war with neighbours, the local government council or his local parliamentarian.

When they drove up at the weekend, he was in the front garden, arguing with a neighbour about branches of a bush drooping over the dividing fence into his property and simultaneously chopping at the branches with a pair of secateurs.

"I know my rights!" Mann bellowed at the neighbour. "Under the law I can cut off anything on my side of the fence as long as I drop the cut branches back onto your property, as the branches belong to you."

The neighbour: "No matter how ugly you make it for both of us?"

Mann: "Well, you're no bloody Robert Redford. So who cares?" He then turned and saw Reed and Meg.

"G'day Meg. So this is your china plate?"

"Dad! That rhyming slang went out of fashion about 30 years ago. Yes, this is David … David Reed … and I have some big news for you. He looks like being my husband." She paused. "Not only that, Dad. We might have a family. That's why we've come to see you."

"Christ! That can't be all. Are you running for prime minister, too?" He turned to Reed and held out a hand. "Glad to meet you, father-to-be. Come on in."

Over coffee and biscuits, he eyed them quizzically, all the while chuckling the chin of Labrador Woofer . "How long have you two been an item, then?"

"Ah, quite a while," said Reed, not wanting to embarrass Meg.

"And what are you going to call the bub if you have one?"

"Um … we've decided to wait and see. Ah…how's life with you?" said Reed, anxious to change the subject.

"Same as ever. Surrounded by nutters out here. You saw that when you arrived. Actually… that guy's not too bad. He's certainly not the worst of them. The moron directly over the road from me has two deranged sons about 12 and 14 that he has never disciplined. When I put the garbage bin out at night for council collection, they sneak out sometimes and tip it over onto the footpath. Then the bloody council workers turn up next morning and refuse to pick up the rubbish. I have to do it."

"How do you know it's them, Dad?" Meg asked.

"Because at least twice I've seen them in their front yard, looking at me and laughing while I'm cleaning up. If I catch them doing it, I'll beat the daylights out of them."

"That might not be a good idea, Dad."

"Well it sounds a damned good idea to me."

"Why not get your local councillor to come and talk to them?"

"Ha! What a joke. My local councillor? Dear old Bernie Castles gets $90,000 a year to park his bum at a council meeting once a week and spends all the rest of the week, days and nights, at the pub. There's no way you'd get him to go and give those kids a lecture."

"I take it you don't think much of the local council," Reed interposed.

"Oh, they're fantastic, mate. I mean that literally. They live in a fantasy world. I'm forever picking up beer bottles, plastic bottles, cardboard coffee cups and potato chip packets in the street. So what does the council do? The milk bar down the road shut down a while ago so now the council – which is forever sending out pamphlets telling us how "green" it is and how "green" we ought to be – has taken away the street's only litter bin!"

Meg: "Dad! You have to stop getting so angry. You'll have a heart attack."

"Don't you worry about that, my love. I really enjoy getting stuck into these bludgers who live off the rest of us. They've refused to do anything about kids playing soccer in the street here instead of at the park just down the road, which is a pest for those of us driving cars. And they slug us with taxes for everything, then splurge the money on festivals to raise public awareness about environmental threats to bottle-nosed something-or-others somewhere in the Congo. What they should be doing is fixing the potholes in the street so our cars aren't wrecked."

"Well, actually, I think we should save the bottle-nosed somethings from the Congo if they are the only ones left in the world."

"Oh god, Meg, don't tell me you fall for that sort of rubbish, too."

"How would you feel, Dad, if a campaign got under way to rid the world of black Labradors. You wouldn't like that, would you."

"Labradors do something useful. If someone came into the back yard in the night, Woofer would soon let me know. And a lot of them make good guide dogs. They even serve with our troops to suss out road mines. So they *are* worth having. Anyway, enough of this argy-bargy, how many kids are you two planning to have, David?"

"Ah ... I think that's a question to be answered by Meg, thanks Bruce."

"What do you do for a living, David?"

"I'm a journalist, Bruce."

"A journalist. So you make up stories to entertain some people and annoy a lot of others. Is that right?"

"Something like that."

"Well I hope you belt the parasites and back the poor."

"Occasionally, Bruce, occasionally."

"I don't buy newspapers any more. I get enough bad news off the TV as it is."

"I won't be able to continue belting those parasites if people don't buy the paper, Bruce. I'll be out of a job."

"Well, it's been interesting to meet you, David. Given the fact you've a bub on the way, I take it you and Meg have been together for quite a while. How many years?"

"Quite a while, Bruce." Then to Meg: "Darling, I think we need to be going. It'll take us an hour to get home."

Back in their car, Reed allowed himself a laugh. "God, Meg, how does Woofer put up with him? He's not a very happy soul, is he?"

"Au contraire, David. I think he is happiest taking on the whole world. He has always been like that. I remember Caroline was a bit upset when he first left, but that soon gave way to relief. She had almost forgotten that life could be enjoyable."

At the *Gazette* next day, Reed approached Butler about changing his role from covering parliament to investigative reporting.

"Why would you want to do that, David? You've been doing a great job up at the House."

"Graham, I'm settling down a bit and I owe it to my partner to have a job with more reasonable hours for at least a couple of years."

"Well, Family Man, you know damned well that investigative work can be quite dangerous. Have you stopped to consider that?"

"I survived Keralia, Graham."

"From what you wrote, I think you were just lucky."

"Oh well. What would you like me to take on? Property writer? Food critic? Religious affairs editor? Art critic? No … that last one might be too dangerous."

"All right, David. All right. Two more months in parliament while I find the right person to replace you and then you can go crime-busting, OK? When you do start that, just mind your arse, all right?"

"Thank you, Graham. I'll be careful."

At home over a dinner of grilled salmon he told Meg of his plans. "Thank you, darling. It makes good sense." Then an afterthought with a smile: "I'll really believe it when it happens. By the way, David, I've found the perfect house for us and as I'm going to spend mostly your money on it, it would be good if you would take a little time out tomorrow to come and have a look at it."

To his satisfaction – and relief – the house she had set her heart on was in the inner suburb of Rochley, only 10 minutes by car from the *Gazette* office. A high front brick fence offered privacy, behind which was a fine garden of roses, ivy, lilacs, a lemon tree and a tall, slender eucalypt, waving in a light breeze. Three bedrooms, two bathrooms, a dining room, a loungeroom, a kitchen and a sunny courtyard at the back were rounded off by a double carport – essential in a city where cars parked in the street were often subjected to "key-ing" by vandals driven by jealousy to scratch cars they could not afford.

"How much do they want for it, Meg?"

"$600,000 darling. What do you think?"

"The important thing is: what do *you* think?"

"I think it will be ideal for us."

"Right. Let's buy it." He hugged her to him and kissed her neck. "Well done, gorgeous."

"The agent told me that if we met the price we could walk in within two weeks. So I will ring him now and say Yes. OK?"

"Right, darling. You realise we are going to have to work for 15 years to pay it off."

"I do. But when the baby is two, I'll be able to go back to work. We can put him or her in nurse care, then crèche, and I can go back to banking."

"Right! Off we go to the pub for a glass of champagne, then back to work."

Back at parliament several days later the phone rang on his mahogany desk.

"David Reed?"

"Yes it is."

"I want to give you a tip. Are we off the record?"

"If you say so. Who is calling?"

"I work in the Department of Finance."

"Yes, but who is it calling?"

"Are we absolutely off the record?"

"I said that. Now what is your name?"

"It's Greg Barrow from the expense supervisory section."

"Yes, Mr Barrow."

"You did a great job on that sex case and I have quite another good story for you I think. Some MPs living the high life at taxpayers' expense."

Reed, a doubtful tone in his voice: "Is that new, Mr Barrow?"

"Well the scale of this is. And it looks like out-and-out theft."

"Go on."

"Well, if you use the Freedom of Information Act to look up certain expense claims going back a year or so I think you'll be very surprised."

"There are over 200 MPs, Mr Barrow. So can you give me some names?"

"Yes. Roy Dalley, Anthony Garund and Martin Leeson."

"Even if I get the request in tomorrow, Mr Barrow, the department can do the usual thing and take three or four months to make a decision about whether to release any documents."

"Don't worry about that, Mr Reed. I'll be able to help out at this end."

"Anything else, Mr Barrow."

"All this is off the record, isn't it."

"Yes. I think I've said that three times."

"Good. As I have a private office, I have taped the call at this end to be sure."

Reed burst out laughing. "Thank you, Mr Barrow. And good day."

That's interesting, he thought. First an anonymous, complicated tip that leads to a ripping sex scandal and now a departmental insider even identifies himself to give me a tip about supposed money shenanigans by three MPs – and all of them Whitaker Government MPs. Some of the people in the halls of power must have decided that the Whitaker show was on the way out and decided to have some credit in the bank with the Opposition. But to be fair, he thought, he should throw a few Opposition MPs names in with the Whitaker three and see what happened. That afternoon he filed requests with the Finance Department for lists of the expenses claimed by Dalley, Garund and Leeson in the past year and for four MPs of the Opposition, though dubious that any information would come through before he finished working at parliament. That would not matter though, as, if there were any sizeable rip-offs of the taxpayer eventually revealed, it would make quite a good story – or feast of reports – in his new role of investigative reporter. To his astonishment, instead of the usual departmental queries about the request, followed by a 50-day delay, within two days he had documents delivered to him detailing a year's expense claims by Dalley and Leeson, with a note to say those of Garund would soon follow. Barrow was one slick operator, Reed thought. He must have had those documents in his drawer, ready to fire.

Starting to wade through the Dalley expense claims, he found the usual lunches at expensive capital-city hotels, light-plane flights to various towns in his sprawling electorate, hire of a community hall for information sessions for constituents, but then Reed came to a $350 payment to Rudimentary Services Pty Ltd with no explanation of the service. The line in the list had been underlined in red, presumably by Barrow. Reed went to the internet and typed in the name of the company. Up popped an advertisement offering nubile young women for physical dalliance at reasonable prices and promising no risk to your health. Bullseye! Reed thought, slapping the table with glee. The headline leaped into his head: Taxpayers pay for Dalleyance. He could hardly wait to tell Butler. Rudimentary. What a pun. It was certainly rude, all right. And he still had 50 or 60 Dalley claims to go. Leafing through them yielded three more payments to Rudimentary Services, all at the standard $350, well above the price that Reed imagined would be standard for a quick visit to a brothel. He rang Rudimentary's number listed on the website.

"I saw your website offering a bit of fun with girls and wondered what it costs."

"It depends what you desire, sir," said a honeyed female voice in reply.

"Well, how much, for instance, for a quickie."

"This is a very upmarket establishment. Sir. We don't do quickies, as you put it. But a standard service, with wine provided, is $200."

"And an upmarket service in your upmarket establishment?"

"The provision of two girls, champagne and a spa bath with them afterwards, sir, costs $350."

"It's a bargain. Thank you very much, ma'am," said Reed, hanging up, smiling. Barrow had underlined Dalley's Rudimentary listings in red, so he must have known the company ran brothels, Reed thought. Apart from salaries, all MPs were given electoral allowances for necessary work expenses, but that did not include banging away in a brothel.

He related the afternoon's work to Meg over dinner. "That sounds much more profitable than bank work. And spa baths thrown in. I might give it a go," she said, laughing and gathering up the dinner dishes.

Next day he began checking the expense papers of Garund, flipping through them quickly, just looking for any red underlinings. There were five, and in each case the sum was curiously large:

$3500, a total of $17,500. All were paid to Bayside Enterprises over the course of four months. A quick search of the phone book showed that Bayside Enterprises was a small firm that built new boats and repaired existing ones. Reed mulled over how to discover what Garund had spent the money on until an idea sprang into his head.

Driving to the yact firm, he approached the manager and asked was there any sort of yacht he could buy for $18,000 or $20,000.

"As a matter of fact, sir, we have a single-mast, 18-footer called the Bluewater which we can build for you for $17,500. It is our most popular product, actually."

"Do you have one in the yard at the moment?"

"Yes, we do. Come and have a look at it."

At the end of a pier the manager indicated a sleek white-hulled yacht bobbing gently. Reed took out a camera and the manager nodded that he could take a shot.

"How many of these do you sell in a year?" Reed asked.

"We build about eight or nine. They are regarded as something special here on the bay. The last one we finished was for an MP."

"Oh, who was that?" Reed asked.

"Sorry, sir. I think that should remain confidential. Business people, and I imagine MPs, can get quite snaky about their private affairs being made public."

"Yes, they can," Reed said smiling. "Well, thank you very much. I'll be in touch."

That night at home on his laptop he looked up Anthony Garund's web page, smiled at the list of 10 pledges, including one promising to campaign for open and accountable government, and noted the one thing he wanted: Garund's home address. It was no surprise that it turned out to be one of the most desirable in Apollo City – Langley's Inlet, a sheltered cove whose steep hillsides were dominated by mansions with steps leading down to individual piers – and yachts.

The next day Reed drove to Garund's listed address, 35 Kingsway Court, Langley's Inlet and was able to look down its sloping driveway to the water far below, and there, riding at anchor near the pier, was a shining white yacht. Reed drove back towards the city to a boat firm he knew that hired out small power boats, then cruised back to Langley's Inlet and took several shots of the boat at Garund's pier. On the stern was painted the name Bluewater and in smaller type underneath: Bayside Enterprises. Reed smiled. Mr Barrow's information was coming up trumps. Now there was only Martin Leeson to check out. That night at home, he leafed through Barrow's documents on Leeson and noted two red underlinings. Payments of $2000 and $2500 had been made out to the National Animal Aid Society whose main work involved offering some support to people who ran rescue shelters for lost dogs and cats. Reed's first reaction was that this was hardly an egregiously offensive use of taxpayer's money.

"What do you think of that, Meg?" he asked over dinner.

"Well, I love dogs, particularly Labradors which never give you any trouble. But I had a cat once that was absolutely obnoxious. It would miaow and miaow to be let out at night, then kill a pigeon or blackbird and leave it on the bedroom floor for my admiration when I woke up. And when did I wake up? At 5.30am when the blasted cat miaowed and miaowed by my bedside, wanting to be fed."

"Yes, darling, but what I was asking you was your opinion on whether it was appropriate for Leeson to be giving money to that society."

"Well, speaking now as a private enterprise banking official and a taxpayer ... hell, no. If taxpayers want to give money to the society they can send individual cheques. But it is their decision. That $4500 he gave had nothing to do with his work as an MP – except perhaps to curry favour with three or four constituents who might happen to work for the society and might spread the good word about Leeson. And even that would be indirect bribery ... Put him in the dock"

"Jawohl, mein fuhrer."

"Stop it! Don't you jawohl me. You asked for an opinion didn't you?"

"Yes, darling. My apologies. A forceful opinion it was. And you've supplied me with just the argument to use in my report."

Reed now waited for Barrow or the Finance Department to supply him with information on the expenses of the four Opposition MPs he had named. When the documents arrived, none of the items had red underlining, Reed spent hours sifting through them, without seeing any curious claims. He would have to go with reports that would look like a concerted attack on the Government, but perhaps the stories would trigger retaliation from that side. He suggested the Dalleyance headline to the sub-editors and they seized on it with delight.

"Boy, aren't we PUNishing the Government!" said the chief sub-editor – to groans from around the large oval desk. Reed's intuition that the reports would trigger a response was soon confirmed, but not in the way he expected. The first phone call that came was not from a Whitaker Government hack but from a member of the public.

"David Reed?"

"Yes, this is David Reed."

"Mr Reed, I've been reading your stories about rip-offs by Government MPs and I've got a ripper of a story for you – a rip-off actually - but it concerns the other side."

"Yes. Go ahead."

"Well, I work for Allstate Car Repairers."

"Yes. Can you tell me your name first."

"In a minute. See what I have to say, first. You've run these stories about MPs ripping off the taxpayer and I know of another case."

"Yes?"

"Yes, a woman came to us with a badly damaged car. She had scraped right along one side by going too close to a light pole. We told her it would cost at least $9000 to repair."

"And?"

"She went away and the next afternoon her husband came back and asked us if we would repair the car, but put on the invoice the registration number of HIS car – AVG310067, not the rego of his wife's car. I thought that was more than curious so later asked the boss who the guy was. He told me: Eric Finnsley."

Reed: "Finnsley, the Shadow Environment Minister? Are you sure?"

"Yes, and I realised the boss was right, because I had seen the guy on television going on about cars being one of the worst polluters and how they all needed to be smaller, there needed to be fewer of them and they should all be electric! Hilarious, isn't it?"

"After that, I made a note of the rego number that Finnsley asked us to put on the bill. Not only that, I made a fax copy of the invoice. Would you like it?"

"I sure would. Two questions: what was the make and colour of the wife's car which you ended up repairing and when was it done?"

"It was a light grey Volkswagen Supreme and we did it about three months ago."

Reed gave the repairer a fax number in his office at the *Gazette* then asked just once more: "Would you please tell me your name. I promise I don't need to use it in the story, but if there are any legal ramifications later I want to have your support."

"Well, I want to see this crook get his deserts, so my name is David Ransell. But you promise you won't name me in the paper? My boss might give me the chop. As it is, he's going to suspect all of us here."

"I promise, David – and thank you. If you'll just fax off that copy to me I'd be grateful and we can stitch up Mr Finnsley."

About two hours later, the invoice copy came in on Reed's fax and he noticed immediately that although it listed Finnsley's AVG registration number, it still had the repaired car listed as a Volkswagen Supreme. Reed knew that Finnsley's car, like all the Government cars, was a black Ford sedan as the Fords were bought under a special mass contract. He then rang Allstate Car Repairers and asked to speak to David Ransell.

"He can't talk at the moment. He's with a customer out in the car yard," said a woman who answered the phone. "Can I get him to call you?"

"No, It's OK," said Reed, now satisfied a David Ransell existed. "I'll call him later."

Despite the evidence of the invoice, Reed realised he had to use FOI again to prove that Finnsley had lodged a claim for the $9000. He rang the Department of Finance and asked to speak to Mr Greg Barrow.

"Can I say who is calling?" came the telephonist's routine.

"Just say it's a friend," Reed responded and when he got through to Barrow reassured him that he had not given his name to the telephonist. Barrow on hearing the details, agreed to intercept, if possible, the FOI request when it came and expedite a reply. Reed lodged the FOI immediately, calling for a list of Finnsley's expenses over the past six months. Two days later the details arrived and Reed laughed when he opened the envelope; normally FOI requests took at least 45 days. He whipped through the claims for accommodation, meals, fuel, home phone, electorate office expenses and then, there it was, a claim for $9000 for repairs to vehicle AVG310067. Attached was a cope of the original invoice and, astonishingly, neither the departmental expense boffins nor Finnsley apparently, had noticed that buried in the middle of the document were the details of the make of the car – a Volkswagen Supreme.

Reed went up to Butler's office, waving the documents. "Got a ripper here, Graham." When he outlined the story, Butler slammed a fist on his desk in satisfaction.

"Terrific, David. And don't forget to get into the piece the comment by the mechanic about Finnsley's rave against cars. I remember seeing that. Isn't it juicy?"

Reed got the impression that Butler was far more pleased to learn that an Opposition MP had been caught with a hand in the till rather than the original three Whitaker Government MPs that Reed had exposed. Butler was the Tories' Tory, he thought. At dinner that night Meg broached the subject of their having talked of marriage.

"At some stage we actually have to start making lists, David. You know ... what sort of ceremony, whom and how many we invite, the reception afterwards ... little things like that."

"Well, my darling, I think such matters are largely a woman's prerogative."

"Oh, rubbish, David. Let's start with the very first question: a full church service with organist, priest, choir and hymns or a civil celebrant in a local park?"

"Which would you prefer, my sweet?"

"It's not a matter of what I would prefer. I'm thinking of your devout Catholic parents as against my separated, atheistic, agnostic or totally apathetic parents. What would they all prefer?"

"Hmmm, yes. I imagine John and Dawn would be more at home in a church than in the park, but they do know we've been sleeping together for quite a while now. Maybe we could find a priest who would preside in the park?"

"Can we stop joking and sort out something definite? How would you feel about a full church service? I imagine quite a few of your friends would like it and my friends wouldn't be too fussed. We've never talked much about this, but do you still have any religious inclination?"

Reed stared out the window at the shrubs in the front yard dappled by dying sunlight. "The only time I think about life, death and any hereafter is when I look up at the stars at night. Scientists now say they can look back 13 or 14 billion years and are getting closer and closer to the time of the Big Bang – if there was a Big Bang. That makes you wonder: could the universe, or universes, with trillions of stars and planets have all materialised from one tiny spot? And did a God decide to trigger all that? And if so, was God in that tiny spot or outside it? And is God a he or a she? We've never been told. So, my darling I don't think I have any strong inclination."

"You sound like Richard Dawkins, David."

"No, my darling. Richard Dawkins says there is no God. I can't prove there is one. Nobody can. But Richard Dawkins likewise cannot prove there isn't one. The only sensible attitude, I believe, is that of the agnostics. So, like them I sit on the fence. And what do you believe, my sweet?"

"I like to think there's a god. I find it hard to believe the universe just happened – out of nothing. Or that it was always there, then suddenly decided to expand. Also, I like to think that there will be a paradise we go to when we die. That would be nice … to meet our parents and friends again and be with them forever."

"Some of our friends I'd rather not spend eternity with, Meg."

"Oh, stop it. Now let's get down to earth. Church or park?'

"No, Meg. You choose. I'd be happy with either."

"Well I know my parents won't care, and while your parents are understanding people, I think they would probably prefer that their little agnostic was married in church, so that's my choice."

"That's really decent of you, my darling."

"Right. Well now your darling is going to make up a list of at least 60 relatives and friends to invite to the reception and that leaves you with 60 of yours to invite. And I will leave you to book the church, find out if I have to become a temporary Catholic, book the reception centre for 120, check it has a dance floor and book a band so we'll have music to dance to."

"Is that all?"

"No. We have to settle the date and it has to be a Saturday, not a Sunday, and not a public holiday."

"And not footy Grand Final day."

"Correct, my darling David. Also, I will arrange my invitations, my bridesmaids and my bridal gown. For the invitations, I need you to settle the date as soon as possible."

"Oui, ma'amselle."

"That's much nicer than Jawohl, mein fuhrer. And now, ma'amselle is ready for bed. How about you?"

"Ready and eager my gorgeous one."

The next day was Reed's last at parliament and he turned on drinks for his friends among the other journalists there and a smattering of politicians from both major parties. Only two turned up from Whitaker's Government ranks. Reed surmised that others he invited did not want to be seen with the hack who had caused the Government so much heartache. An hour or so of sinking beers and scotches, then a chorus of "For He's a Jolly Good Fellow" but with substituted lyric "For He's a Jolly Good Wanker", then handshakes all around and that segment of his career came to an end.

At the office next day Butler eyed him curiously. "Do you still think life will be quieter as an investigative reporter?"

"Well, Graham, I asked for the change not because I want a dull life, but because the hours will be more reasonable now that I'm on the way to being a family man. So, have you anything interesting lined up for me yet?"

"As a matter of fact, I have. As you know, we now have quite a few Somalis in Apollo, refugees from the hell of their home country. And we've run a few reports of racial abuse of them – two attacks at rail stations, abuse in milk bars and in the street. Now I've had a letter from the Somali ambassador suggesting some of the attacks are organised, so I think there could be a good piece in looking into that."

"Does he say who he thinks is behind the attacks?"

"No, David, he doesn't. It will be up to you to find that out if it's the case."

Reed mulled over where to start, then asked the Police Department for a list of addresses of Somali victims of recent attacks.

"Can't give you that. Privacy laws," said the departmental officer. Reed explained why he needed the list. "Sorry, can't help," was the response. Reed shrugged, went back to the *Gazette* office and on his computer trawled through the files and was able to retrieve the names and suburbs of nine individual victims, most of whom had been attacked and robbed on suburban trains. He then marked on a city map crosses showing where they were attacked and their home addresses. As refugees in a strange land, the Somalis naturally had largely clustered in two northern suburbs so the crosses he marked were closely bunched. That gave him a good indication of where he should start interviewing people and hanging around rail stations to wait for possible action – a practice, it occurred to him, that perhaps the police should have been following.

In the street in Kellenpark near a rail station he approached an African carrying a briefcase. "Excuse me sir. I'm doing a report for the *Gazette*. Can I ask you: are you a Somalian?"

"No, I'm an Australian now," the black man shot back, smiling.

"Sorry. I get that. But I'm investigating attacks being carried out on Somalis. Have you experienced any physical aggression in your time here?"

"Only from my wife, man. She's really scary," he retorted, laughing, and waved Reed away. Reed decided first to confine himself to trying to interview the nine known victims of attack, a process that took him nearly three weeks to complete, because the newspaper reports of attacks on victims had listed only their suburbs and not street addresses. He had to approach any Somalis in streets in an area, tell them what he was doing, and ask if they knew the street address of any of the nine reported victims. Finally he had the addresses – some vague – of seven of the nine. After finally speaking with these seven he noticed a few common factors: robbery wasn't always the motive – some victims had been carrying mobile phones and money but were bashed yet not robbed – several of the attacking thugs arrived and escaped on big motorbikes and they mouthed racial abuse including "nig-nog", a local adaptation of "nigger". None of the victims had been able to give police a registration number of one of the motorbikes, but in all cases the attackers were white. Reed realised he was coming to the Somali ambassador's view that the bashings were the work of an organisation, possibly a bikie gang. He had noticed that some of the attacks were near train stations so decided to spend a few days just sitting in his car in the nearest main street to two of the stations.

Butler rang him: "Are you having any joy on that story? Otherwise you had better pack it in and look for something with a bit more meat."

"I'd like a few more days, Graham. I know it's been slow going, but this will be a cracker story if I can break it."

"OK. Take a bit longer and then we'll size it all up."

In late afternoon on the Thursday, two Somali students with backpacks of books got off a train and came into the street where Reed was parked a couple of hundred metres away with his driver-side window down. Around the corner roared two Harley-Davidson bikes, all gleaming chrome and thunderous exhausts, with jeering mid-thirties male riders to match. They slowed almost to a stop near the two students, reached into black saddlebags and, producing spray cans of paint, daubed the students from head to waist in white paint

"Only whiteys in Apollo!" the bikies bellowed. "Only whiteys!" then gunned their bikes. Reed grabbed for the camera he had left on the seat beside him, but the racist pair roared off. He just had time to catch one number plate – BOGAN23. Why would the rider identify himself as bogan – that is, a person of no class – Reed wondered. Then he realised. Of course. It was a triumphant declaration of disdain for the more civilised slice of society. But for Reed it was a valuable clue. His next stop would be the Motor Registration Office to try to persuade some official to give him the addresses of anyone with a BOGAN motorcycle number plate. The portly bureaucrat behind the front counter listened to his explanation but gave him a stern brush-off.

"You may have the best of intentions, Mr Reed, but we are bound by privacy laws. Sorry about that." Reed turned and made for the door.

"Mr Reed!" Reed turned and went back to the bureaucrat.

"If you report that I helped you, I'll deny it flatly. But here's a suggestion. If you go to the police in the area you just might find a cop prepared to help you. They have the power to look up registration details on their computers."

"Thank you, sir," said Reed, offering a friendly salute. He realised as he left that he should have thought of that avenue in the first place and for a brief while bureaucrats went up in his estimation. At the Winston police station the young constable on desk duty was sympathetic.

"The Bogans. Oh yes, we know them. There are 20 or 30 of them. Some only kids of 18 or so. They've got a club down by the river, but I think they're pretty harmless. Have you got any evidence that they have been wog-bashing?"

Reed mentally winced at police use of the word "wog" but related the incident of the paint daubing he had seen.

"Just sounds like a prank to me, mate. Did they attack the two or just drive off?"

"A prank? I'd hardly call it a prank, officer, when the students' clothes were ruined. It was a racist attack. How would you like your kids to come home from school covered in paint?"

"I don't have any kids, mate, and if I did it's none of your business. Do you want to sign a statement and have us try to prosecute the bikie you saw? Can you provide the names of the students? No. And No. I see. Well there's not much more to be done here is there?"

Reed was going to explain that he wanted a bigger story than just one act of paint-throwing, but could see he was not gaining any sympathy so asked for the address of the Bogans' club, which the officer, while shaking his head in silent derision, did give, adding, "I suppose you'd soon find it anyway. Try to keep out of trouble, OK?"

Reed drove to the river, pulling up near the club, a fortress with high, black steel walls and gateway adorned with a caricature of a devil. He mulled what to do next and decided the only course of action was to spend time following individual Bogans when they left the fort. It was two days later, on a Saturday, before there was any sign of action. Individual Bogans rolled up and were let in through the great steel gate and at about four in the afternoon, 15 or 20 of them roared out in a cavalcade and took over the riverside highway in an intimidating phalanx, led by a beefy figure whose handlebars carried a small flag with the letters SAJ. Sergeant-at-arms, Reed assumed, and found it amusing that these toughs had abrogated the title of the figure responsible for security at parliament, a figure whose origins dated back to 14th century England.

At a major intersection the gang blatantly rolled through red lights, three of them giving the finger to one motorist who dared to blast his horn in protest. The group cruised into the parking lot of a riverside pub and flowed into the main bar, Reed following. Normally such a bar would be crowded and noisy on a Saturday afternoon, but now as the group commandeered stools and tables, the other drinkers became silent and watchful. Reed bought a scotch and soda and sat where he could observe the Bogans while pretending to be reading a paper from the shelf behind him.

When a barely-dressed young woman came on screen on the large TV set at one end of the bar hoots and drumming of beer pots on the bar went up from the Bogans, but Reed noticed that one young member of the gang did not join in. In fact, although he was wearing the regulation Bogan gear he appeared to be drinking by himself, which Reed thought quite odd. About half an hour later one of the roisterers play fully punched the youngster in the shoulder and handed him a beer, but the about-25 -year-old did not respond with a grin but just took the beer. Reed wondered whether for some reason the greenhorn was on the outer, and decided to wait and try to follow him home. Three drunken hours later the gang began to break up so Reed headed for the car park, saw the younger Bogan come out and trailed behind him and nine other gang members as they headed south-west towards their fort. But after about 10 minutes the youngster waved to his companions and peeled off into the suburb of Linfield where he pulled up at a rundown single-front weatherboard house, leaving his motorbike – *not* a Harley, Reed noticed, but a much humbler make – on the street. Reed thought that odd and decided to sit and watch for a while.

To his surprise, the youngster emerged within minutes no longer a Bogan, no longer in the devil-adorned black leather jacket and now carrying a blue helmet also denuded of any devil. As Reed, at the end of the street, gunned the motor to follow, he rang Meg to say he might be late for dinner. "Quelle surprise!" she said sardonically, then laughed. The part-time Bogan rode only about eight blocks, pulled up at a much more impressive house, went up and rang the front doorbell. A young woman answered, gave him a hug, came out, hopped on the motorbike with him and they set off. Reed couldn't believe his luck: the girlfriend of this "save-the-world-for-the-whites" Bogan had black hair with a magnificent sheen, black shiny eyes, firm prominent breasts and … he could hardly believe it … beautiful *olive* skin. She was probably Asian, perhaps African. A Bogan gal she was not.

There's no doubt about the power of sex, Reed though and he smiled as he followed them for about six kilometres until they stopped at a café, then he went home. Tomorrow being a Sunday would be the time to have a chat with Mr Half-Bogan when he might get a chance to catch him on his own. And he did. Meg wasn't exactly thrilled that journalism was wiping out any chance of a weekend together, but as he left at 8am he promised her a dinner at C'est Magnifique, Apollo's best French restaurant. Back at Half-Bogan's single-fronted house he waited, listening to classical music on the car radio and just before 10am the quarry emerged on his motorbike, but again without devilish regalia. Reed followed him for two blocks then pulled alongside, beeped the car horn and indicated to the young man to pull over, which he did, probably thinking Reed a plainclothes cop.

"Thanks for stopping, mate." Reed said. "I'm not a policeman. Just a journalist. But I'd like to talk with you about an important matter."

"Like what?"

"My name is David Reed. Would you like to tell me yours?"

"It's Henry."

"Just Henry?"

"Yes. For now, it's just Henry. What do you want?"

"Henry, I was in the pub the other night when you were there with the Bogans and you didn't seem to be joining in very much."

"So?"

"So now I happen to know that you also have a girlfriend who is … how shall I put it? … not exactly a Snow White. I don't think the Bogans would like that, do you?"

"You are a real snoop aren't you?"

"Yes, Henry. That's my job. But the way the Bogans treat people of colour is becoming a serious public issue and I think you could help me to bust the whole thing wide open."

"What? And get myself maimed for life?"

"We would arrange to see you are well protected until the whole thing is over."

"You and what army?"

"The Apollo police force."

"Look, Mr Reed, I have been thinking of getting out of the Bogans. I joined them a couple of years ago for the fun of mass motorbike rides. But you don't understand. They don't like people to just walk away. You have to have a good reason, like moving interstate for instance.

"My paper could arrange that for both you and your girlfriend if you were willing to help."

The youth looked warily up and down the street but it was deserted. "Just suppose I agree. What do I have to do?"

"Have you actually witnessed any attacks by the gang on African or Asian migrants?"

"Yeah. I was in a group on the way to the pub one evening when the leader saw two blacks walking up to Werrigal train station. Four of the guys actually rode their bikes up onto the footpath and formed a square around the two so they couldn't move. Then five others got off their bikes, they all shouted abuse at the blacks, knocked them to the ground, took a laptop one was carrying, laughed, got back on the bikes and rode off."

"Do you remember the names of the four?"

"Of course I do."

"And the other five?"

"I think so."

"Well, Henry ... by the way can I now know your second name?"

"It's Addison."

"Well, Henry, if you were prepared to go to court and tell that story just as you have told me, we could wipe out the Bogans, you would have done a remarkable, honourable thing and you and your girlfriend could get on with your lives. What about it?"

"I'll think about it. It's a bit scary. And I'd have to ask Adisa. I can't just throw her into such a scheme without even asking her – and her parents."

For a moment Reed considered offering the prospect that the paper might even offer finance for the young couple to re-locate, but realised that if that became public, in court it could be depicted as a bribe to persuade Addison to give evidence. Anyway, such a proposal would probably have Butler hitting the roof, so it would have to wait. He gave Addison his office phone number and persuaded him in turn to give his home phone number. Reed promised to be in touch but in fact was surprised the next morning at the office to get a call from Addison: "I've talked with my parents and with Adisa. They don't like the idea at all, but she does. They think I'd be crazy, but she thinks it would be good for race relations in Apollo. And not only that, she particularly likes the idea of me getting out of the gang and us going off to live together. So there you are."

"I agree with her, Henry. It would be good to break up a bunch of racists."

Addison agreed to come into the *Gazette* office the next day after work and there Reed taped a long interview about the attack that Addison witnessed and evidence of other attacks he had heard about and racist comments of the sergeant-at-arms. Reed took the tape to police headquarters and asked to speak with a deputy commissioner. He did not want to risk dealing with someone from the lower ranks like the dismissive cop at the Winston police station. The deputy he spoke with listened to the tape, asked if Addison were prepared to go to court and promised Reed that the young couple would get full protection. When Reed reported all this to Butler, the news editor held up one thumb and winked, his silent way of offering congratulations.

The trial of the nine Bogan attackers lasted for three weeks, the nine were all found guilty and each sentenced to four months' prison. Even the sergeant-at-arms was fined $10,000 for incitement to racist violence and got six months' prison. Henry Addison and Adisa were given elaborate protection and the *Gazette* revelled in Reed's reporting of the case, running a picture of him every day with his byline. In retrospect, that turned out to be a mistake. The paper's report of the guilty verdicts and sentences carried the booming headline "BOGANS GO DOWN", again with Reed's small photo next to the headline. As he left the *Gazette* office that afternoon, two heavily-built men approached.

"David Reed?"

"That's right."

Reed saw a large clenched fist coming at him and that was the last thing he remembered until he came to with a traffic warden pumping his chest with both hands and saying, "Hang in there, mate. There's an ambulance on the way. The bastards were kicking you on the ground until I hit one of them with my traffic sign and they buggered off."

As the ambulance took him to hospital, Reed thought: "Christ, this town is even more dangerous than Keralia." But he took satisfaction in knowing that although his attackers were probably another couple of Bogans, the Whitaker Government had announced that morning a ban on any bikie fortresses throughout the state. There would be no more racism indoctrination, well, not by Bogan sergeants-at-arms anyway.

Butler came to see him in hospital. "What's the damage mate?"

"Apparently they kicked in three of my ribs, but the docs say I'll be all right and be out of here in a couple of days' time." Reed was actually astonished that Butler would take the time to come to hospital to see him, but refrained from saying so.

"Well, it was another great story, David, but I thought you said you wanted a quiet life."

Reed was determined that was not going to be the last word. "I'm getting married next month, Graham, so there goes any prospect of a quiet life." He rang the bedside bell to summon a nurse.

CHAPTER 6

With his ribs strapped, Reed soon was able to leave hospital, the only temporary drawback being that whenever he laughed, he felt a stab of pain. "No jokes for a week or so, please Meg," he said when finally propped up in bed at home. He had been able to give the police a brief description of the thug who had asked his identity, but there was no word of any imminent arrest. The medics had told him he could be back on his feet within a fortnight. So from his bed he booked the local Catholic church and priest for a wedding in the middle of the following month, a reception at the Apollo Plaza Tower Restaurant overlooking the city and the bay, booked a band and MC and checked these details with his mother Dawn. A local printer was able to produce invitation cards within three days, taking the details over the phone, and with some relief Reed handed 60 of the cards to Meg and began the tedious business of sending out his share, ringing friends to find out whether they could come and getting their home addresses. After signing 21 cards he could not think of anyone else he wanted or needed to invite.

"Forty-two of my friends will go through barrels of booze anyway," he told Meg. "I'll still be paying for this wedding at Christmas time. But you're worth it, darling, every cent," he added quickly.

"David. Could I just remind you that I'll be paying half of the bill?"

"I don't think you should do that."

"Don't be absurd, David. Sometimes you are an old trog with master-of-the-cave ideas. It's my wedding, too, and I'm paying my share."

"Oui, madame."

The wedding went off superbly and even Meg's irritable father Bruce seemed to enjoy himself – at least not getting into loud disagreement with anyone, which David had half expected. He and Meg had decided to wait until the northern hemisphere summer to have an extended holiday, so the honeymoon consisted of one memorable night at the Plaza Tower in a luxury suite.

"Mmmm … that was delicious," Meg said as he slowly withdrew.

He kissed her breasts softly. "Would you like some more?"

"Are you up to it? How are your ribs? Are they hurting?

"No, my darling. They're fine."

"Anchors aweigh then!

"The main mast is all set, me hearty."

"Oh, David. Full sail ahead!"

Later as she lay entwined in his arms and legs she asked: "When I have this baby, you realise I'll have to give up work for some time?"

"Of course, I do. Why do you raise that?"

"Well, after a certain time, we won't have my salary coming in."

"Of course we won't. But I think on my salary now we can afford for you to get on with the family business – and have two kids if you wish."

"There's no immediate worry about expense. Under the new

industrial agreement the banks have signed up to, I get a year's paid parental leave."

"True. But I'll bet that means all our bank fees will go up."

"David! Don't be such a scrooge! Come on, get up. Time for breakfast. I'm hungry after all that bed activity."

Three weeks later, the wedding over, news editor Butler couldn't suppress a scowl at first, when Reed said he needed two weeks off, then grudgingly wished him a happy honeymoon. Three days later David and Meg were sitting in the afternoon sunshine on Piazza San Marco, sipping chianti and looking across the bay at stunning San Giorgio Maggiore.

"Mmm...I could stay here for a year," Meg murmured.

"I think you might get bored with pizza."

"Oh David, if I were not madly in love with you and on honeymoon, I'd say 'Don't be so banal.'"

"Sorry about that. In recompense, can I offer you a ride in a taxi?"

Slipping down the Rio di Palazzo in the gondola, they came to the Bridge of Sighs.

"It's 400 years old, Meg, and still standing," David said.

"Yes, David, I can see that."

"Know why it's called the Bridge of Sighs?"

"Didn't criminals cross it to be executed?"

"No, Lord Byron made that up. In reality, crims did cross it from their cells to face a grilling, but not necessarily death."

"How do you know all this?"

"I looked it up before we left."

"Clever boy."

"Thank you, my darling."

"David, what about we turn about and find a restaurant. I'm getting hungry. I'd just love a plate of stracciatella alla romana."

"Romana what?"

"You mean you didn't look up Italian food before we left?"

"OK, stop teasing."

"It's eggs, parsley, parmigiano-reggiano cheese (parmesan to you) nutmeg and butter in a beautiful sea of chicken stock."

"And after that?"

"Why, panna-cotta of course, with superb strawberries on top."

"Now you're making me hungry. You're so lovely I could eat you."

"You can lick me later."

"Promise?"

"Promise."

Lying back in bed that night, sated and smiling, he looked across at her and said: " I feel as lucky as Hylas."

"Hylas?"

"Yes, Meg, Hylas. He was a friend of Hercules."

"Mmm, so what was lucky about being a friend of Hercules."

"Oh , no, he just got lucky because one day he was beside a river and five naked nymphs dragged him into a pond and raped him. How lucky can you be?"

"Is that a recurring fantasy of yours?"

"No, Meg. You are my recurring fantasy."

"That's more like it. Now roll over and go to sleep."

"Yes, commander."

The remaining holidays flew, their only contact with the troubles of the world a riffle each day through the pages of the International Herald Tribune. The lovemaking was entrancing, but at the end of the second week, Reed was ready to go home, itching to know what the latest news was in Apollo City. He realised then that journalism was an addiction.

Out in the suburb of Paradisia where Meg's truculent father Bruce Mann lived, it was anything but paradise that day. A group of young car hoons had decided to take up burn-offs in his street. Bruce came out yelling and wielding a garden scythe which was a quite inadequate weapon against swerving sedans. When he realised this, he went back inside to jeers but emerged with a plastic box of large nails and scattered them across the road in front of his place.

"Try that, you mugs!" he yelled at them. The youths left their cars at the top of the street, advanced towards him, but stopped about 10 metres away and began taunting him: "Silly old bugger. Where's your nurse?", circling fingers beside their temples to indicate insanity and making masturbation motions. One unzipped his trousers and pulled out his penis so Bruce was in no doubt about the "wanker" insult. Being Bruce, he responded in kind, undoing his belt, pulling down trousers and underpants and "mooning" the group. This hilarious but provocative moment was interrupted suddenly by the loud wail of a police siren as a cop car roared into the street, responding to the phone alert of a neighbour who had witnessed the whole charade. The youths ran to their cars, jumped in and fled leaving the police to deal with one angry, semi-naked Bruce.

"What the hell do you think you are doing?" a sergeant said as he stepped from the police car. Bruce tried to explain.

"We didn't see anyone roaring up and down in cars," the sergeant said to one of his companions. "All we saw was one elderly man with his penis hanging out in public, didn't we?"

"That's right, sarge," said the second officer.

"Well I think we're going to have to charge him with public indecency, aren't we?"

"That's right, sarge."

"You fucking coppers are all the same. Can't see the hoons when they're right in front of you, complete with rubber marks on the road. What a joke."

"Did you hear that, Constable? This miscreant also used offensive language. I think we'll have to charge him with that also."

"Quite right, Sergeant."

"Right, Mr Public Exposure, get into our patrol car. We're off to the station to charge you."

Reed almost burst into laughter when Meg rang him to relate the drama, saying that she would have to put up a bond to get bail for her father. Then he cautioned her: "Let's get him out on bail, Meg, then try to keep it all quiet. Tell him if he tells nobody, we'll keep mum, too. When the case comes up it'll be in a suburban court and probably not be noticed. But if there's any gossip in advance I can well imagine seeing in the opposition press the headline "*Gazette* man's dad-in-law moons police in public".

"Is that all you are worried about, your reputation?" asked Meg. "What if he goes to jail?"

"Frankly, darling, it might be about time he had a spell there instead of fighting with the rest of the world."

"That's really unfair, David. I know he can be something of a bore, but he had a right to protest about kids roaring up and down his street. That's quite dangerous, for one thing."

"Ok. I agree you're right about that. Let's just organise bail for him and hope it all goes quietly away later on."

"Thank you. By the way, darling, I don't think you're so famous that that headline you imagined would make Page 1 anyway."

"Ouch."

They both laughed and arranged to go out to dinner that night, but over chicken breasts and guacamole at a nearby restaurant, Meg had a change of heart.

"David, as I said, Bruce is a bit of an old bore, but he is my father and I wonder if you could give him some help. Talk to him about taking life easy at his stage."

"Me! Help Bruce! Darling, how could I possible do that? I couldn't imagine getting in five words every 10 minutes. And how could I help him even if he did listen for that long?"

"David, yes, he is a bit cranky, and a lot older than you, but you're better educated, you've been around the world, had lots of experience. Please give it a try."

Reed chewed at hairs on the back of a hand, plucking them out one by one with his teeth, a curious habit he developed when under stress. She pulled his hand away.

"All right, Meg. He's an old idiot and I don't know what on earth I'll be able to say to him, but just for you I'll give it a go."

Meg put up the $500 bail money for her father that afternoon, having phoned in sick to her bank. And after dinner David headed out to Paradisia, mulling as he drove what on earth he could say to the old grump that could possibly be useful.

He was a journalist, not a bloody psychologist. At Bruce's door he pressed the bell and when it was jerked open, stepped back in alarm when confronted by Bruce wielding a cricket bat.

"Oh, it's you. I thought it might be those bloody kids out to annoy me again. Come on in, David. Would you like a beer?" Mann added, indicating that Reed take a sofa seat in the front living room.

"Meg asked me to come and see you," Reed said, adopting an apologetic tone.

"Yeah. I don't know what she's worried about. I'm in a bit of shit, but I can look after myself."

"Are you going to hire a lawyer, Bruce?"

"Nah. It's all straight-forward. I don't need a mouthpiece."

"Offensive behaviour to police can cop you a sizeable fine, Bruce."

"That's if I'm found guilty, mate. As I said, it's all straight-forward. I didn't bare my bum at the cops. I didn't even know they were there. I was ridiculing those hoons in cars."

"But according to the police you swore at them and insulted them."

"Jeez, David. It's a sad day if the cops get all upset at hearing the f-word. The poor little petals."

"Bruce, I hope you won't take that attitude to court with you. You need to be particularly polite to the prosecutor and accept everything the magistrate says. Otherwise you might even find yourself in the slammer for a month or two."

"Wouldn't worry me unduly, mate. Couldn't be much worse than living in Paradisia. Par-a-dis-ia. Huh. I wonder who the local council moron was that gave this dump its name. It oughta be called Helluvahole. If I had any real money, I'd be out of here like a rocket."

David sucked on his beer stubby, reflecting that this, as he expected, had been a wasted journey. But at least he had done as Meg wished. He finished the beer, got up, shook hands, and headed to the door.

"Good luck, Bruce. Thanks for the beer." Driving away, he puzzled that such an apparent drongo could produce a charming, intelligent, well-educated daughter as Meg. Her mother must have been the power in the family, he decided. And he hoped that his marriage would last longer than had those of Bruce and his father Jim.

One of Reed's regular pleasures when in Apollo was lunch at the male-only Apollo Men's Club, at the up-market end of the city's main thoroughfare. You had to have a university degree to be eligible for membership – and you had to be voted in by a majority of the membership after being nominated by at least two members. The chief financial officer at the *Gazette* was a member and had agreed to nominate Reed and persuade another club member also to agree to the nomination. Reed heard later that in the full membership vote he scraped in with a very narrow majority. The Club was quite suspicious of media types. One well-meaning but perhaps narrow-minded minister in the Whitaker Government had moved to force the club to take in women members on the ground of equality, but retreated under heavy fire when it was pointed out that the city's three women-only clubs would then be forced to take in males. The AM Club, as it became known, was also famous for having in its gardens the city's oldest and largest tree, a magnificent monster. About a year after Reed joined the club the tree was found to be dying. Experts were called in to determine if anything could be done to safe it. After examining it for some time, the experts came up with the solution: it needed watering. Reed wanted to give a light-hearted short report to a *Gazette* columnist, but thought he should check first with AM Club officials. They referred the matter to a committee and the answer there was no. For the first time in his career, Reed was censored. He had to laugh.

It was through the club that he picked up his next significant assignment. Leaning back in one of the club's fine leather chairs, legs outstretched, he was reading a copy of the *Gazette* when he overheard two club members talking in chairs behind him.

"It was quite hairy for a while. Three Aradale residents were giving us the shits, threatening to go to the local council about stuff we were putting in a disused quarry near them, but we bought them off," said the grey-haired one.

"Why did you have to do that?" asked the other.

"Well we wouldn't want a damned court case, would we? Much easier to throw them a few thousand dollars."

"What was the stuff being dumped in the quarry?"

"Just a chemical used in the manufacture of polymers and some drugs."

"Why did the residents care about that? What was the chemical?"

"Hydrogen cyanide, but we reckoned it was quite safe once covered with soil."

"I thought cyanide was fairly dangerous."

"Well nobody's died yet." Joint laughter.

Reed also thought cyanide could be quite dangerous and wrote the words hydrogen cyanide on part of the newspaper he was reading, tore off that part and pocketed it as a reminder to check.

He walked over to the barman, pointed at the club member who said his company was burying the drug and said: "Albert, I just forget the name of that member sitting on the left. Can you remind me?"

"It's George Redwood. From Belport Chemicals I think. You should know him, he's on the club committee."

"Oh, that's right, of course. Thanks Albert."

A Wikipedia check at home on Reed's laptop gave him full details on hydrogen cyanide. Highly poisonous, a concentration of it in the air could kill a human in 10 minutes. It was even used by Nazi Germany to kill prisoners in extermination camps and is still used in gas chamber executions in some states in the US. Reed could hardly believe his luck – eavesdropping onto a first-rate story, but on reflection realised publication would damage the reputation of the Club and perhaps even jeopardise his membership. Well tough luck, he thought. He had a duty to save people from possible injury or even death. And he could live with not being a member of the club. Next day he rang Aradale council and asked the whereabouts of a disused quarry in the suburb.

"You can't dump anything there," said a council clerk. "It's no longer used."

"I realise that," said Reed., "but I think someone has been secretly using it and I want to check."

The clerk gave him directions. That evening, when he knew residents would be home from work he began visiting houses surrounding the quarry, asking owners if they had been aware of any dangerous chemicals being dumped in the quarry.

At several houses, people just shook their heads in puzzlement, asking what he knew. Reed did not want to alarm them at this stage so just shrugged and moved on. But then at one house, the male at the front door glared at him, said "Piss off. Mind your own business," and slammed the door in his face. He kept moving down the street and eventually encountered two other uncomfortable denials that left him thinking Redwood's boast had been true. He was wondering whether he would have to have the paper engage a chemicals specialist to dig in the quarry when a flush-faced woman came hurrying towards him.

"Are you the reporter who spoke to my husband about the quarry?"

"Yes, I have been asking people about it."

"I'm sorry he was so rude to you. I've just had a big argument with him. You see, you are right. There was a nasty chemical being dumped in the quarry about two years ago and some of us complained to the company. But we were paid off by them. I felt really bad about it at the time, considering we have young kids, and I wanted to go to the council but my husband wouldn't listen. He wanted the money instead."

Reed got out his pocket tape recorder. "Do you mind if I get your name and tape your story so I have evidence? Then I can write it up and we can force the company to do a big clean-up – and your husband can still keep the money." The woman agreed, giving her name and running through the detail again.

Reed: "How did you know in the first place that it could be a dangerous chemical?"

"When the big truck first started coming, my husband went up to the driver and asked what he was dumping because the quarry was supposed to be closed. The driver said he thought his company had got permission, and although the loads included a pretty dicey chemical, it would be all right as it was being covered by soil. Jerry, my husband, asked him what the dicey chemical was and he said it was a form of cyanide. Jerry got angry at that and asked the driver for the name of the company doing the dumping. He then talked to a couple of our neighbours and they arranged to go and see the company. The next thing a fellow from the company turned up at our place with two thousand dollars in cash for Jerry. Two thousand dollars. I said to Jerry, does that make it worth risking the health of us and our kids? He got really angry and told me to shut up ... oh, please don't put that bit in the paper."

Reed: "I promise I won't."

He then approached the company's public relations manager, but was handballed to another PR firm in the city which promised to get back to him, but did not. Reed waited 24 hours then rang the PR company again but again got a brush-off. He decided to run with the story, including the refusal to comment at the end. The story didn't make Page 1 of the *Gazette* but got the splash across the top of Page 3: "COMPANY BUYS SILENCE ON POISON DUMP". And it listed the company's six directors. The same afternoon a Whitaker minister jumped onto radio to lambast the directors, but within 48 hours Reed, the minister and Darryl Sheridan, the *Gazette*'s editor-in-chief were in for a nasty shock.

It came in the form of emails to all three that the six directors were taking joint action for defamation in that they had in no way been responsible for any dumping of dangerous material. News editor Butler summoned Reed to his office, stubbed out his large cigar and threw a printout of the email on the desk in front of Reed.

"What the hell do you make of this? That story was watertight, wasn't it?"

"I think so, Graham. Our company lawyer looked at it before we went to press. I can produce a witness to the bribery and we might be able to find the truck driver who did the dumping. What we have to do first is hire a chemical analyst to dig into that quarry site and provide evidence that there is cyanide there."

"Might have been an idea to do that before running the story, David. We'd better hope there is poison there or the paper will be up for about six million dollars."

The *Gazette*'s lawyers were ordered to organise the chemical check and within a week there was good news: yes, the site was seriously contaminated. Two days later writs served on the *Gazette* by the six directors stated that they had never sanctioned any cyanide dumping at the site and in fact knew nothing about it until reading of the allegations in the paper. The *Gazette* ran a small item on Page 17 noting that the directors denied any involvement and had issued writs.

"It's not like you to just be poking at the lamb chops instead of gulping them down? Are you worried about that poison case, darling?" Meg asked at dinner.

"Don't know at this stage, Meg. It turns out bloody George Redwood is no longer with the company so it's possible he organised the dumping, not the present directors. If so, we're in deep doodoo."

Reed realised he had to act to get the paper off the hook. After discussion with the *Gazette*'s lawyers, he went back to the home of resident Harry Dalray whose wife had admitted to taking a bribe.

"What the fuck do YOU want?" snarled Dalray when Reed knocked and identified himself.

"Harry, you were originally really pissed off about the cyanide?

Are you happy for the company that did it to get away with it and not only that, but make a pile of money out of our paper when we did the right thing and exposed it?"

Dalray glowered at him, but, after a long pause, said: "What do you want now?"

"Will you tell me exactly who it was gave you the two thousand dollars? And was it a cheque, or cash?"

"It was a guy called Redwood. And it was cash."

"One other question: do you happen to remember the name of the trucking company that was dumping the chemicals?" "Yes. I'll never forget because, given what they were doing, it was a sick, sick joke. The name on the trucks was Cleanup."

"Would you be prepared to go to court and say so, to see the chemical company get what it deserves?"

"I'll think about it." With that, Dalray shut the door in Reed's face.

Cleanup had a large depot in an eastern suburb. Reed realised that if he wanted to interview several of its drivers, the only logical path was to approach the Transport Employees Union, explain the whole issue to the union secretary and persuade him to advise the drivers to talk to him. That worked and as each truck left the depot, Reed, waiting outside the gate for a quick chat, soon found a driver who admitted to having been involved in the quarry dumping. Now he had the ammunition he needed to approach John Reilly, the manager of Cleanup.

"Ah, Mr Reed. I read your original article in the *Gazette* and now you're being sued. I figured you might show up here sometime. Now what do you want?"

"Look I know you are not responsible for what Belport Chemicals did if they told you the chemicals would be made safe at the quarry. But whom did you deal with at Belport? Was it George Redwood?"

"Yes it was. Why?"

"Did you deal with anyone apart from Redwood?"

"Yes, after Redwood left Belport, the company's managing director Greg Hedley sent us trucking orders and organised our payments. That went on until about three months ago, but then we stopped getting orders. Hedley thought the quarry site wasn't a good idea."

"You say this is all off the record, Mr Reilly, but if you were prepared to tell all this in court, it would leave your company looking blameless. Think about that."

"I'll think about it."

Reed reported back to Butler who called in the company's lawyers.

"Well, Mr Reed," chortled the legal team leader, "I think you may have found the sauce to save your bacon." The legal three laughed. Even Butler smiled. But because of the backlog in the state's courts, Reed endured three months of tension, waiting for the defamation trial to come on. When it did, the six directors gave evidence that they were distraught to be accused of corruption, particularly when the issue involved public safety. But then the defence brought on John Reilly, manager of the trucking firm Cleanup with his evidence that Belport's managing director had known about the dumping long after George Redwood had left the company.

"Should not the directors of Belport have known that their managing director Hedley was involved in this activity after Mr Redwood left, even if Mr Hedley did put a stop eventually to the activity?" asked the judge. "Isn't it the role of company directors to keep abreast of what their executives are doing?"

And with that question, Reed knew that he was home safe. The counsel for the six directors went into a long repetition of his claims but the fire and indignation had gone from his delivery. He knew his case had been cooked.

"Meg! We've won!" Reed bellowed into his mobile. "I'm off to a celebration in the board dining room with the execs, but on your way home from the bank buy yourself a fine new dress. You and I are going to celebrate at the best restaurant in town."

At the celebratory drinks with *Gazette* executives in the board dining room, Reed was toasted by editor-in-chief Sheridan, but News Editor Butler had the last, sour word: "You were bloody lucky, Reed. If that resident Dalray hadn't spilled the beans, if the union hadn't helped you, and then the trucking company we'd have been six million dollars into the shit. And I think we'd have been looking for another special investigative reporter."

"Well, Graham, going on what that judge said about senior executives being responsible for what goes on underneath them, perhaps we've all been lucky." Editor-in-chief Sheridan, standing near the pair, roared with laughter. Reed bowed to Butler, moved away, and soon the function broke up. Dinner with Meg was a delight and so was bed that night, but three days later came an unpleasant surprise: the Apollo Men's Club notified him by letter that a hearing of the club's committee had decided to revoke his membership on the ground that he had injured the club's reputation with his accusations against George Redwood. Reed had to laugh at the brazen absurdity of the decision: Redwood, of course, was still a member of the committee and would have organised the expulsion vote.

Reed sent a letter in reply: "Dear Sirs, I would not want to be a member of a club which retained Mr Redwood as a member after what has been proved against him, and definitely not a member of a club which would allow such a miscreant to organise a vote to expel a decent member."

He then gave copies of the club's notification, and his response, to the *Gazette*'s social gossip columnist Deborah West who, being a strong feminist, filled a third of her column with savage delight. After work next day, Reed went with several colleagues to the nearby pub for a few relaxing beers where conversation turned again to the future of journalism.

"I suppose it'll survive in some form," said foreign editor Bruce Temple, wiping a moustache of beer foam from his face.

"That's pretty pessimistic, mate," Reed retorted. "When we switch across fully to e-readers, the industry will save a fortune. Just think: no pine forests to grow, no factories needed to pulp them into paper, no huge printing plants needed, no need to truck the papers to newsagents who take their cut – and take extra to deliver to millions of houses. We're talking billions of dollars, Bruce."

"Yes, I know that, David. And I know the big proprietors have already moved into electronic delivery and put up pay walls. But I'm talking about the human side of the industry, the journalists, your job, mate."

"How so? People are always going to want news, news dug up that somebody doesn't want made public."

"I think you might be overestimating the public's view of the public need-to-know, David. Remember when we had reading rooms in newspaper offices. Experienced, knowledgeable former librarians used to check every word on a proof of every page of the paper before it went to press. They couldn't just spell, they knew when any prime minister first took office and the year he was booted out. If they doubted any fact in a story they knew where to check it. And what happened? Just to save money, when computers replaced typewriters in news offices, the owners sacked those readers. Sacked the lot. Reporters were supposed to rely on spellcheck – and that was useless if the reporters had constructed ungrammatical sentences. Today in any newspaper you can find misspellings, laughable ones. Kids come to newspapers to be cadets and they can't spell! Did you see in today's *Gazette* that some union officials were "grabbling" with the problem of declining memberships. Grabbling? Not grappling?"

"I don't think, Bruce, that a few misspellings will stop the public from wanting to know what's going on in the world."

"You don't get it, David. When everybody has an e-reader, it's your job that will be at stake. Electronic devices love pictures, particularly video. And with a fingertip, the users can zip from item to item. There won't be room for your investigative pieces taking up two full newspaper pages. Young people are even crunching the English language into txt. U no – lifes gr8." Temple drew the image of that last sentence in the air with a finger to make his point.

"Not only that, David, with e-readers, people won't rely just on the *Gazette* for news. They'll be able to search for news in English-language papers and web sites across the globe. Also, with Twitter, Facebook and websites, many politicians, for instance, prefer to communicate directly with their audience, rather than through the filter of a newspaper reporter. Even in your area, David, will the media need to have investigative reporters when we have online amateurs divulging secret government documents and other news to the world? Why governments are now bringing in laws so that any blogger or tweeter has the same right to protection of sources as trained journalists have. The news media soon will be drowned out by crap."

"Gee, Bruce, that's a dismal picture you are painting. Why have you stayed in the game?"

"Well, I'm a lot older than you, David. So papers should last until I retire. I started off as a kid delivering newspapers in the morning, then selling the afternoon paper on street corners after school. Evening papers are dead now – killed by television news. See what I mean about the future?"

"I used to deliver morning newspapers as a kid, too, Bruce. It was great fun. The milkman used to do his round before dawn in the suburb I lived in, so every now and then there would be two or three bottles of milk lined up on a veranda ledge when I came past an hour or so later. The papers were all rolled tightly and bent at one end to maintain the roll, so they made perfect boomerangs to knock the milk bottles off the ledge. Strangely, I never did get caught doing that."

"What a disgrace, David Reed. I think I'll pass the news of your destructive behaviour on to our excellent columnist Deborah West." Both roared laughing and went back to the bar for more beers. Meg rang on his mobile. "David, I rang my dad to see what was doing about the court case and it turns out the hearing is tomorrow. Lucky I rang as he's not the sort to volunteer anything. I'm going to take a sickie from the bank to go to court to support him. Do you think you could come, too?"

Reed paused in thought. "Meg, I don't know if that's a good idea. If some suburban court reporter sees me there waiting, he or she might get curious and your dad could end up with publicity he might otherwise have avoided."

"Oh, I don't think you're quite that much a celebrity yet, David. I think we could risk it."

"All right, Meg. You're the boss."

"The boss? Oh, don't be ridiculous."

"Yes, boss."

"I'm going to hang up. See you at court."

"Yes, boss."

Reed told Butler he would be late in next day because of a possible interview. As it turned out, Bruce Mann managed to constrain himself in court, told the magistrate he had been grossly and unfairly provoked by the car hoons when all he had tried to do was curb dangerous behaviour, and apologised for swearing at the police. Reed smiled to himself: crash-through Bruce had taken his advice after all. The magistrate read Mann a lecture, imposed a $200 penalty for the abuse, and said he had been lucky not to earn a conviction.

Reed spent 10 days investigating a suspected housing development scam after a sacked employee contacted the *Gazette* with allegations, but could find no evidence to support the employee's claims, then came home one night to dinner and to a broad smile from Meg.

"Darling, I have had another check-up with the doctor and our bub is in great shape. Fingers and toes are all there, and it's a good weight."

David gave her a big hug. "Darling, you're such a clever girl."

"Well thank you. Though I have to admit that you've had a small hand in it."

They had decided early on not to ask the medicos what sex the child was, but to wait for the birth. Reed hoped it would be a boy, but kept that to himself. Whatever it would be … that was life. One thing he realised: they would need a new four or five-seater sedan. Their present two-seat sports jobs would have to go. At work next day, he faced a minor drama. The reporter at the next desk to his, Ashton Robertson, had had a long struggle with alcoholism but the *Gazette* management had been very tolerant, recognising that it well might have been caused by the need for reporters often to drink with interview subjects to establish a confidential rapport. But when Butler emerged from his office and snapped at Robertson this day, demanding to know how a story was shaping up, Robertson stood up, shouted "Fuck you, Butler!" and hurled his laptop at the news editor. Butler reacted typically, calling up two security officers from the ground floor and ordering them to eject Robertson from the building.

Reed was shocked at this, as the laptop had actually missed Butler and crashed onto a desk beside him. He followed the security officers down to the ground floor where they put Robertson onto the street and told him not to try to re-enter. Reed went up to him and said, "Ashton, you're a bit of a mess. Are you going to go home?"

Robertson: "Nah. I'm going to the nearest pub to forget that bastard and wipe myself out." And he did. Reed went with him and sat with one beer as Robertson downed scotch after scotch until he was incoherent and probably had no idea where he was. Reed then phoned the *Gazette* personnel office to get Robertson's home address, called a taxi, gave the driver $50 and piled Robertson into the back seat, asking the driver to take him to the address and leave him at the door.

"Butler can be an absolute bastard," Reed told Meg when he got home that evening. "Robertson has been with the paper for 20 years, held down important positions, cracked some big political and crime stories and finally succumbed to the booze. I've felt like throwing my laptop at Butler at times."

A week later there was still no sign of Robertson at the office. Reed felt he could not ask Butler where Ashton was, but, encountering editor-in-chief Darryl Sheridan in the lift, asked him if there were any news of Robertson.

"Oh, haven't you heard, David? I'm afraid the poor man is being detained in Ravenswood mental centre. He embarked on a booze binge again, went berserk in the street outside his flat, shouted abuse at everyone passing by and stripped off all his clothes. A psychiatric assessment has deemed him a risk to the public and to himself and he has been detained. This was all done privately of course, as is proper in such tragic circumstances. "

Reed was stunned. No notice of this had been posted at the office for the staff. He decided to go to Ravenswood that evening after work to try to see Robertson. The clinic staff were accommodating, but told Reed he could speak to Robertson only through a grille in the door to his room. "Don't expect too much," a staff member warned Reed as they walked down a corridor lined with what looked to Reed not like rooms, but cells. At "room" 19, the door having that number in large letters, the staff member rapped on the dark oak and called, "Mr Robertson, a friend to see you." Reed looked into the cell and discovered the walls were padded. It was just as well. Ashton was standing at the far end, punching at the padding, shaking his head and stamping a foot. When Reed called, "Ashton! It's me. David," he showed no sign of hearing, but kept just punching at the wall. Reed called several times, with still no response.

"You see, Mr Reed, he is badly affected," said the staffer.

"Is he likely to recover?" Reed asked.

"Who knows? The psychiatric report was rather bleak, I gather. It is not for me to say, but he is a seriously disturbed man. People in his condition often die here."

Reed shook his head sadly, turned and left. Journalism, he thought, can be a superb game and, for some, a treacherous trap.

He was late getting home that evening and Meg noticed that he was quiet and withdrawn. He told her of the Ravenswood visit.

"Look," she said with slightly forced cheerfulness in her voice, "We see your mother quite often because she's here in Apollo. But we haven't seen your dad for a couple of months. Why don't you see if he'll have us at the farm for the weekend. You know. Herefords, dingoes, echidnas, wombats and all that. Get away from the city and journalism for just 48 hours."

"Don't know about a whole weekend with him, darling. What about we make it a night and one day?"

Reed did, telephoning Jim to check that he would be there and they would be welcome to come. The farm was nestled in a eucalypt-clad valley nourished by two creeks and with a high, grey-rock peak at its back and as they drove up on the Friday evening, instead of the boom of a shotgun blasting rabbits, as Reed would have expected, they heard the thunder of an orchestra.

"What on earth is that?" Meg asked as they neared the farm gate.

"That, you should know, my darling, is The Anvil Chorus from Verdi's *Il Trovatore*. And being broadcast, I might add, at about 120 decibels."

"God, I wonder what the neighbours think?"

"Well, you might not have noticed but any neighbours are about six kilometres away."

They pulled up beside the farmhouse but no Jim Reed emerged to greet them. David knocked on the door, but no response. When he looked in the window there was Jim, sitting in front of two enormous loudspeakers, waving a hand to conduct an imaginary orchestra and singing along with the chorus. David just opened the door and they walked in. Jim waved to them then just went on conducting and singing to the end of the Chorus. David and Meg both put fingers in their ears to protect their hearing.

"Hello, people," he said finally in the stunning silence. "It's my new disc, The Greats of Classical Music. Just enjoying a bit of culture in a way that you city slickers never can."

"Oh, I don't know about that, Dad. I think they would just about hear that back in Apollo City."

"Do them good if they could. They're mostly peasants down there." And then an afterthought: "Not you two, of course."

"Thanks, Dad. I must say, as we drove up I couldn't help noticing all the Herefords herded up against the far fence in your bottom paddock. I don't think they like Verdi very much."

"Well, I'm not breeding them to be members of the National Orchestra. They're just meat, David. Just meat, and very good meat at that."

"Just watch out Dad that the Animal Protection League doesn't get onto you. And, by the way, you're likely to go deaf eventually if you keep playing records at that level and then you won't hear any music at all, Verdi or otherwise. "Hmmm ... you might be right there. I'll tone it down a little."

Throughout the evening they had to endure lots more Verdi, including yet another chorus … The Gypsy Chorus from *La Traviata* followed by the Brindisis from the same work and De Miei Bollenti Spiriti, also from *La Traviata*. After a merciful break for dinner, which consisted of off-the-farm Hereford steak and garden tomatoes and potatoes, David was allowed a non-musical half an hour in which to bring his father up to date on his newspaper career and his evolving family life and then Jim returned to his records. After enduring ear-throbbing Polovtsian Dances from Borodin's *Prince Igor*, The Jewel Song from Gounod's *Faust* and Song to the Moon from Mascagni's *Cavalleria Rusticana*, Meg signalled to David that she could stand no more. They stood up, David tilted his head to rest on his two hands, indicating s-l-e-e-p, and they retreated to the bedroom. That was not quite the end of the torture, however. Huddled under a heavy, winter quilt they still had to endure Wagner's O Star of Eve from *Tannhauser*, Rossini's Overture from *The Barber of Seville*, and Bizet's Pearl Fishers duet. The house stopped vibrating. Silence, glorious silence, ruled. David lifted his head out of the quilt, lifted it off Meg's face and kissed her.

"Can you hear me?" he whispered. "I almost enjoyed that final duet from under here. Almost."

"Shsssh," she giggled. "You'll wake the Herefords. Go to sleep."

Next morning, after a quick cereal breakfast, they shook hands with Jim and left for the city. Behind them, echoing to the hills, was Gounod's Je Veux Vivre, from Romeo and Juliet.

David closed the farm gate, got back in the car and as they moved off slowly down the gravel road, began to sing Sartori's Time to Say Goodbye. Meg burst out laughing. "I'll bet the Herefords would like to hear that."

At home that evening Reed was reading a newspaper while eating the shepherd's pie prepared by Meg. She rapped him on the knuckles with a teaspoon.

"David, it's pretty rude to be reading the paper while having our meal. Did you used to do that with comics when you were a boy? I'll bet you weren't allowed to."

"Sorry, Meg. I was just catching up."

"Well, you can do that later in bed."

"I'll have better things to do then, Meg."

"Well, you just might not, Mr Smarty."

"Sorry, Your Highness. I won't let it happen again."

"Can we ignore the political crisis in Subcutania or wherever and talk about such mundane things as getting ready for this baby. We are going to have to go shopping for a pram, a safety cot, blankets, a car cradle, the replacement cars. When are we going to do all this?"

"Ah, how about next weekend?"

"Well, we won't get all that done in one weekend, will we."

"No, but we can get at least one of the cars, and trade in the sports."

"Hmmm. Male priorities. First get the cars!"

"Well, darling. Without the cars we won't be able to go anywhere, will we."

Dessert was a whole baked pear with ice cream. Reed stabbed at the pear with a sharp, pointed knife to secure it for slicing but it skidded out of the small bowl and the knife nicked his left hand, triggering the cry "Jesus Christ!"

"Such language! And in your case, futile," Meg chuckled.

"You've often told me you don't believe there's a God, so why call out to his Son?"

"Gee, thanks, Meg. You're so sympathetic. It's quite touching."

"Well, I don't think you are bleeding to death, dear boy, otherwise I would call an ambulance. You don't even need a sticking plaster, thanks to God."

"Look I know we married in a Catholic church to please your parents but do you really believe there's a heaven somewhere out there beyond our universe with millions of good people all somehow clustered around God the Father, Jesus, Mary and the Holy Ghost? If all those millions have been raised up again, what do they eat? What do they drink? And what about the millions of baddies down in Hell? Who keeps the fires burning all the time? And why don't they all get incinerated instead of enduring hellish pain forever? Oh, and those in Purgatory. I nearly forgot them. Who decides when they've served their time or do they never get out of there?"

"All right, Mr Atheist. We've been over all this before. I just think it's rather amazing that people say that they saw Jesus raise Lazarus from the dead, and then there's the issue of Jesus's body disappearing even though a big rock was put in front of the cave."

"Couldn't some of those apostles have decided that there was a good living to be had promoting Christianity? They could have rolled back the rock. They had three days to do it."

"David, life's fun with you ... most of the time. I just like to think that when we die that's not the end, that there is something else. Even if I do end up living with you up there for eternity. That's if they let decent atheists in."

"No, Meg. I'm not an atheist. I'm an agnostic. Even Richard Dawkins couldn't prove that there is no God. We just don't know.

It does all seem highly improbable to me, but then once upon a time so would nuclear power, the internet and putting a man on the moon. Maybe one day an Apollo Government will send a super-rocket to the end of the universe and humans will find out for sure whether or not there's a heaven."

"My darling David, there's one thing you can be pleased about."

"What's that?"

"As you are older than me, and men don't live as long as most women, you'll be the first to find out whether there is a heaven or not."

David put down the offending knife, cupped one hand under his chin, looked into her blue-green eyes and smiled. "Let's go to bed, my goddess."

CHAPTER 7

Butler called Reed into his office. "How long is it, David, since you broke the news of the big voting security scam? About nine months, isn't it? Well, you mightn't believe this, but the legal system has finally got off its arse and two guys from the Security Bureau are about to be charged. I wouldn't want to go public with my opinion and cop defamation or contempt-of-court charges, but isn't it amazing that the Whitaker Government has taken so long to act, given how much detail we published at the time. Anyway, thanks to a phone call from a top official I won't name, the charges will be laid tomorrow. What this means for you, of course, is that you are going to be out of action for the paper for a few days giving evidence to the preliminary hearing and after that about a bloody fortnight or more giving evidence at the trial.

"Sorry about that, Graham. But we did get a nice big scoop out of that, didn't we? And I did get the house I was renting fire-bombed. So I'll be glad to give any evidence that helps send the bastards down."

As it happened, Reed did not have to spend much time in the witness box. After his original expose, the Government had sent its own investigators into the Voting Security Bureau, and through computer records was able to establish who was responsible for checking death notices and then deleting names from the voting rolls. Under heavy questioning, a 25-year-old official cracked, and admitted he had been paid by an older fellow official to leave names of deceased on the rolls and to hand over a list of the names.

The older man, 58, was a member of Whitaker's Democracy Party and that's how the "deadies" continued to vote. No wonder, Reed, thought, as all this emerged in court, that the Whitaker Government took nine months to get it all to trial. They were probably hoping to get the next election out of the way before the trial began. For the day of sentencing, Reed sat up in the press gallery where, as also applied in the Parliament House press gallery, the initials of long-dead reporters were carved into the oaken desk lids. Odd, he thought, that nobody had ever, as far as he knew, been charged with contempt of court or contempt of parliament. Some schoolkids never grew up. The judge donned his wig, read a long, stern rebuke, to the two offenders and sentenced the 23-year-old to a year's prison. The 58-year-old, as organiser of the corruption, was far more culpable, he intoned, and sentenced him to seven years jail. A middle-aged woman in the court, probably the accused's wife, let out a cry of anguish and collapsed, sobbing. Reed felt sorry for her. Presumably she had nothing to do with the crime, but she, too, was now being punished. Not only that, he thought, but there were other people in the Democracy Party who obviously knew about the racket. Why weren't they also in court? Back at the office, he suggested to editor-in-chief Sheridan that that issue would make a good editorial for the paper. He then rang Meg's mobile with news of the sentencing. "Those bastards who almost ran us down in the Verada have been put in the slammer, so when we get home, darling, let's go out for a champagne dinner."

"I'm already home, David. I took an early break from work, and I have a surprise for you."

"Well, what's the surprise?"

"It won't be a surprise if I tell you now. You'll see it when you get home."

"Oh-oh. This sounds like trouble if you won't tell me now."

"No darling. No trouble. This surprise is going to bring new light into our lives."

"Really. Can't wait. See you soon."

He swept their new sedan into the carport at Rochley, strode into the kitchen, hugged her and said: "Well, where is the big surprise?"

"Oh. Wasn't he in the courtyard?"

"He? He! Don't tell me you've got a lover!"

"Silly boy. Of course not." Going to the front door, she called: "Here, boy!" Into the lounge room bounded a large Labrador with shiny black coat, nuzzling his soft nose against her leg, then lying down in a doorway. "Tutu, I want you to meet David. David this is Tutu."

"Tutu? Why is he called that. Too, too big? Too, too friendly? Too, too hungry?"

"No, Silly. I named him after Desmond Tutu. Black, highly intelligent, strong and loyal."

"Oh, I see. But I hope he's not going to take up residence in doorways. I can see what will happen. One day I will trip over him, whack my head against that cupboard's sharp edge, collapse on the floor, get face-licked by Whatshisname then die."

"God, David. You are such a pessimist. Labradors are the gentlest, smartest dogs going. I'll train him to stay outside if you wish."

"No, darling. I'll get used to him. We'll just need to be careful of that baby that's bound to pop out soon. Won't we, Tutu. Now are we going for that champagne dinner I promised you?"

"Oh, David. You men never remember anything important, do

you? Pregnant women, particularly very pregnant women, don't drink alcohol do they?"

"Talking of babies, Meg, it's way past time we decided on names for the bub even though we're waiting until the birth to discover the sex."

"If it's a boy I'd like to call him after you, David."

"We can't do that, Meg. Just imagine you calling out one day, 'David, would you go and chop some more firewood. I'd just sit there, look at the 14-year-old and say 'She means you'. And he'd just sit there, too, and say, 'No, I think she means you.'"

"Oh all right. Let's call him Desmond."

"You've got to be joking. We have a guest and our son comes in with the dog and you say 'I'd like you to meet Desmond and Tutu'. Come on. Let's call him after your Dad – Bruce. And if it's a girl, call her after your Mum, Caroline. OK?"

"We will see. Now, why don't we try that new French restaurant in the city. I think I'd enjoy a lamb noisette."

"Lamb noisette. Noisy bleating lamb is it? Yes. Pardonnez moi. Very crass of me. But I do remember on one assignment to France ordering cuisses de grenouilles and discovering when it arrived that it was frogs legs. Yuck. I never forgot the name. And you know, I think that's why the Poms long ago started calling the French the Frogs."

At the restaurant, David immediately ordered a bottle of champagne, French naturally, but Meg settled for iced water.

"Meg, sweetie, would you order for me, please? My French isn't that polished. Just order anything you think I'd like."

"David, my love, if you bother looking at the menu, you'll see that they do provide translations in brackets after each item. So go to work. By the way, I have some more news for you."

"We're not getting a cat, I hope."

"No, just a new human. The baby is due any time within three weeks as you might remember, so I have told the bank I am starting my six months parental leave from next Monday."

"I think you've been amazing to stay at work this long."

"So do I." She paused, then "David, having children is just about every woman's dream and I think it will be wonderful for both of us. But being permanently at home for a year long could become rather stultifying so I'll be happy to help you in your work any way I can, such as research perhaps. I'm quite good on the computer."

"Yes, darling. If I can think of anything you can do, of course I'll come knocking."

"As I've told you before, I've always thought journalism a fascinating profession ..."

"No darling. An occupation, not a profession. Lots of journalists, some of the best, have never been to university."

"... oh all right, a fascinating occupation, but you've never actually talked to me much about it. For instance, what's the proudest thing you've ever done as a journo?"

He repeated the story that he had told in Keralia of having been given the job of a sacked father of five – and refusing to take it, instead walking out after calling the managing director responsible a capital C.

"Fortunately I landed a job in Britain, telling them I wanted superior experience. I felt good about that. Stayed there for four years."

"Good for you, darling."

"Well, I felt really good when I heard a little later that the pricks were so embarrassed that they gave the father-of-five his job back on the magazine. If it had been me dumped, I would have told them to stick it, but then, I don't have five kids."

"Maybe one day you will, my darling."

"Hey. Easy there, sweetheart!"

"And now my great love, the other side of the coin. Is there anything you remember as the thing you are least proud of so far in your profess … in your occupation?"

"Why do you want to know that? It's odd. A trooper in Keralia wanted to know just that, too."

"Well, it's an obvious counterpoint, isn't it. And I'd like to know all sides of the man I'm going to spend the rest of my life with. We have rarely got around to deep conversation in all the time we've been together."

Reed bent his head and stroked his eyes thoughtfully. "Yes, Meg, you're right about that. It's been hectic one way and another, I know. The worst thing I've done? Oddly I think of it every now and then. You might remember Robert Gilverry, president of the National Development Party. Well he became very ill and was in hospital. All the media were trying to see him to determine whether he would be able to continue in politics or would have to resign his post, but he had given instructions to hospital staff that he wanted to see only his relatives as he had a mobile phone to keep in touch with political colleagues. I thought I could get a scoop on his views on his political future if I could get to see him, so told a fib at the visitors' desk and said I was a relative. When I got to his bed, Gilverry said, 'Who are you and what do you want?' When I told him he shouted 'Nurse! Nurse! Get this mongrel out. He's a journalist. Out! Out!' I shot through before the staff could find out which outfit I worked for, as that probably would have meant the axe for me. On reflection I realised what a lousy thing it was to do. Worse than that, I did not know at the time that Gilverry was in hospital to be treated for brain cancer. He never came out."

Meg took his hand on the table. "You weren't to know that at the time, darling. Don't let it eat away at you. I'm almost sorry I asked."

"Thank you, darling. Now on with the lamb noisette."

Four days later Meg shook him awake at 3.30am. "Darling. Darling. Call an ambulance! I think the baby is coming."

The ambulance arrived within 20 minutes and half an hour later Meg was in a maternity ward, alternating between groans, gasps and the odd yell. "Keep pushing! Keep pushing!" exclaimed the midwifery nurse as David watched, marvelling at the female experience of producing a new human. The groans went on for another 40 minutes. The nurse looked to David. "I think she should stand up for a while. That will help the process." Helpless male David just nodded.

The nurse summoned help from a colleague and lifted Meg from the bed to stand up against a wall. The groans, the grunts went on, but suddenly the midwife exclaimed "It's coming! It's coming! That's the girl! Keep on pushing!" The two staff slid Meg back onto the bed and David watched fascinated as the head of the child emerged. "That's it, darling! That's it!" he cried. "Keep going!" Three more screams and the shoulders emerged, then the whole child.

"What is it? What is it?" cried Meg.

"It's a boy," announced the midwife. Meg burst into tears. David rushed to kiss her, saying "Well done, darling. Well done. He looks great. He looks to be over three kilos I'd reckon. And he has 10 fingers and 10 toes."

"Oh, David. Give him to me."

"The nurses are just bathing him, darling. You'll have him in a minute."

The midwife put the tot in Meg's arms and she cried again, this time tears of happiness.

Meg went home three days later, then four days after that David asked her would she could manage if he returned to work. Meg looked down at the baby at her breast, smiled, and said, "Of course I'll be all right, David. I've got young Bruce here to look after me. And Tutu, of course. And I can always call on Caroline to come and help."

At the *Gazette* he passed a dull two months, puzzling over what major issue to tackle next. One of the problems of being an investigative reporter could be finding something worthwhile to investigate – particularly at a time like this, with Christmas holidays for the whole nation looming. This country always goes quiet at Christmas, he thought, except for drunks crashing cars and groping girls in bars – hardly the material for an investigative reporter.

But then, sometimes luck is just around the corner, as he discovered. Walking out of the office to go to the adjacent car park for his VW, a tall, lean character in dark suit and matching tie came up beside him.

"David Reed?"

"Yes, why?"

"I recognised you from your photograph in the *Gazette*. I think

I have a good story for you. Can you spare the time to go and have a coffee?"

"What is the business about?"

"It's about nuclear weapons."

"And?"

"And the fact that our country has decided it needs to have them."

"What? Do you really know about that?"

"I work in the Defence Department. Coffee?"

"Ah … yes. Let's go to that café just across the road."

Selecting a discreet table for two in one corner, Reed asked the stranger: "What coffee?"

"A long macchiato, thanks."

Reed signalled a waitress. "Long macchiato and a weak latte thanks." Then to the stranger: "Now you know my name. I need to know yours."

He got the common response. "If I give you my name, do you promise to keep it off the record?"

"Unless evidence comes about that you have lied to me, I will."

"My name is Alistair Bradling. Alistair is a-*i*-r."

"Can I see your driver's licence, Alistair?"

"Why so?"

"So I can verify your name."

Bradling laughed. "Oh, of course!" and produced it.

Reed: "Ok, Alistair. What evidence do you have that the country is planning nuclear weapons?"

"Well, they have already started."

"You're kidding. Where have they started?"

"Out in near-desert country in the far north, with only one dirt-track road through it, the Government is building a plant to make N-bombs. Defence already has long-range missiles, as you know, to carry standard explosives. So they will get nuclear warheads."

"Where exactly in the north is this plant?"

"You've heard of Ngarringan? Well it's about 260kms northwest of there. There's now a large settlement of caravans to house the technicians, a cookhouse and a canteen. There's even a small library."

"What do they do for water out there?"

"They've sunk wells, but all the food and items such as milk have to be trucked in."

"Now look, Alistair. Why are you telling me all this and risking your job at Defence – if you do work there."

"Oh, David. What a cynic! Still, I guess in your work you have to be careful. My reason is simple: I just happen to believe the world should never have gone down the nuclear path, not even nuclear energy, which is dangerous. If enough countries develop N-weapons it could end one day in the obliteration of the human race."

"Well, Alistair, the fact is about a dozen countries now have nuclear weapons and nobody has used one since people saw the horrific mass slaughter when they were first launched against Japan. Many people see them as a deterrent against further mass slaughter with rifles, rockets and standard bombs."

"It sounds like I've come to the wrong guy."

"No, you haven't. If the Government is secretly building

N-weapons out in the desert then the public has a right to know that. So I'm going to check out the road from Ngarringan. Like another coffee?"

"No, thanks. I'd better get going."

"One last thing: why didn't you just leave the Department when you found out what they were doing?"

"I figured if I did that, then tried to alert the media, people perhaps would think I was just disgruntled and making it all up."

The next morning at work, Reed rang the Defence Department to check Bradling did work there and it was not all a hoax. "Could I speak with Alistair Bradling, please."

"No worries," said the telephonist. Reed smiled at the adopted Americanism. "No worries? That's what you think, sweetheart," he said to himself.

The phone rang. "Alistair Bradling here."

Reed recognised the voice, said "Sorry. Wrong number," and hung up. He went and outlined the potential story to news editor Butler and pointed out that it was such a long trip that he might be out of contact for anything up to a fortnight. He then had the unpleasant task of relaying the same news to Meg, but she took the news cheerfully, having now long been accustomed to the life of a journalist.

"Don't worry," she said. "Bruce Junior and I will look after the house."

Reed decided against taking a photographer. A guy with all that gear would immediately alert any guards at the plant. It took him three days of driving and sleeping at hotels just to reach Ngarringan where he found the only other road leading out of the town – a dirt road. An encouraging clue pointing to Bradling telling the truth was that this road was marked with large tyre tracks, suggesting big vehicles were using it. He figured he had a three-hour drive to the plant, so refuelled the car then enjoyed coffee and cake at the general store, rang Meg on his mobile to tell her where he was, and sat reading a magazine until 3pm. He wanted to arrive at the plant, if there was one, at dusk. His main aim was to get quick pictures, swing around and burn back to Ngarringan where he could start asking questions of the locals. About 400 potholes later he drove up over a slight crest and saw in the distance a large steel building, glittering in the dying sunlight. It boasted two large satellite dishes and an aerial mast that had to be 30 metres high. Well, he thought, that had to be rather strange for an outfit supposedly working on dry-land agriculture. Clustered around the building were about two dozen caravans and two smaller buildings. It all tallied with Bradling's description.

When he got within a kilometre Reed took out his camera and, shooting through the windscreen, took several snaps of the settlement, noticing three large trucks parked near by. Then, as he drove up close, he saw what he had expected: a uniformed guard in a small sentry box.

As the road obviously ended at the settlement, Reed got out as the guard approached and said: "Good day, mate. Is this the end of this road?"

The guard: "It looks like it, doesn't it?"

Reed: "What's the name of this town? I've just looked and it's not on my map."

Guard: "It's not a town, as you can see. It's just an industrial research site."

Reed, pretending ignorance: "Oh, which company runs it?"

"It's run by the Government."

"Oh, I see. And what are they researching?"

"It's agricultural research."

"Agricultural research way out here in the desert?"

"Yes. And what, may I ask, are you doing out here driving on a road to nowhere?"

"Oh, I'm an artist and particularly interested in native rock art, particularly the ancient work. So when I'm on holiday I love driving into the Outback looking for such pieces. I came to Ngarringan, saw this dirt road leading off into the desert and thought I'd see where it went and whether there were any rock caves. But it looks like I've struck a dead end here."

Reed got back into the car but as he did so, the guard looked into it and saw the camera lying on the front passenger seat.

"Have you been taking any pictures?" he snapped.

"Oh, yes. I stop to take snaps of any birdlife I see on my bush drives. That's another of my special interests."

Reed now swung the car around to head back to Ngarringan, braked, leaned out the window with the camera, snapped a shot of the guard and the settlement and roared off down the track in a cloud of dust. He did not stop in Ngarringan, figuring the guard might come after him to try to seize the camera, but went on to the next town that had a motel and booked in for the night. Next morning he went to the small post office, took the sim card from his camera, bought a registered-post envelope and mailed the card to himself, c/o the *Gazette*, Apollo City. He then put a spare card in the camera and headed back to Ngarringan, dropping first into the lone café for coffee and a meal, chatting with locals about his "search" for native rock art and sounding them out about the strange plant at the end of the dirt road.

"Jeez governments are brilliant at wasting taxpayers' money," said one greybeard. "Fancy experimenting with dry-land planting. As a matter of fact, I went all the way out there once just to have a look at that factory and I didn't see any crop anywhere. The only thing you could grow out there is cactus. The only reason Ngarringan exists is because it's sitting on a small field of opal. When that's all been dug up, the place will die."

At the hotel that evening, Reed drank and talked with the men at the bar. Ngarringan was still very old world, with the males lined up at the bar and the few women there conversing at two tables. Talk with the men yielded nothing new but he then went and introduced himself as a tourist to two women sitting at a table.

He gave out the rock art spiel one more time then mentioned the "dry-farming" factory at the end of the dirt road, expressing some puzzlement and ridiculing the idea.

"It's not funny, you know," the youngest of the two women said.

"Oh, why's that?" Reed asked.

"Well, I happen to know what's really going on there," she said. "My brother was working there in the canteen and he said that whenever the scientists went into the big plant from their caravans they were all dressed up in those white suits like astronauts wear, complete with helmets and gloves. It was like something out of Star Wars."

Reed: "Is your brother still working there?"

"No. He decided it was all very odd and he now works over the road here at the garage."

Reed: "I'd like to have a chat with him. What's his name?"

"Gregory. Gregory Allin."

Reed thanked the two women, ordered a round of drinks for them, headed across to the garage where Gregory was behind the counter, told him of the conversation with his sister and asked him about the factory.

"Very weird – and scary," said Allin. "I'm sure some of the work they were doing involved radioactivity. I wasn't allowed to go in there, because I was told it was not safe, but I saw a big sliding door open several times and inside there was all sorts of elaborate gear and, in a couple of places, small radioactivity warning signs with, you know, those three triangles in a circle. And at times big trucks turned up and barrels were unloaded from them that carried the same signs."

Reed: "And did the staff all wear protective suits?"

Allin: "Yes, they did. It was quite weird."

Reed: "Gregory, I'm a reporter with the *Gazette*, in Apollo. Now that you are no longer working at that plant, is it OK if I report what you have told me? I think the people of Ngarringan and other towns in the area are entitled to know what is going on out here."

Allin: "Sure. Doesn't matter to me. What I've told you is the truth and I'm not tied to them any more, so go for your life."

Reed: "Is it OK with you if I take a shot of you to go with the story?"

"Fire away."

Reed: "By the way, what exactly was your job there?"

"I worked in the canteen."

Reed headed out of Ngarringan but then took a wide, circuitous route back to Apollo just in case any posts had been set up on the main highway to look out for him. After several hours he had to pull over, shut his eyes and rest, starting out again at daylight. And it was late at night again before he hit Apollo. He rang Butler at home, told him what he had discovered, promised a full briefing in the morning, found Meg and Bruce snuggled up on the living room sofa and put his arms around them both .

"This is dynamite," Butler told him next day. We have to be sure we've got it right or the ridicule will be very damaging. What if it turns out to be a dry-land farming research station after all?"

Reed: "I have two witnesses – Bradling and Allin. One in the department and the other who worked at the plant."

Butler: "From what you tell me, Bradling won't have his name on the record and Allin was just a canteen worker. We need more than that if we are going to alarm the entire nation. The fact is, somehow you have to get Bradling to go on the record."

Reed rang Bradling. "Can we meet again at the café at lunchtime for one more chat?"

Bradling, quietly: "If you must."

Reed: "One o'clock then."

To his relief, Bradling turned up – and on time. "What's the problem? When are you going to run the report?"

"The problem, Alistair, is that the paper won't run it unless I can put your name to it. It's too hot a story to be credited to Mr Anonymous. You did tell me you don't want to be associated in any way with the production of N weapons so why not come out and tell the nation what's going on?"

"But there's my problem, David. If I reveal such secret information, I could end up in prison. So might you."

Reed: "I don't think the Whitaker Government would dare, Alistair. They'll be too busy trying to explain away their nuclear policy. The only risk you run is the immediate sack and the Government might even think twice about doing that. But even if they do, as I said, you don't want to be working for such an outfit. So what do you say?"

"I'll think it over."

"Don't take too long. The more you delay, the nearer the N weapons will be. In fact I remember one minister telling me in private conversation at a dinner a couple of years ago that if the nation ever needed nukes it could build them in about six months."

"I'll think it over."

Reed raised his wine glass: "Good luck!" Bradling smiled and left, leaving Reed to pay the drinks bill, but it was not wasted money. The next afternoon a letter addressed to him arrived at the *Gazette* office and in it a typed note:

"To David Reed of the *Gazette*. This note is to authorise you to use my name in revealing nuclear issues at a so-called dry-land farming research plant in the far north of the nation. Signed: Alistair Bradling."

The note carried his handwritten signature and underneath that the scribbled: "David, you are quite a powerful advocate for the public's right to know. I hope you will help me to find a job!"

The *Gazette* hit the streets the next morning with a huge headline: "N-BOMB NATION", with underneath it a large Reed photo by-line and the tag line *Exclusive*. Television and radio stations blared the news to millions as soon as the *Gazette* hit the streets but from Prime Minister Whitaker and his Cabinet came rigid silence until noon when finally Whitaker announced that "minor nuclear research" was taking place at the plant and there was no cause for alarm or wild speculation. But editor-in-chief Darryl Sheridan did get a call that afternoon from a male claiming to be an "insider" of the Prime Minister's Department warning him of "unpleasant consequences" for the print media if the story went any farther. "Such as?" queried Sheridan. "Such as a new law providing for print media to have to have a licence from the government," came the response. Sheridan's response to that was blunt: "Bugger off" and he hung up. Media in nations bordering the Pacific all ran with the *Gazette*'s story, some approving, several hostile at government direction.

Butler to Reed: "Fantastic effort, David. Now, how do we follow it up?"

Reed scratched an itchy neck, stared out the window, then: "Why don't we poll our readers on whether they think we should have nuclear weapons or not?"

Butler: "Good idea!"

Reed: "Yes, but to make it fair dinkum, let's print a coupon which allows the reader to tick Yes or No, but in which they also have to put their name and address – which we promise not to make public – and which they have to mail back to us so we can check they are not some political group. That way we are more likely to get honest responses instead of some organised fakery."

"Wouldn't work, David. Most people wouldn't go to that trouble. We'll get one of the polling companies to run an extended poll of 2500 people. That should give us a good idea."

"Yes, Graham. As long as the polling company is fair dinkum."

Ten days later the *Gazette* published the results of the poll: 53% in favour of N-weapons to protect the nation, 42% against,

5% undecided. Butler admitted to Reed that he was astonished at the result. "I thought a strong majority, particularly young people, would be anti-nuclear, David."

Reed: "Maybe they've realised that so many countries now have N-arms that it's the only serious form of protection."

Five days after publication of the poll, Reed sardonically remarked to editor-in-chief Sheridan that it was curious that not only was there no further threat of newspaper licencing from the Whitaker Government, but in fact the defence minister had given an interview to one television station on why it was necessary to move towards nuclear defences and also why it had been wise to try to keep the development secret for as long as possible.

"Yes, David. As you well know, that's politics," said Sheridan. "I also have some good news for you. You have done such an outstanding job for the paper recently that I have asked the travel editor to organise for you and your wife a fortnight anywhere you would like to go and all you have to do is give us a travel piece on return. Have a good time!"

"You and your wife" thought Reed. Perhaps. Bruce was only four months old but was breastfeeding well. But would Meg be up to it?

"Absolutely!" was Meg's response when he went home and put the proposition to her. "Where are we going to go?"

"Well, darling, my dear old dad Jim when he was young got a motorbike and he and his brother travelled all around western and eastern Europe when the East was under the heel of the communists. I'd particularly like to go back to the Czech Republic and Germany and see how they've changed if that's all right with you."

"Why those two, darling?"

"Well, Meg, I believe a lot of the great architecture of Prague survived both Allied World War 11 bombing and communism so I would like to see that and my Dad still talks about Berlin's notorious Checkpoint Charlie, the point at which you had to be checked by Communist military if you wanted to go into Eastern Europe. More to your interest, I'm told Berlin has some of the world's most magnificent art."

"All right, darling. Book the tickets. And don't worry about Bruce here. As long as my breast milk lasts, he'll be happy."

Two days later, and after a 10-hour flight, they were walking the streets of Prague, Meg propelling Bruce's pusher, looking at ornate old buildings, many adorned with superb statues. A guide shop for tourists directed them to a hill on the edge of the city where they entered the fascinating underground bunker built to protect Communist leaders, doctors and other specialists in the event of a nuclear attack. The whole hill has been hollowed out to a vast cavern 60 metres down, with a maze of corridors separated by 30cm thick steel doors. Shelves in the corridors still held hundreds of gas masks and anti-radiation suits, automatic rifles and military caps. Guards allowed tourists to don some of the gear and take photos. David gave his camera to Meg, dressed in a full military outfit, held a sub-machine gun across his chest and commanded "Shoot!" The tunnel full of tourists laughed.

The next day they visited the King Charles bridge over the river Vlata, built in 1357. The camera was busy again, capturing the bridge's 30 or so huge sandstone statues, mainly of Christ and his crucifixion. Then there were the living human troopers at each end of the bridge, dressed in medieval uniform and carrying flag-adorned spears. This is the bridge that St John is said to have been hurled from for refusing to reveal details of a confession thought to involve adultery. His body was recovered and is in a silver tomb in nearby Prague Castle. A recent moment of glory for this bridge was that, to the admiration of thousands, the hearse of the Czech liberation hero Vaclav Havel passed over it for Havel to lie in state in Prague Castle. The 12th century castle is also famous for the fact that one rebel bishop was locked up in its black tower and spent the rest of his life playing the violin. Good King Wenceslas was buried in a chapel there in 929 and knights once jousted in the castle's main hall. In the 17th century, under Protestant rule, some Catholics were defenestrated from a high window, but are said to have survived – because they landed in rubbish in the courtyard.

David and Meg kept marvelling at how much glorious ancient architecture had escaped the Allied bombing of the war, with David making brief notes for his travel article. That afternoon they took a bus to Kunta Hora, about an hour from Prague.

"It was once just about the biggest silver-mining town in Europe, Meg," David said. "And they used to mint heaps of silver coins here, I've read." After visiting the triple-spired church of St Barbara, they entered a mining museum where they saw how a "minter" used a 5kg hammer to make coins by striking a circle of sheet silver against a metal mound. The head of the hammer was carved and so was the metal mound, simultaneously forming the images on both sides of the coin.

"Gee, I could do that at home," quipped David.

"And the TV news would have great delight in later announcing '*Gazette* reporter binned'," retorted Meg while cuddling Bruce.

From the mint they were taken by a guide to a nearby disused silver mine 260 metres deep and, with lamps and helmets, walked down and along small tunnels. Ancient pumps that brought down air and took away water were still there. Even horses were used to operate a circular lift that brought silver ore to the surface. The horses could be used for only two hours before becoming exhausted.

"How sad. No Animal Lib in those days," said Meg.

David: "This is all going to make good copy for my article."

"Do you ever think of anything else?"

"Only my undying love for you."

"Ho. Ho. Ho."

The next day they visited an ancient Jewish synagogue.

"What are those slits in the side walls for?" Meg asked an official.

"Those slits allowed bowmen inside to defend it, madam," he replied.

That night, after finding that their hotel had a nursing service to look after Bruce, they enjoyed a night of stunning opera – Dvorjak's Rusalka at Prague's splendid National Theatre.

"The ballet was as superb as the singing," Meg remarked as they left. "I read on the internet that Prague has more than 50 million tourist visitors a year. No wonder. It's a magnificent city. You know, the first tourists were pilgrims, coming to see the city where St Wenceslas was martyred."

David began to sing: "King Wenceslas didn't look out on the Feast of Stephen …"

Meg: "Oh David, you are such a peasant!"

The next day, on advice from a tourist office, they visited the Southern Bohemia city of Tabor, once occupied by the Hussites, a Christian movement led by Jan Hus who became a leader of the Protestant Reformation. On the wall of one building in the city they saw a relief depicting a cannon on a cart and asked a passer-by what it meant.

"Don't you know?" he replied to David. "We invented artillery! The Hussites to defend themselves bolted cannon onto their farm carts which meant they could be quickly moved to where they were needed."

Meg: "I wonder if years from now N-bomb maker Robert Oppenheimer's visage will be carved into New York buildings?"

David: "That's if H-bombs leave any New York buildings to be carved on."

"Oh, David. Think of little Bruce."

"All the little Bruces will have to work to see their world stays sane."

The next stop was Ceske Krumlov ("City of the Bend"), so named because it is built on a virtual island because a major river winds through it forming more than semi-circle. To repel enemy invaders, the ancients had only wooden bridges across the river that could be burnt down to deter an oncoming army. That didn't stop the city being decimated by The Great Plague.

On the bus drive back to Prague, David pointed out to a fellow passenger next to them storks in a field. "Aren't they splendid," he said.

"Not if you are a farmer there," the passenger replied in heavily accented English.

"Why's that?"

"They build nests on top of your chimney and when you light fires in winter, up goes the chimney and perhaps your house. Fortunately there is one – what do you call it? – remedy."

"What's that?"

"All the farmers have to build higher fake chimneys beside their houses and that costs money. But the storks do move into them and nest there."

The next day David and Meg took the train to Dresden. David warned Meg not too expect too much.

"Right at the end of World War 2, the head of Britain's Bomber Command Sir Arthur 'Bomber' Harris organised a 1300-bomber raid to flatten Dresden in retaliation for the Nazis' blitz on London. A huge firestorm destroyed the whole the city centre. So I don't know whether much interesting is left of the place."

They were pleasantly surprised to find a city with five museums, magnificent bridges over the river Elbe, and fine food everywhere. Bomber Harris's planes burnt out the 200-year-old Frauenkirche (the Church of Our Lady) and when it cooled down, it collapsed. A taxi driver told them as they passed the superbly rebuilt cathedral that it was only restored, using much of the old stone, after the Communist regime collapsed in 1990.

Meg then astonished David with this request: "I want to see the Historiches Grunes Gewolbe."

"The Historiches what?"

"Don't worry about the name, David. I'll tell you when we get there."

And she did. "It's a Baroque treasure chamber, David, with a magnificent history. It was badly blitzed in World War 2 but has been astonishingly restored."

"Yes, but what IS it?"

"It's a treasure chamber, as I said. It was built around the 1720s by August the Strong to show off the finest arts. I read about it before we left home. August was rich and powerful and built the chamber to show off his treasures to selected guests. It is one of Europe's oldest museums."

Leaving baby Bruce with a child-minder at their hotel, together they walked through the musem's Ivory Room, White Silver Room, Silver Gilt Room, Room of Renaissance Bronzes, Jewel Room and finally the Hall of Precious Objects.

"There's another splendid collection of treasures, David. And they're all just upstairs on the second floor."

There in the Dinglinger Hall they came upon a huge work that triggered a stunned "Wow" from David. "That," said Meg, reading from a museum pamphlet, "is the Grand Mogul Aureng-Zeb of Delhi."

The figure of the bearded mogul with jewelled crown, jewelled belts and clutching a jewelled staff, sits astride a splendid throne atop golden steps. In front of him, in a row on either side, are helmeted warrior guards and rising above them bejewelled shades, the whole work an outstanding example of Baroque jewellery art.

Meg: "Just takes your breath away, doesn't it, David." And, again reading from the pamphlet: "It was created by Johann Melchior Dinglinger and his workshop in Dresden between 1701-1708."

"Yes, darling. It's a humdingalinger."

"Oh, David. It's a waste of money sending you here! Next stop is Berlin isn't it?"

"Yes, my love. It should be really interesting because it not only had the life bombed out of it, but it was then also divided between Commies and the West."

"I know that, darling. *Everybody* knows that."

"Well, I'm particularly interested in that because my Dad went through the famous Checkpoint Charlie in 1961 when the Wall had just gone up. He and his brother on their motorbike had to face a grilling there from armed guards when they were going through to East Bloc countries. American and Soviet tanks faced each other at that point."

"Righto, David. First stop: Checkpoint Charlie."

After booking into their Berlin hotel, they hailed a cab, this time taking Bruce in the pusher.

"Checkpoint Charlie!" Meg announced emphatically to the cabbie. He smiled and off they went. At Friedrichstrasse they got out and Meg burst out laughing. The once-grim checkpoint has been turned into a comedy act with two lavishly uniformed actors waving flags outside a little hut and waiting for tourists to take photos – at a price.

"What would your Dad make of that, David?"

"Oh, he has quite a sense of humour, Meg."

The cabbie took them to a surviving part of the Berlin Wall where a long series of photographs depicted the rise of the Nazis, the wartime devastation of the city, the ensuing division and finally unity and democracy.

The next day they visited the Brandenburg Gate, the 17th-century Charlottenburg Palace, the Bundestag and the National Gallery with its grand collection of 19th century art. David asked a grey-haired gallery guide: "How did all these splendid paintings survive the bombs of the Second World War?"

"We took them all down, sealed them, and hid them in coal mines," he said.

The next visit was to the vast, heart-wrenching Memorial to the

Murdered Jews of Europe, a couple of hectares of huge grey stone blocks, dozens of them taller than any human. Meg, wheeling the pusher down a path between some of the blocks, asked to David.

"What do you think they represent?"

"Coffins."

"Yes, that's what I thought, too. God, it's sad isn't it."

"There's a Jewish museum here, too, Meg, on Lindenstrasse. Could you bear to take that in, too? A guy at the *Gazette* told me it's one of Berlin's must-sees."

"All right, David. It's been a big day, but let's go."

The museum covered Jewish life in Germany from the year 950. But the room that chilled both David and Meg was The Memory Void, an installation of several thousand metal film reels lying in a long corridor, looking like screaming faces, and representing some of the millions of Jews who perished under the Nazis. A sign requested onlookers to remain silent. It was hardly necessary.

On their way to the exit they passed a wall on which were listed the names of Nazi concentration camps: Auschwitz, Belzec, Sobibor, Treblinka, Majdanek and Chelmno. David hugged Meg. "We are so lucky to live in a relatively civilised era, darling."

"Yes, we are, sweet. Now I need a good coffee, somewhere."

"One last comment then, darling. You have to concede that the German people have not tried to hide the nation's hideous past. They direct tourists to these museums, memorials and synagogues. And there are now more than 100,000 Jewish people living in Berlin again. Hitler would be aghast! By the way, Meg, we'd better have a quick coffee because we've been away all day. I know you left a bottle of breast milk for Bruce, but he might be missing an actual warm, soft breast, don't you think?"

"He might be missing it, David, or is it you?"

"Touche!"

"That reminds me, David. We'll need to get a good night's sleep tonight as we are off to Spain tomorrow."

"Touche encore!"

They had agreed to go to Barcelona, rather than Madrid, because Meg was fascinated by the work of Antoni Gaudi and friends had said that his work La Sagrada Familia (Temple of the Holy Family) started in 1882 was in the category of "see it and die".

Booked into their hotel, they took a cab to the top of one of Europe's greatest walks, the Ramblas, got the pusher out of the boot and set off to show Bruce the town. Being a Saturday there were scores of Spaniards rambling along the wide street, buying at book stalls, fruit stalls and flower stalls, stopping to listen to buskers, clowns and beggars. They spent half an hour just strolling.

"Right, Meg. It's Gaudi time. According to my little map, his temple is more than 25 blocks from here over on the north side of the city, so we'll need another cab."

As they drove up Carrer de Sardenya, the distinctive Gaudi towers of the huge temple loomed into view – eight of them.

"Let's walk right around it and then go in," said David. Hey, look there. There's another tower going up. I wonder how many they'll end up with."

At the entrance, he asked a uniformed official just that. "At least two more are planned," the official said. "We have to raise another 50 million euros to complete Gaudi's vision."

"I thought the Spanish Government was hard up for money," David countered.

"The whole temple is being built with private donations from around the world," the official said. "Countries such as Japan have given millions."

Gaudi's stone figures were all grim and angular. "Like something out of Star Wars," Meg commented. But inside the temple, they gasped at the sight. A forest of grey and white pillars soared up to meet a network of windows surrounding a blazing great circle of white light. Biblical figures crowded ledges inside and outside the temple.

"You were right, Meg. It was worth coming to Spain just to see this. But I don't know how long it will be the Holy Family Temple. It'll be Gaudi's Cathedral."

"There's one other Gaudi delight, David. Remember I told you about Parc Guell. It's a magnificent park he designed on the top of a hill in the north of the city. Another cab fare, I'm afraid, but you'll love it."

"How do you know? Have you been there before?"

"No, darling. I just looked up pix of it on the internet. Let's go."

At the entrance Gaudi placed a large, tiled dragon. "Look out for the monster, Bruce," David joked as he hauled the pusher up the white steps to the court above where Doric pillars held up a ceiling covered with tiled mosaics. On the floor, several men had laid out rugs with rows of small ceramic figures on them – for sale. But just as Meg and David came by, a uniformed figure swept in, shouted at the men who swept up the figures with their rugs and ran. At the very top of the park, Gaudi had ordained a serpentine row of beautifully-tiled seats where you could sit in the sun and look over the whole of Barcelona.

"Why don't we have something like this in Apollo?" Meg sighed.

"Because we didn't have a Gaudi, my love. Now … back to reality. We fly out tomorrow so I offer one last pleasure before we go."

"Oh, yes, David. And what would that be?"

"One of the guys flogging material on the Ramblas gave me this leaflet about a guitar concert here in Barcelona tonight at the Catalana Music Palace. Look at this pic; it's worth going tonight just to see the theatre. Isn't it beautiful? And classical guitarist Xavier Coll will be performing. How about it?"

"Looks and sounds good. Yes, let's go. I guess madame childminder at the hotel won't mind one more session."

At the concert, guitarist Coll was so overpowering that David began swaying in his seat to the rhythm, so much that Meg gave him a sharp elbow in the ribs – just as the item was ending.

"Ah, Spain," David sighed. "It's moments like this I will always remember."

CHAPTER 8

Twenty-hours of flying from Barcelona brought them home to Apollo City. Bruce had one crying fit lasting about 20 minutes soon after take-off and no amount of cuddling or breast-presentation would mollify him. A businessman in a seat opposite them, typing on an iPad, looked daggers across at Meg who pulled a disdainful face in return. He then buzzed for a hostess and asked if something could be done about the noisy child.

"Sorry, sir," said the woman. "It's a fact that children sometimes find the changing air pressure during the climb out of an airport uncomfortable. I don't think we can ask the parents to leave the aircraft, do you? And we don't have a crying room. Perhaps you could wear the TV earphones for a while."

The businessman scowled, ignored her suggestion, and went back to typing. David let out a hoot of laughter. Almost a day later, after landing in Hong Kong for fuel, they were home and ready for a long sleep to overcome jetlag – that's if Bruce and Tutu allowed it.

Back at the *Gazette* office, Reed printed out from his computer the travel article he had written during their holiday and laid it on editor-in-chief Sheridan's desk. Sheridan did not even look at it, handing it back saying: "I'm sure it's fine, David. Just give it to the travel editor."

Waiting to be given a new assignment, Reed saw Apollo's police chief interviewed on TV saying that the city's drug problem was out of control, with gangs having found quite clever ways of smuggling heroin and cocaine in from Mexico. He needed a much-enhanced drug squad, he said, and intensified surveillance at the port. Only the next evening, at home in Rochley, Reed fed Tutu, then took him for a walk, taking with him a ball-thrower to give the dog plenty of exercise. Only a block away, an ambulance came wailing up to the foot of a tower of public housing apartments. It was followed by a police car.

"That'll be another drug overdose, I'll betcha," a neighbour tending his front garden grunted to Reed. Reed nodded and walked on to the long, narrow lane near by where he would usually make Tutu chase the ball about a dozen times. But this time when he flicked the ball, Tutu rocketed after it but did not come back. Reed called him several times, then went to find him. Around a curve in the lane he came across the dog licking a man lying face down. Beside him was a small plastic bag and an injection needle. Reed shook him to revive him, but got no response, so ran back with the dog to the ambulance and the police. The ambulance driver shook his head, saying, "We're already dealing with a bloody overdose up there," indicating the high-rise flats. "We'll come and get the guy in the lane."

Reed noticed the police wagon's driver was still sitting in the vehicle and went up to him.

"I heard your chief on TV saying the city drug problem is getting much worse. Do you think there are many dealers around here?"

"Of course there are," replied the cop. "I reckon there's a hundred bloody dealers up in that tower. Do you know how many drug needles get picked up in the streets of Rochley every month? About three bloody hundred. Three bloody hundred, mate."

Reed had noticed that a black sedan was pulling up almost every

evening across the street from his and Meg's house. A scrawny
male in his 30s, always in grubby jeans and a brown jumper, would
wait in the street, then go to the sedan, sit in it for a while, then exit.
Reed had retailed this to Meg and asked her to keep an eye on it and
tell him of any odd events.

"That black sedan has been back every afternoon of the past
four days," she told him a week later. "The guy in jeans must want
something badly. Twice he was standing in the cold rain waiting.
Yesterday I went down to the bush near our front gate, made sure
I was hidden, and watched from close up. Street Guy handed a
50-dollar note through the window to the driver, who handed a
10-dollar note back. Then the driver must have pushed the boot-
release button, because the boot lid sprang open. Street Guy went
there and in the boot was a shelf with a line of small white packets
on it. He took one, slammed the boot shut and headed for the high-
rise block."

"Certainly looks like a drug drop, doesn't it," David said.
"Check the car one more day, get the number plate if you can, and
I'll pass it all on to the cops." Two days later Meg had the number
plate and David signed on to a government website called Crime
Campaign and left all the details. Nothing happened and the black
sedan kept coming and Street Guy kept handing over money. David
became irritated and emailed the details to a member of the drug
squad at central police headquarters, asking if anything was being
done to check out the sedan. About a week later he got an email
reply. The driver of the sedan, he was told, had been checked out
and he was selling cigarettes. David read this and snorted. Why
would Street Guy stand in the cold rain sometimes just to buy a
packet of cigarettes when he could just go around the corner to a
small shop and buy a packet? And why would Black Sedan drive

John Kiely   209

up to Rochley almost every afternoon just to hand over a packet of cigarettes? Laughable. Two days later Meg reported that the black sedan was no longer calling.

"What a surprise!" David grunted sardonically. "I guess he has just run out of cigarettes." Then seriously: "For the next couple of weeks, Meg, if someone knocks at the front door just go to a window and check who it is before opening up. I'm serious. Sometimes these low-grade nutters are driven to take revenge without considering the consequences. I'm sorry now I took the whole thing up with the cops. If people want to kill themselves with smack, should we care? We let millions kill themselves with cigarettes."

"Yes, David. But the difference is that smokers don't rob houses and bash people just to get the money for some smokes. And they don't leave poisonous used needles in the street for kids to pick up and play doctors and nurses with them."

At the office, Reed had no important investigation lined up, so wrote a short opinion article about Rochley's drugs, illegal drug dealing across the whole city and calling for government action to strengthen the city's Drug Squad. The response from the Government was a studied silence.

After work, having a gin and tonic in the bar two doors from the *Gazette*, he was hailed by member of parliament Ronald Laxmoor, whom he had encountered before when investigating MPs' expenses. Laxmoor had given him some useful tips about whom to check among the Opposition.

"Hi, Ronald. How's life guiding the uninformed masses?"

"Same as ever, David. And how is life misleading the uninformed masses?"

"That's our role, Ronald. That's our role and we are performing splendidly."

"It must be dull sitting in your parliamentary office all day answering the complaints of the never-satisfied."

"No. It can be quite fun, actually."

"How's that?"

"Well, take yesterday. There I was in the office and my secretary takes a call from a woman constituent who demands to speak to me. I take the phone. 'Mr Laxmoor,' the woman says, 'Prime Minister Whitaker has been sitting up the telegraph pole outside my house and staring in when whenever I head for the bathroom. I want you to tell him to get down.' While she is still listening, I wink at the secretary and command her to get the prime minister on the phone immediately. Then I say loudly 'Is that you, prime minister? Good, well you have to get down off that telegraph pole immediately or we will have to call the police and have you arrested.' Then I said to the woman, 'That should fix it.' And she hung up. See, David, political life isn't all argument about taxes and the cost of living."

"Some of your parliamentary friends, Ronald, treat all of the public as if they were like her ... off the planet."

"Oh, that's a bit harsh, David."

"No. You promise to bring in budget surpluses, then give us a stunning deficit."

"You journos should be in our shoes. The public say they want us to be economically responsible, but at the same time they want us to deliver all sorts of fancy new programs. And in fact, you journos lead them on ... complaining sometimes about our profligacy and at other times decrying the lack of new programs to solve all of society's problems. Like another G and T?"

"No, sorry, Ronald. Got to be going."

Back at the *Gazette* tower, editor-in-chief Sheridan called Reed into his office and handed him a piece of paper with a name and phone number on it.

"Got a call from this guy in the Darling Ranges. He claims there's some dodgy business about the setting up of a large solar panel farm. Can you look into it? He seemed to know what he was talking about, but obviously it's a tricky area politically."

"Sure is, chief. But we're used to that, aren't we."

Reed rang the tipster, Harold Ronaldson, to get his address, some of the detail he was offering, and to arrange a time to see him. Ronaldson was happy to see him that evening.

Then he rang Meg. "Darling, I'm going to have to be away for a couple of days. Going to the Darling Ranges to look into the setting up of one of those solar panel outfits which a local is claiming is dodgy. Will you be OK with Bruce?"

"Yes, my sweet. I'm sure that Bruce will look after me. And he is great entertainment. Even keeps me awake at night, as you know. But give me a ring when you get there and when you are leaving. OK. By the way, aren't you coming home to get a change of shirt, underwear and socks?"

"No. I'll just buy a set before leaving the city. Bye, bye."

"Bye."

When he drove to the ranges, Reed was expecting to see a farmer but Harold Ronaldson had just a modest house on only four hectares of land. It was, he told Reed, a weekender, a refuge for him and his wife to escape the pressures of work in Apollo City. Behind their house, on a vast slope facing north and catching the sun all day were hundreds of solar panels, making that part of the range look like something out of Star Wars.

"We used to love it out here," Ronaldson said, looking out from his front veranda. "That slope was covered with tea-tree and eucalypts, we had birds galore and, yes, the occasional wild dog."

Reed: "Now it's all glass and metal."

"Actually, David, I have come to accept that. I'm a scientist myself and I realise that we had to move to new sources of electricity. Even if the world isn't heating up, and there's quite a debate about that, eventually we are going to run out of coal and we are going to need permanent sources of power such as wind, sun and waves. So many of our tree-clad hills may have to shine, so to speak. But actually we also have plenty of arid areas in which to put solar farms. No, David, what I'm actually angry about, and why I rang your paper, is that some solar spivs have ripped off the Government with this scheme and unless that sort of dodge is eradicated, the public won't accept these new forms of clean energy until it is too late. Anyway, that's enough for a minute. Come on in, meet the wife, and have a cup of tea or a glass of wine." They moved inside.

"Harold, is it OK if I tape our conversation? It helps to ensure accuracy."

"Go ahead."

"Thanks. Now what led you to suspect anything dodgy about that solar field?"

"I became suspicious when the company that built it boasted to the stock market that its profit from the work was $8 million, so the bill to the Government must have been at least $12 million. And $8 million is one hell of a profit for a field that size. I know because I have a science friend in another company that also is working on solar farm production. He said his company would never gouge that much profit from a field that size. It was ridiculous."

"So, apart from that, how have you been able to satisfy yourself that there is something faulty about the field?"

Ronaldson went to a cupboard in the dining room and returned with what looked a cross between a camera and a semi-automatic pistol.

"This baby tells me the truth," he said.

Reed: "What is it?"

"It's a pyrheliometer."

"A pyro what?"

"A pyrheliometer. You can use it to check the power being generated by an individual solar panel, giving you the units of kilowatts to each square metre. Handy, eh?"

"And what did you find out there on the hill."

"I checked with the other solar company what the power output approximately should be from each panel in this field and, after I quietly checked about two dozen of them, it transpires that they are producing about a fifth of what they should."

"So, what do you make of all that?"

"Well, I figured that for the company to make so much profit from putting up a third-rate field, they must have conned the Government somehow into shelling out millions more than the system was worth. So the next question was: why was each panel delivering such a poor power output."

"And what did you find?"

"Can you turn off the tape recorder for just a minute?"

"Why. What's the problem?"

Ronaldson did not answer but reached over and clicked it off.

"Well, David. The answer to that last question could mean legal trouble for me, so you'll have to think about that. Here's the answer: I went into the field at night and prised loose one of the solar discs, took it to my friend who works in the solar panel industry and asked him to check it out. Then I took the disc back and placed it in the panel from which it came."

"And the result of your friend's check?"

Ronaldson reached over and clicked the recorder back on. "Turns out all the panels in that field are el cheapos mass-produced in Asia by el cheapo labour and near-useless. The discs have a special mark on the edge and I was able to walk around the field one evening near sunset and check that the discs are all the same, from one end of the slope to the other. Thousands of them."

"Why didn't Government experts pick up the fact that the field was producing hardly any power?"

"I guess the Government either didn't think to do that, or just doesn't have enough experts in the field capable of checking out all its projects. Who knows?"

"Ronald, this might seem an odd question, but why did you approach the *Gazette* rather than take the issue to the Government?"

"Oh, come on, David. You know what governments do. Do you think they want to advertise that they have blown $12 million on a shonky project?"

"Hmmn. I guess you're right about that. Well, if we are going to blow this open, we'll have to use your name and evidence. OK?"

"OK."

"And I will have to take your claims to the energy minister and give him right of reply."

"OK to that, too, David. Ask him if he had his own experts check the field output after it was built."

That night Reed stayed at a small pub five kilometres from Ronaldson's property and next morning headed back to Apollo to approach the company that built the solar field. At the office of Greenpower he showed his press card and asked to see the managing director.

"What is the issue?" asked the blonde secretary at the front desk.

Reed: "I would like his response to some questions about the solar field your company built in the Darling Ranges."

The secretary walked down a corridor, leaving Reed standing at the desk, and returned within two minutes. "The MD is very busy. He asked me to ask you, what is the issue?"

"The issue is that I have evidence the field does not work properly."

"Just a moment, please." She walked down the corridor again, and returned shaking her head. "The MD says he is not interested."

"Not interested? Really."

"Yes, not interested in silly gossip. Thank you, Mr Reed."

The next stop was the office of Energy Minister Lyall Rusfeldt, but when Reed outlined Ronaldson's claims to Rusfeldt's media adviser he was told the minister would be in touch. But four days later the minister hadn't been in touch and when Reed rang the adviser to find out what was happening, the media man said Rusfeldt's response was that Reed should get in touch with the company Greenpower. Reed burst out laughing, told the adviser what the company's reaction had been, hung up, then strode into editor-in-chief Sheridan's office.

"Right, we publish," was the chief's response. "And make sure you include high up in the piece the reaction of Rusfeldt."

"Of course I will chief," Reed laughed. He was back at his cubicle only five minutes when his desk phone rang.

"Hello. David Reed here."

"Ah, Mr Reed. Print those lies about a solar field and we might have to get somebody to attend to you. Got it?"

"Who is this?"

Laughter at the other end. "Never mind who I am. It's what I am. I'm an expert in seeing that people who cause trouble for my friends live to regret it – that's if they live."

Reed slapped a hand over the mouthpiece, signalled frantically to a colleague near by, pointed at the phone and said "Trace!" The colleague nodded and rang the *Gazette* switchboard to ask for a trace on Reed's phone. But almost immediately the line went dead. Sheridan rang police headquarters, told them of the threat, and requested a temporary tap on the *Gazette*'s switchboard to pick up any further threat, but there was none. The solar rip-off splashed on the front page, along with Minister Rusfeldt's absurd response, and Prime Minister Whitaker had to weigh in, reproving Rusfeldt and ordering a commission of inquiry. To Reed's astonishment, PM Whitaker also contacted Sheridan and asked if he would accept a security guard for Reed for a couple of months to ensure his safety. Sheridan consulted Reed, then accepted. David went home, told Meg of the threat and that for a while they might be shadowed by a security officer.

"Good God! I thought you'd be safe once you gave up going to wars," Meg exclaimed when told of this. "You just can't resist the thrill of it all, can you? But ... (she gave him a hug and kiss) it WAS a great story, darling. I'll call in nanny Beryl and you can take me out to dinner!"

"Yes, my sweet. In the meantime, what about we have a nice glass of red?"

He slumped into the lounge sofa, picked up a literary magazine, began reading and let out a groan.

"What's wrong now, David?"

"Modern poetry. It drives me nuts. Just listen to this. 'The refuse collectors have been on strike for weeks. The rats link arms and dance with melancholy and the cats have turned themselves into aromatic troubadours.' Really! Is that poetry?"

"I think it's rather nice."

"It doesn't even rhyme!"

"Well, what is **your** idea of good poetry?"

"I'll tell you. *'The Assyrian came down like a wolf on the fold*

And his cohorts were gleaming in purple and gold

And the sheen of their spears was like stars on the sea ... "

Meg interrupts: "Yes, I know. Old Byron. *'When the blue wave rolls nightly on deep Gallilee.'"*

"Well, darling. **Old** Byron, as you like to call him, could call up the most powerful images and make them rhyme as well. Which makes the works so easy to remember."

"True, David. But I don't think modern poets can keep on eulogising the Assyrians and other ancients."

"I don't think dancing rats are the answer, Meg."

"Oh, I like the image of dancing rats ... tails wagging, whiskers flicking."

"Meg, enough! That's Beryl at the front door and it's time we went to dinner!"

Two months later, the commission of inquiry brought court charges against Greenpower. The court ordered confiscation of company assets to reimburse the Government for the cost of the solar field and finally the grey-uniformed security officers living in a car outside the Reed house day and night vanished. Meg had noticed them there, but knew well why they were there, so had made no comment.

Over dinners of black satin duck with egg noodles, David reached out to take Meg's hand: "I had some good news at work today."

"What was that?"

"Sheridan has authorised a good rise for me … another $200 a week."

"Great. We can certainly use that."

"Also, believe it or not, I haven't forgotten it's your birthday the week after next."

"I know, darling, because you keep the date in your diary, don't you."

"Yes, I do."

"Well, here's a test. Can you tell me how old I am?"

"Er … umm … 29, coming up 30!"

"Oh well done. Good guess!"

"I raise it now because at such a milestone you deserve a big party. What do you say to that?"

"I say, thank you. But how big?"

"Well, I think we should also celebrate my pay rise by inviting about 40 of our friends to a champagne dinner-dance at Eagles

Roost. Their restaurant/ballroom on the top of the tower is a great venue at night, looking out over the whole glittering city."

"Forty of us? It will be a glittering bill, too, David. Do you think we can afford it?"

"Got to have some fun in life, darling. Let's do it."

"All right. Let's start now on the list. There's your parents, Dawn and Jim and mine, Caroline and ... oh, dear ..."

"Oh dear, what?"

"I hope Eagles Roost has long tables if we are going to invite Caroline and my dad Bruce. They'll have to be at opposite ends of the table."

"I agree. We wouldn't want Bruce getting into an argument with someone over politics and ending up baring his bum at them."

"Don't be unkind, David. That theatrical event with the police was a one-off."

"I sure hope so."

"Well in turn I hope your dad Jim doesn't bring along a tape recorder and start playing Beethoven at full blast to amuse the other guests."

"I'll make sure he doesn't."

"Just to indulge in a bit of feminism for a moment, David, it's interesting isn't it that we both have sane, sensible steady mothers but slightly loopy fathers."

"In your case, I object to the word slightly."

"Thank you, David. Now whom else are we going to invite?"

"Well apart from a couple of our friends from the street here I thought I'd invite about five journo mates and their wives. What about you?"

"There are a couple of friends from the bank that I'd like to invite, and a few of my old uni girlfriends and their husbands. I think that looks like only about 30 all up, David. Why not settle for 30?"

"OK. Thirty it is. I'll ring Eagles Roost and book us in."

The party went splendidly, with no bare buttocks or Beethoven but lots of cabernet sauvignon, pinot noir and shiraz because it was mid-winter. David, however, when it was time to address the party about what a splendid wife and mother Meg was, ordered a bottle of Dom Perignon for every guest.

"The best wine to honour the best possible wife," he announced as the bottles were popped by staff. "By the way, all you drivers had better order taxis when the night is over."

"Hear! Hear!" bellowed Meg's father Bruce, picking up his bottle and swigging from it.

When David finished speaking, Meg stood, holding a glass of sparkling. "Thank you all for coming to enjoy this night with me. Now I'd like to say a few words about my David."

"Hear! Hear!" bellowed Bruce again.

"Thank you, Dad. Now, about David … One of the commonest things said about journalists is that in the public's estimation they rank lower than used-car salesmen or money-lenders. But we all know that, in fact, without journalists revealing the true world we live in, we would be at the complete mercy of unscrupulous politicians. My David has at times risked his very life to bring to us news that we have to have to run a democracy. I am so proud of him for that, but also grateful that now that he is a father, he is taking a very responsible attitude to the issue of risks. I am so glad for the sake of our little son that David is now tackling sloppy politicians and corrupt businessmen rather than Keralian terrorists. It is also very comforting to have him roll into bed beside me every night rather than getting on my Ipad another hello from some war front. It's much warmer! So, a toast to my David!"

The whole room clapped and raised glasses "To David!" And Bruce, of course, roared out one more "Hear! Hear!"

A fortnight after the party, Meg was devastated to receive a letter from her bank notifying her that although she was due to return to work in three weeks' time at the expiry of her parental leave there would not be a position for her. The person who had filled in as a casual in her position had been given permanent status and thus she was no longer required. A cheque totalling her superannuation was enclosed.

She rang David at work. "Can they do this to me? It's outrageous! I get parental leave for having a baby and when I want to go back to work, I'm sacked! Can we do something?"

"I don't know, darling. I'll talk to our industrial relations reporter and get back to you. We might be able to embarrass the bank into keeping you on, but we'll have to be careful. For one thing, as your husband, I'll have to stay right out of it, publicly at least."

At home that night he had some positive news. "Don't cash that superannuation cheque yet, darling. The IR reporter Greg had a good idea. Because of my position it wouldn't be wise for the *Gazette* to take up the story, so he is going to phone the industrial relations reporter on Channel 6, who happens to be a woman which is a plus, and tip her off about your case. He won't give his name but will pass on your name and phone number and the name of the bank. We'll see what happens."

"Oh, you clever monkey, David."

"No, Greg is the clever monkey. He thought of doing it. And the channel will leap on it because it's a feminist issue – discrimination against a mother who wants to work. Yippee!"

Curiously after Channel 6 rang Meg, arranged an interview, sought comment from the bank, then gave plenty of pre-publicity to the issue before running the case top of their public affairs evening program, the bank refused to relent.

"All right, Meg," said David. "We'll call in a lawyer and take them on."

"Do you think that's a good idea? It could cost us heaps and I could always look for another finance job when Bruce is a bit older and we can leave him with a nanny."

"No, darling. The bank signed up for parental leave and now they are abusing it. We'll get a good lawyer and I'll bet we can get feminist activist Geraldine Grayer to go into bat for us. She knows the law backwards and loves a fight. When the bank hears she's in the fight they'll probably roll over. You watch."

Three months later Meg's case came up before the Court of Civil Rights. Four TV stations had crews at the court steps to film Meg and Geraldine going in together while two grim bank executives watched. But David's hunch proved correct. The judge called the case, the bank's defence lawyer asked to make a preliminary statement and announced that the bank wished to drop the case and offer Ms Greer reinstatement. Meg's lawyer turned and raised a querying eyebrow to Meg: did she want to go back and work for them? Meg turned to David and raised both eyebrows.

"It's up to you," he said quietly. "Do you think you'd enjoy going back there?"

"I'm not worried about that. The thing is: we've won." She turned back to the lawyer and nodded.

"My client indicates that she will accept the offer, Your Honour."

That wasn't enough for Geraldine Grayer. On the steps outside, addressing four TV cameras, she launched into a searing attack on organisations such as banks run by all-male boards, people who thought they could treat women like dirt. She ran through detail of the feminist fight in various nations until eventually one TV group called a halt saying they would miss the evening news if they did not leave. There was just time for Meg to be asked how she felt about the result and she declared she would be happy to return to the bank and the court case had been worth while in setting a mark for all women needing parental leave. David signalled to her to call it quits, she nodded and headed for their car.

At the office three days later David swung around to look at News Editor Butler on hearing him cry out "Fucking hell!"

"What's happened?" said a nearby reporter.

"The bloody Whitaker Government is planning to set up a media commission with the power to hold hearings from people who claim to have been offended or insulted by a media report. And if the commission decides in their favour, the paper or radio or TV station would have to print an apology. Can you believe it? We already have defamation law, contempt of court law and contempt of parliament law. If this commission is set up we'll spend half of our time before it. Imagine not being allowed to insult a politician! It's the bloody end of democracy."

Reed: "What can we do about it, Graham?"

"You, David, can write me an editorial giving Rolf Whitaker hell for this insidious scheme. Start by outlining the great struggles early writers, poets and then newspaper owners had to finally get to the acceptance of free speech we now enjoy. Start with the bloody Magna Carta."

"Right, chief. I will."

Reed didn't know it, but he was about to start a long, arduous battle against repression but after having opened fire with the Magna Carta editorial he decided a week later to test existing defamation law by taking on Whitaker's Media Relations Minister William Kerley who had lashed out at all the media in a long tirade in parliament three days after Whitaker's announcement.

He wrote this item for the *Gazette*'s main gossip column: "People alarmed at the Whitaker Government's push to muzzle the nation's entire media will have noticed that, ironically, it is the so-called Media Relations Minister Kerley who is trying to shut down any critical communication in the media. Well, we have a fascinating story to tell about this minister. We were at a party of a few journos only about five months ago and the minister had been invited. At one point discussion came up about businessman John Elfridge on trial for alleged defrauding of shareholders. Our media relations minister loudly announced at the party: 'The only thing to be decided about John Elfridge is the number on his jail door.' As you know, Elfridge was found *not* guilty. So our minister feels that he should have enough free speech to find someone guilty whether they are or not. But that doesn't apply to the rest of us."

A month went by and there was no response from Minister Kerley. Reed went to the nearby Crusaders Arms hotel and bought drinks for seven of his office mates. When the first set of drinks was lined up on the bar, Reed lifted one of them high and announced the toast: "To free speech!" The bar room echoed to a roar of "Hear!

Hear!" which flattered David, but did give him a jolting reminder of Bruce's bellows at the party held for Meg's 30th birthday.

One of Reed's roles at the *Gazette* was to interview prospective cadets, to check their education, query what prompted them to wish to become journalists and ask a series of questions designed to reveal whether they already had a keen interest in public affairs. Each January when not overseas he would quiz about six or eight promising youngsters. This year there were nine and as the paper needed only four, he quickly selected the leading quartet, three young men and a lively 18-year-old blonde Kylee Simpson. Each cadet was asked his or her primary interest and was then attached to a relevant senior reporter, whether covering politics, crime, industrial affairs, health or finance. The cadets would then go out with their guardian to interview people or to a crime scene or to a business official, write their version of the issue and have it checked by the senior, who after filing his or her own report, pointed out any errors in the cadet's version. David found Kylee Simpson quite amusing and told her that she would be "attached" to him for the six-month training period.

"I like that idea," she replied with a cheeky smile.

"Hmm, what have I got here?" thought David. He was not long finding out. At the end of the fourth interview he took her to, in each case explaining to the interviewee why she was there to listen and take notes, it had been a long day but as he headed back to the office with her, she said: "David, what about a glass of red at that pub?"

"I don't think that's a good idea, Kylee."

"Don't you like a drink?"

"It's not that, Kylee."

"Well, what is it then? Don't you like me? I thought we were getting on well."

"Yes, I like you. And yes, we have been getting on well. But I don't think it's a good idea."

"Oh, I see. It's because I'm a young woman. The feminists have got you running scared from having a drink with me, eh?"

David braked hard, swung the car around, hit the accelerator and said, "Right, a glass of red it is."

"That's the stuff. A real gentleman."

David laughed. "We'll see about that." They had one pinot noir then he said, "I have to go. Got a story to write – and so have you." As they pulled into the car park at the *Gazette* she leaned across and gave him a light kiss on the cheek. "Thank you for a lovely afternoon."

"Hey! Get in there and start writing," he said. "I want to see that story by 6:30."

"Yes, commander."

Two days later she turned up at the office in a pair of black plastic tights which emphasised dramatically the curves of her backside and long, smooth legs. "God," he thought, "she certainly would be quite delicious in bed." Then he shook his head to shake away the thought, but in succeeding days it kept coming back and Kylee did nothing to dispel it, continuing with the tights, only sometimes switching from black to grey, but always offering wide smiles from bright red lips.

"What about taking me out for a quick dinner," she said at the end of one day. "I'd like to talk about my career, what area I should aim to work in and what you think of my work so far."

Reed hesitated, thinking of Meg waiting at home with Bruce, but gave way with a nod of agreement. Kylee laughed and took hold of his hand.

"I will have to ring my wife and tell her I'll be late," he said.

"Of course," she replied laughing.

After dinner of pasta, sticky date pudding and three pinot noirs, Kylee smiled at him and said, "Will you drive me to my flat?"

Reed paused again, then nodded again. At the flat she leaned over, put a soft hand on the back of his neck and said, "Come on up for one last drink."

"Eh? What would your parents think of that?"

"Parents? My parents don't live in my flat. I'm independent."

"Independent? How can you be independent on a cadet's salary? How do you pay for the flat, let alone living costs?"

"Well, my parents do pay my rent, but that's all. And they know I'm grown up enough to lead a sensible, independent life, so they leave me to it."

"All right, Kylee. One drink or I'll be over the driving limit and have to stay the night. And no shenanigans, eh. I'm twice your age and any funny business with a cadet could cost me my job."

"Funny business? What do you mean, David?"

"You know damned well what I mean – funny business in bed."

"Oh, David. I haven't had years of experience like you, but so far I have always found it exciting, not funny. Exciting and delicious."

"Ms Simpson. Stop it!"

"All right, Mr Reed. Pinot noir?"

"Yes please, Ms Simpson."

As they sat on opposite sides of a small table, Kylee slipped off a shoe, raised her foot under the table and with her toes gently massaged his genitals. He could not resist it and said nothing. God, for an 18-year-old she sure was up for adult pleasures, he thought. What would one quick fling matter? She would have to keep silent about it or her career might be over, too. She got up, took her drink to the bedroom and began to undress. He thought again of Meg and how long their relationship had been. And he thought also of editor-in-chief Sheridan who was a Catholic and something of a moralist. If this kid happened to blab that she had had a fun night with him he could find himself fired, or, just as bad, back on the shipping round. No, best to pass and head home to Meg who was always a pleasure in bed anyway.

"Sorry, Kylee," he called. "I have to get going. See you at the office." He grabbed his jacket and headed downstairs to his car, hoping that the girl would not try to take it out on him for the rejection, with gossip at the office.

"Big night at the office?" Meg queried in greeting. "What's the story?"

On the way home he had realised he would face some such question.

"No one story. I just realised I had to go through all my files and clear out a lot of rubbish. The stuff builds up ridiculously."

"Well, darling. Have you had any dinner?"

"Yes, sweetie. I'll just get myself a banana and a beer and then let's head off to bed."

"A banana and a beer. What a bogan diet before bed!"

"Well, sweetheart. You married a bogan. Sorry 'bout that. I'll try to reform."

Both naked and warmly tucked under the doona, they embraced. "Would you like to make love to me, bogan boy?"

"Mmm. What an excellent idea."

Later they lay gratified, but still clinging together.

"Thank you, bogan boy," she said. "Talking of boyhood, what adventures did you have as a boy. Care to tell?"

"Well, let's see. Where do I start. Hmmn. Here goes. My parents were quite poor, you know, and one day when I was about seven or eight I was sent to school in a pair of shorts which had a big patch my mother sewed on the bum where I had torn them. At school one kid saw the patch and, pointing at it, began bellowing 'Cinderella! Cinderella!' Other kids began joining in the cry. I bunched my right fist and let the instigator have it right in the face. He began bawling but that was the end of any cries of 'Cinderella'. It was an early lesson to me to stand up for yourself."

"I see, tough guy. Any other dramas in your childhood?"

"Oh, lots. When I was, I think, about 10, a group of us boys in my suburb used to play cricket in the street. One day a girl called Shirley asked us if she could play too. We said yes. She didn't even know how to bowl but we showed her. Down the road was a paddock with a small metal shed. One of the kids had a great idea: take Shirley down to the shed. She happily agreed. In the shed, I said to her: 'You show us yours and we'll show you ours.' She pulled up her dress and pulled down her knickers. 'There,' she said, 'now show me yours.' We all laughed and ran away."

"Bogans indeed," said Meg. "Any other sexual excitements?"

"Let me think. Oh, yes … During the war there were a lot of Yankee troops camped in a big park near our place and one day a mate and I were just wandering through a pine plantation at one end of the park when we saw this Yank with his pants down lying on top of a woman who was mostly bare and was groaning. We couldn't help laughing and when the Yank looked up and saw us he shook a fist and yelled 'Fuck off!' We fucked off, having had a practical lesson in human intercourse."

"Yes, well, as you have proved many times with me, darling, you did learn something that day. By the way, with the Government banning smoking in cafés and hotels and legislating that all cigarette packets have to carry scary pictures of what cigs do to your lungs and heart, it's a wonder anyone still smokes. You've told me you did smoke when young, haven't you."

"Yes, I had my first cigarette when I was about eight. One of our street gang nicked a box of matches from home and six or so of us went to a local wood yard where we built a cave in a wood heap, stripped bark off some stringybark logs, wrapped it in newspaper to make cigarettes and puffed away. But somehow the wood heap caught fire and we ran for our lives. The whole wood yard caught fire and next thing fire engines roared up with sirens bellowing to put out the blaze. We never told our parents. That didn't stop me smoking. When I became a copyboy on the *Gazette* at 16 everybody smoked, even the women. So I started, too. I've told you how at 17 I signed up for National Service in the Air Force and farmer's son Kanga bullied me into giving up smoking. I haven't smoked since and I often think 'Thanks, Kanga, for my good health.' Now, darling, I have rambled on and on. What about one of your childhood dramas?"

"Another night, darling. I think it's time we went to sleep."

At the office next day, news editor Butler called him into his office.

"David, we've had a call from a woman who says she is a nurse at East Boundary Hospital and claims a surgeon there is losing his mind but won't stop operating despite a couple of mistakes. Could you look into it? Here's her phone number." He handed Reed a slip of paper.

"And her name, Graham?"

"She wouldn't give it to me, oddly, yet gave me the number. I rang it back and she answered, saying 'Hello, Gail here.' So I guess her name is Gail. "I thought it best not to push her but to leave it with you. So I just said 'Sorry, wrong number' and hung up."

Reed: "OK, Graham. I have a contact in Telemetry Directorate so I might be able to get her name and address from him, but I'll try ringing her first."

He had to ring the number four times that evening before getting an answer, a very quiet "Hello?"

"Gail?"

"Yes. This is Gail. Who's speaking?"

"My name is David Reed. You rang us at the *Gazette* and I'd be happy to help you."

"Oh. Why ring me, Mr Reed. Why not take up the issue with my hospital?"

"We can't just approach your chief and say we've heard one of your doctors should not be operating. We have to have some evidence to present so we know what we are talking about. For instance, at first of all we have to have the doctor's name. And we need some evidence from you about the mistakes that have happened."

"I would lose my job if I did that and I have a child to support."

"Well, will you give me the name of the doctor and some detail about the mistakes and I promise I will not reveal your name or phone number to the management."

"How can I trust you not to do that? What I read about journalists is that they are in public opinion on a level or below used-car salesmen."

"Gail, if you think all that, why did you ring our chief? I know why, actually. Because you know that it's the despised journalists who are prepared to try to uncover such despicable behaviour. Sometimes in life, Gail, you have to have the courage to do the right thing. I promise you that if the hospital management came to realise that you might have tipped us off, even if there were no proof, and if they took any action against you, we would make their life hell until they reinstated you. We have the power to do that. And if even that did not work, we would help you to find another job."

"I'm no fool, Mr Reed."

"Please call me David, Gail."

"I'm no fool, Mr Reed. I want you to send me a letter detailing the promises you have made me, including about finding a new job, and mail it to Post Office Box 2279, Milhurst. Include your phone number and if I am happy with your promises, I'll get back to you. OK?"

"OK, Gail. Just tell me one thing: which hospital is it?"

A long hesitation then, "Apollo General." And she hung up. He realised he would have to run the promissory letter past news editor Butler, so drew it up and took it to him, explaining the background.

"Well I hope we *can* find her a new job if it all blows up," Butler said. "Better make damn sure we find somebody else on the staff to back up her claims."

Reed posted the letter to the Post Office box and waited for a phone call. When it did not come after two days, he rang her number in the evening but the number rang out. He tried again for the next two evenings and still there was no answer. "Odd," he thought. When he got the same result after two more evenings, he decided on action. He stood on the front marbled steps of the hospital and as uniformed nurses left he would ask "Gail?" Repeatedly women either smiled and nodded the negative or even laughed, offering such remarks as "Good try, but no!" The second day he did this, a hefty, uniformed security officer marched down the steps: "What do you think you are doing harassing our staff? Do you want me to call the cops?"

Reed realised his ploy was not going to work. "Sorry, officer. I work for the *Gazette* and one of your staff, Gail, offered us some important information. She seems to have gone missing, so I'd better go in and talk with your management. OK?"

The guard waved him in, directing him to the manager's office. A secretary at a desk outside the office demanded peremptorily what business he wanted with the manager.

Reed: "That's confidential, but important to the reputation of this hospital. I'm sure the manager would want to know that. By the way, can you tell me his name, please."

"Roger Allerday."

"Thank you. And would you mind now telling him?"

She got up, went into the office and several minutes ensued before she returned, waving him in.

"Mr Allerday, I'm David Reed from the *Gazette*. Thank you for seeing me."

"What is this supposedly confidential but important information about our reputation, Mr Reed?"

"It's not your present reputation, Mr Allerday. It's something that could badly damage it if true."

"Well, don't keep me in suspense. What is it?"

"One of your nurses has claimed to us that one of your surgeons has been making damaging mistakes affecting patients possibly because of an apparent absent-mindedness."

"And the doctor is?"

"She would not say. She appears to be afraid of being sacked if she goes public."

"Nonsense. That would be most irresponsible. Corrupt in fact. What is her name?"

"Her name is Gail. She would not give us her surname, but I suppose you don't have that many Gails who work in the operating theatres."

Allerday pulled out a leather-bound volume and ran his finger down a list of names.

"You are right, Mr Reed. We have one Gail. Gail Renaldor. She has been with us, let's see, about eight months. I don't know that that would make her an expert on all forms of medical operations."

"But if she saw a surgeon repeatedly pick up the wrong instrument, or worse still, begin to operate on the wrong breast before being alerted, she would not have needed years of experience to know that something was badly wrong."

"Is that what she is saying?"

"As I said, she has given me only limited information as she wants a guarantee that she will not be punished."

"Well now that you media have some whiff of something that might be wrong, I guess I will have to grill her anyway. Right?"

"Well Mr Allerday, if you put it like that, yes, you will."

"Can I have your guarantee that you will not publish until you hear from me?"

"Sorry. I don't think I can do that for two reasons. Your board might decide to break the news where it would have less impact than on the front page of the *Gazette* or you might decide to take some action and tell nobody about it."

"You don't seem to have a very high opinion of our integrity, Mr Reed."

"Sorry, Mr Allerday. The caution comes from long experience. However, I do realise that you will need some time to interview Ms Renardor and then a series of doctors. So I will hold off naming the hospital for the time being – in the hope that I will hear from you about what action has been taken."

"I have given you Gail's surname. I hope you will have the decency not to publish it, as she was not prepared to give it to you when you phoned her."

"Fair enough. She will remain just "a nurse".

"And this interview, is it off the record?"

"No, Mr Allerday. You did not ask for it to be off the record and you saw me taping it."

"Get out of my office, Mr Reed. You have just reinforced the view I have of media creeps."

"Thank you, Mr Allerday. I hope your investigation is timely enough to lead to someone's life being saved." Reed walked out.

After consulting Butler and two of the *Gazette*'s lawyers who specialised in libel, he waited a fortnight then wrote a short article that a major Apollo hospital was investigating allegations by a staff member that an ageing surgeon feared to be suffering mental disability was endangering patients with some disastrous results. Three days after that he received a call from Allerday.

"Reed? This is Allerday. You will be no doubt pleased to know that 78-year-old surgeon David Kopyanski has been declared redundant by our management in the interests of patient safety. That is all I can say."

Reed: "I suppose now, Mr Allerday, the hospital will be facing some court actions alleging negligence?" The phone went dead. Reed rang back the hospital.

"Could I speak to nurse Gail Renardor please." He was put through to Ward 14.

"Hello. Nurse Renardor here."

"Gail, this is the dreaded David Reed here. I just want to thank you for taking such a principled stand for patient safety. Kopyanski has been made redundant as you know. But I just want to tell you that if the same thing should happen to you, ring me immediately and the *Gazette* will make damned sure you are reinstated pronto. OK?"

"OK Mr Reed. And thank you."

CHAPTER 9

"Bloody hell!" Butler's bellow resounded through the newsroom.

"Another boatload of 257 bloody refugees (as he sounded the word he waved two fingers of each hand up and down to indicate quotation marks thereby also indicating his view that true refugees they were not). So that's about another 200 houses we have to find, another 200 jobs and in the meantime, another 200 welfare pensions. At this rate we're going to take in 30,000 a year."

He pointed at Reed. "David. Into my office. I want you to get to the bottom of who are the people running these rackets."

Butler slumped into his oak and polished leather chair, leaned elbows on his wide brown desk and said: "You can take all the time you need on this. I want you to get the individual stories of these characters, but, more importantly find out how much they are paying, whom they are paying and what the Whitaker Government is going to do to block the traffic."

Reed nodded, but responded: "A lot of these people know they are risking their lives in shoddy boats, so it could be that they have been in fear of their lives. Some of the countries they are sailing from are not exactly splendid democracies, are they."

"Maybe so. But do you really think our taxpayers should be providing housing, food and spending money for all the world's unhappy people? I don't. These countries with crummy dictators, who make sure their own families and friends have piles of money and spend their holidays on the Cote d'Azur, guzzling the finest wines of Bordeaux, but drive out of the country anyone who criticises them, should be made to take them back."

"All right, Graham. But you realise this is going to take quite some time and a lot of dollars."

"That's my worry, David. If you come up with a good expose, our readers will love it, our circulation will stay up and the advertising dollars keep rolling in. You know all that!"

Reed went home to tell Meg of the assignment and that he expected to have to go to some northern countries to chase down refugee smugglers. "I know I promised you to stay in a safer role now that we have Bruce, darling, but I will be careful. And I don't expect any serious trouble."

"Oh well, darling. I expected you couldn't resist the thrill of the chase indefinitely. So do be careful. And keep in touch every couple of days. Promise?"

"I promise." He gave her a long, strong kiss and hug.

First he approached the office of the federal minister of immigration for permission to interview some of the latest 257 asylum seekers to hit the northern shore, asking for the minister's media officer, Simon Traveldor.

"Hi, Simon. What are the chances of interviewing some of the latest boatload of asylum seekers for a *Gazette* feature article?"

"Are we off the record, David?"

"For the moment, yes, Simon"

"Well the answer, David, is: sorry, no way. Already had instructions from the minister who expected media calls as soon as he heard of the boat."

"But if you don't let us try to find out who is behind all these boats and how they can be stopped, what's the idea?"

"The idea, David. Is that our department's boys will do that."

"Well, there's another aspect, Simon. If you let me talk to some of them I can relate some of their horrifying stories and gain public sympathy for them. What would the minister say to that?"

"I don't know, David. I would have to put that to him. My first reaction is that there's no way we would know what questions you were going to ask and what you would publish. I'll have to get back to you."

Reed waited two days, but when there was no reply he flew to the port of Safebay in the far north of the country, where the latest arrivals were being held in a detention centre. From about 4.30pm he sat waiting in his car about 100 metres from the main gate which was manned by two armed immigration officials, estimating that there would a change of all the staff around 5pm. And there was. Illegal entry men and women clung to the steel-netting fence of the centre, looking out at the world, as Reed studied the workers driving out at the end of shift. Finally he saw a possible target, a woman who looked in her late 20s, leaving alone in a sports car. He followed her into Safebay township and was delighted to see her pull up and go into a café. Going in, he ordered a long macchiato and sat at a comfortable leather bench near her.

"G'day. I'm up here from Apollo," he said. "What's life like in Safebay?"

"Not bad," she replied, sipping a latte. "Why do you ask? Are you just on holiday, or coming here to work?"

"Just visiting. What do you do in Safebay? Are you working, or minding a family?"

"Cripes. Do you think minding a family isn't work?"

"Oops. Sorry. Didn't mean that. Of course I didn't. Was just making conversation."

She laughed. "That's all right – just the feminist in me. No. I'm not married. I work at the refugee detention centre. What do you do?"

"I'm a journalist, actually. But just on holiday. I thought it would be good to explore the north. How do you find working among the refugees?"

"It's very trying, actually. You hear so many tragic stories of hate, cruelty, murder. I sometimes wonder how long I will be able to tolerate it."

"My name is David Reed. Can I ask you yours?"

She brushed long, black hair back from her face, studied him for a moment, smiled and said, "Margaret Clarendon".

"Hi Margaret," he smiled. "Perhaps you could help me to help those people behind the steel wire."

"Oh yes? In what way?"

"I'd like to get some of their stories to the public. That could help them immensely."

She paused, added another spoon of sugar to the remaining half of her latte and stirred it for nearly a minute. "Hmm. How do you think I could possibly help you do that?"

"Is there some way you could get me into the centre to interview some of them?"

"No way. Not possible."

"That's a shame. I can tell from what you have said that you would like to see them get some help."

"That's true. But even if somehow I could bring you in, the minute you published something I would get the sack."

"Well, what about this: I give you some sheets of paper with lists of questions. You talk to some of the detainees, get their names, where from, their religion, why they fled, what kids they have, any torture or killings they know about, how much they paid for a seat in the boat and whom they paid. Then bring those papers out to me. The publicity could arouse a lot of public sympathy, Margaret."

"Depends which stories you decide to tell, doesn't it? They're not all victims of religious or political persecution according to some of the stories I have heard."

"Well that's probably true. But all we have to do is give a fair balance."

"Look, I think I have a better idea. Once a week, a group of the men are taken to the local oval to kick around soccer balls to give them some exercise. At the same time some of the women with kids are allowed to go with female guards to the park near the detention centre where the kids can play on the swings and slides. I think you could probably talk to a few of them without any trouble."

"Are most of the women wearing burqas? There's no way they'd talk to a Western stranger."

"Oh, you'd be surprised, David, at how modern some of them are in outlook. And no, they don't all wear burqas. Give it a go."

"What about the female guards, though."

"I'll word them up to make it easy for you, but please do the right thing when it comes to what you publish. Meet me here again tomorrow evening and I'll fill you in on progress."

The following evening Margaret turned up for another long macchiato. "I spoke to my three women colleagues and they at first were very doubtful, but finally agreed with this proviso: if anything goes wrong with what you publish they will all say they have never seen you. OK? Go to the park tomorrow morning, about 10 o'clock."

Reed: "Deal. Thank you, Margaret."

At the park, on time, he found eight women: two of them uniformed guards, three women in western dress, one wearing a burqa and two fully veiled with niqabs and clutching prams and surrounded by four small children. Not to alarm the women, he approached one of the guards.

"My name is David Reed. I spoke yesterday with Margaret Clarendon and she said I could come here and talk with some of the detainees about their experiences. Could you help me with that?"

"Yes. Margaret warned us," the woman replied.

"Do any of these women speak English?"

"Some speak a little, but I can speak Arabic and can translate for you."

"Could you start by asking one of the women wearing a niqab to give you the story of her background and her escape to Australia and does she expect to be freed to live here."

The guard spoke to the woman for about five minutes then turned to Reed:

"She came from southern Afghanistan. Her husband had a farm. The Taliban came and demanded that he join them. He refused. They set fire to the farmhouse so the family had nowhere to live. They had heard of other neighbours who had fled to south-east Asia so sold the land, the cattle and camels they owned, fled to Pakistan and paid to fly to Aronelia. There they were told they could not stay but as they had money and jewellery, could pay a smuggler to get them on a boat for Australia. Otherwise they would be put in prison or shipped back to Afghanistan. That's what they did."

Reed: "Ask her what the reaction of immigration officials here has been."

The guard chattered again in Arabic and came back with this answer: "They asked her and her husband for the exact location of the farmhouse so they could get an official in Afghanistan to check their story that it was burned down and that Taliban were active in the area. They have not heard of any result."

Reed: "How long ago were they asked that?" More Arabic ensues.

The guard: "She says about five months ago and they have heard nothing."

Reed: "I'd like to talk with her husband. Is he over there with the soccer players?"

Guard: "He's the tall guy dribbling the ball along the ground right now. By the way, he speaks some English."

Reed waited until the ball session ended then approached the tall, bearded husband.

"Hello. My name is David. I am a writer and I am doing an article on refugees and their stories. I have been talking to your wife. Do you mind if I ask you about your troubles?"

"No. Go ahead. My name is Ahmed Hajrah."

"Ahmed your wife has told me why you came to our country. It was quite brave of you."

"We had no choice. It was run or die. There were even murders all around us. A friend tell me that if we get to your country we and our children will be safe. Then I hear of a man in Aronelia who could find a boat to escape to here if we pay enough."

"Ahmed, you speak reasonable English. How did that come about?"

"My father, now dead. He a university teacher. He encourage me to English so I could leave farming and perhaps be trader for foreign companies."

"How much did you have to pay for the boat?"

"I pay 420,000 – 10,000 of your dollars for whole family to escape. Cattle and land sold."

"Would you mind telling me whom you paid for the boat places in Indonesia?"

"If I tell you and we are sent back to Afghanistan he might try to have someone kill us all."

"Ahmed, I promise I will not reveal where I got the information."

"You promise?"

"I promise. I would not dream of putting you, your wife and children in danger."

"All right. His name Abdul Ralinghan. He in the port of Barianta."

"How long have you been here in detention?"

"I not sure. I think maybe eight months. They checking I no terrorist. I tell you I no terrorist. We came here get away from terrorism."

"Ahmed, why didn't you take your family to a refugee camp in your country instead of coming all the way to end up stranded here?"

"You no understand. Government there angry about refugee camps. Hardly any food. Nothing to do all day. You may be there for years. Bad as prison. Dreadful."

"Well, you seem to be being fed properly here. And they even let you play soccer outside the camp. But you and your family may be here for quite a while longer until our country is sure you are no terrorist."

"Perhaps you tell them I good man?"

"Sorry, Ahmed. I'm afraid my word wouldn't mean a thing."

"You a writer. You should have influence."

"Sometimes, yes, Ahmed. But in this case, no. I have to go now. Thank you for talking."

Ahmed held out both arms in a gesture of despair. Embarrassed, Reed turned and walked away. He realised that if he were to satisfy news editor Butler he would have to track down smuggler Ralinghan and expose him. He returned to Apollo City, told Butler, then Meg, what he planned and booked a flight to Daronka. There he sought out Asim Kadir, the *Gazette*'s local correspondent to alert him to what he was planning to do.

Kadir: "Be very careful, David. For a start, I wouldn't go near the cops. You never know which of them might be benefiting from the smugglers and they could soon have you warming a cell on some fake charge."

"Thanks Asim. I'll keep that in mind."

From Daronka Reed took a small plane to Karsuma where he booked into a tourist-packed beachside apartment block close to the main docks. At the front desk he asked where he might hire a Bahasa translator to help with his work and was given the name Hutomo and a phone number. The desk agreed to call the translator and ask him to come to the block. Within half an hour Hutomo arrived, heard Reed's offer of a week's work and nodded agreement.

"Hutomo, I want to track down one of the people who is charging refugees a lot of money, putting them on broken, old boats and sending them out to sea to die. Will you help me? I will pay you well."

Hutomo: "That is risky. We will have to be careful. But I know where there are quite a few asing."

"Asing?"

"Sorry, Mr Reed. I lapsed into Bahasa. Asing … foreigners."

"It's not just foreigners I want to talk with, Hutomo, but refugees."

"Yes, I understand that. If you get a taxi we can go there now."

The taxi took them to the northern outskirts of Karsuma where in an open field 40 or 50 green tents had sprung up. Between the tents children played with balls or just sat in the sun.

"How long have they been here, Hutomo?"

"Five or six months that I know of, Mr Reed."

"OK. What you need to do for me is to approach parents until we find a family who have been offered a boat, who have paid the fee, and expect to be going soon."

Reed waited in the taxi while Hutomo went from tent to tent chatting with the men in them. After an hour, just as a dejected Reed began to believe the project was a failure, Hutomo came running back, waving excitedly.

"Mr Reed. Mr Reed. I have found them!"

Reed shook his hand. "Well done! Let's go see them."

At the tent he met husband, wife and two children. Through Hutomo, they told him they had paid to board a boat in three days' time. The money had been paid to boat organiser Aysor Asodelta.

Reed: "Hutomo, tell him I will give him 50,000 rupiah if he lets me take a picture of him and his family, and tells me where I can meet Asodelta."

Hutomo: "That might be very dangerous, Mr Reed."

Reed: "I'll take that risk, Hutomo. And don't worry. I'll take a taxi to see Asodelta and I won't ask you to come."

"Thank you, Mr Reed."

"But can you think of a translator who might be prepared to go with me?"

"I have some friends, Mr Reed. I could ask them."

"Now will you ask the father where I can find Asodelta."

Reed handed over the wad of rupiah to the refugee, Hutomo got the Asodelta address in southern Karsuma, wrote it down, and handed it to Reed, adding: "If you get to see Asodelta, please do not tell him where you got this." Reed nodded agreement.

Back at the hotel Reed sat in the front lounge enjoying an icy glass of cendol, a combination of coconut milk, rice flour and sugar, when the desk clerk called him across and handed him a phone. It was Hutomo.

"Mr Reed, I have someone for you. He is young but he will be expensive. His name is Dawentra. But if you see Asodelta, do not reveal that name. And Dawentra will want to be paid in cash."

Hutomo then gave a phone number where Dawentra could be contacted and hung up. Reed immediately dialled the number and to his surprise, Dawentra answered. He agreed to Reed's offer and turned up at the hotel next morning.

"Can I be paid now, please?" he said. Reed smiled, went to the hotel desk, handed over his credit card and returned with a stack of rupiah. Dawentra took the money, counted it quickly, then went to the desk clerk, asked for an envelope to put it in, put his name on the envelope, then indicated to the clerk to put it in the hotel safe. He returned to Reed smiling. "Now we are ready," he said.

They hired a taxi, Dawentra handed the driver Reed's note listing Asodelta's address, and four minutes later they pulled up outside a quite imposing house facing the sea. At the steel-grille gate stood a male, obviously a civilian sentry.

"Dawentra, tell him we need to see Mr Asodelta about paying for a family to go on one of his boats."

"Yes, Mr Reed."

The sentry nodded, indicated to the taxi driver to pull to one side past the gate, then retired to the house, returning within a couple of minutes to invite Dawentra and Reed to enter. In a lushly furnished lounge room a bearded, surprisingly tubby man lay stretched back in a leather armchair. The sentry introduced Dawentra and retreated.

"Mr Reed, this is Mr Asodelta," Dawentra said.

Reed, nodding to the man, offered a handshake which was ignored.

"Dawentra, tell him there is a family I became friends with when working as a journalist in Pakistan. They have written to me saying they desperately want to come to my country and could I help. As I have heard that Asodelta can help families get on a boat, would he help and how much would it cost."

Dawentra rattled this all off to Asodelta who held bunched fingers to his mouth and betrayed no reaction. He eventually broke the silence with a question.

"Mr Reed, he wants to know how many are in the family."

"Tell him four. Mother, father, two children."

Asodelta ruminated then snapped an answer to Dawentra.

Dawentra: "He says the cost would be 100 million rupiah."

Reed scratched his head, stared at the ceiling while calculating and said: "That's about $10,000 of our money. I suppose that's about right. It concurs with what we've heard of about other boaties. Ask him whether he will have a boat ready soon."

Dawentra did. "He says he can buy a boat any time he needs one."

Reed: "I'll bet he can. Most of the ones used are rust-buckets. Half of them don't make it to their destination."

Reed took out his mobile phone and pretended to be fingering a calculation but actually held it so he could snap an image of Asodelta spread out in the chair.

"Tell him thanks and we will be in touch within a couple of days about getting the family aboard."

Reed gave Asodelta a farewell wave and with Dawentra headed for the taxi.

HE GETS PAID TO SHIP DOZENS TO DEATH shouted the *Gazette* front-page headline over a large photo of Asodelta the next day. Butler won't be very happy about that, Reed thought when Meg had transmitted to him a photo of the page. The article tended to generate sympathy for the boat people. Then again, it did undermine the boat system. As his hotel faced a delightful park and beyond that the ocean beach, Reed decided to spend a couple of days in Karsuma before taking a flight home. He particularly wanted to experience the country's puppet theatre of which he had heard much.

But the day proved not exactly relaxing. A police officer called while he was having lunch at the hotel and asked for details about

Asodelta. God, news travels fast, Reed thought, if the cops already know what has appeared in the *Gazette*. But he obliged, detailing the whereabouts of the family paying to get on the boat – and Asodelta's address. He decided not to mention translator Dawentra's role to protect the young man from unnecessary stress. As evening approached he ordered a taxi to take him to the puppet performance, leaving in plenty of time to have a few drinks beforehand. But only a block from the hotel he noticed a motorbike rider cruising beside the taxi and looking in at him intently. To his horror he suddenly saw the man draw a pistol. Fortunately he was in the taxi's back seat and instinctively threw himself flat on the seat before the gun blazed. Two shots smashed the left and right-hand side windows then the motorbike roared away. The taxi driver screeched to a halt and began shouting at Reed.

"It's not my bloody fault!" Reed shouted in return. "It's your bloody criminals!" The taxi driver obviously did not understand, but pointed despairingly at the smashed windows and held out an open hand. Reed realised he was asking for money for repairs and broke into a laugh. The driver began shouting and pointing to his open hand. Reed, glad to be alive, nodded, drew out his wallet and thrust a bundle of notes into the hand. Reed slid out of the cab and ran back to the hotel in case Asodelta's killer turned around for another attempt. Despite knowing that Meg would be furious when she read it, he filed a report on the murder attempt to the *Gazette* which happily splashed it on the bottom half of the front page as "Our man escapes refugee gang's murder bid". But as soon as he had lodged the report he packed his suitcase, headed for the airport, booked on the next plane to Apollo and spent three hours waiting in the lounge for flight time. Yes, Meg would be angry, he thought, but Butler no doubt would be delighted.

A decidedly sour Meg did greet him when he walked in the front door. "Hello, Mr Dramatist. Glad to see that you are still alive. Did it occur to you at any time that you might end up leaving me a widow with a one-year-old son to look after? I thought you had promised to give up reckless projects."

"I do apologise, darling. I had no idea that I would end up being shot at. It was supposed to be a simple investigation. But look, darling. Before you married me you did know that journalists don't have dull lives. I don't want to sit at a desk every day and write dull crap attacking or praising politicians. I couldn't bear it. Look, I'm going to make it up to you."

"How so?"

"There are places and things I've always wanted to see in the United States. What's say we take a holiday there?"

"With Bruce?"

"Of course, with Bruce. For him, we don't even have to pay air fares. He just sits in your lap or mine."

"When do you want to go? And can we afford it?"

"I'll just tell Butler I need a break to recover from the shooting and we'll go ... let's say ... in a week's time? And, yes, we can afford it."

They decided on three weeks to be spent in Chicago, New York and Washington. Ten hours flying took them to Los Angeles and four more to Chicago where they collapsed into their hotel beds for nine hours sleep – well, nine for David but only four for Meg before Bruce was whimpering that it was breast time for breakfast.

Eventually awake, over a late breakfast, David took Meg's hand. "There is one thing in this town we really must see, darling."

"What's that."

"The Bean."

"The Bean? What's that?"

"Just that, a huge silver bean in Millennium Park. It's huge. A brilliant, silver sculpture weighing over 100 tonnes."

At the park, they walked up to the monster and ran their hands over the glowing surface. The "bean" was arched so they could walk underneath the centre of it. David lifted Bruce out of the small pram they had hired from the hotel and drew a tiny hand up to touch the metal monster while Meg took their picture.

"David, what is it supposed to be? Surely not all this metal and effort just to produce a bean."

Reed laughed. "No, darling. Sculptor Anish Kapoor titled it Cloud Gate, but the Yanks degraded it to a bean. That's the Yanks for you. Even so, it's magnificent, isn't it."

The next day they took in the city's Art Institute, the entrance graced by huge green bronze lions and the splendid building housing more than 200,000 paintings, textiles and sculptures, ranging from Grecian urns to Impressionist works. At one point they came across a Van Gogh "The Bedroom", a tablet announcing that it was produced during a stay at an asylum.

"I'll bet the old Van had a right old time there," commented David.

"Don't be so vulgar, David. The poor man is dead."

"True. Dead a long time. Nevertheless, quite famous. I wouldn't mind that."

"Really? I think I'd rather be alive than dead and famous."

"Yes, darling."

The next day they took a water taxi from Navy Pier, cruising all the way down the Chicago River. A woman guide briefed the passengers on the history of various buildings, pointing out that the Great Fire of 1871 had destroyed the city but led to a massive burst of new architecture led by Frank Lloyd Wright. However, what caught David's eye was the severe rust eating away the steel holding up nearly all of the bridges under which they passed.

"It looks like you are going to have a similar crunch of a lot of your bridges," David told her, pointing to the rust on the huge old spars. The guide curled her lips in derision, but remained silent. At South Wacker Drive they passed the 110-storey Sears Tower, once, but no longer, the tallest building in the US. David held Bruce up high. "Look at that, mate. Don't go climbing it. It's a long way to fall and you might miss the river," he said loudly. The woman guide glared at Reed but said nothing, but Meg read her thoughts and told David quietly: "You are not the one providing the tour guidance, David. Better leave it to Her Majesty there."

The next morning was spent wandering through Lincoln Park then it was back to the hotel and a taxi to the airport for New York. The flight to New York was delayed for an hour because the airline they had booked was having trouble with several of its planes. If the aircraft landed with a bit of a bump, as aircraft often do, some of the seats would jerk free of their floor rails and slide forward as the plane braked. They did not learn of the reason for the delay until disembarking (safely, as it happened) in New York.

"Have you ever been to New York, Meg?"

"No, darling. This is my first visit. What about you?"

"Yes, I came here in my mid-twenties on my way home from working for some time in London. I'll never forget it."

"Why not? Did you have trouble?"

"No. But it was funny. I had been told by other journos that there was an outfit called Driveaway and you could be given a car to drive to some other part of America if you had an international driving licence, which I did have. I went there and they gave me a Chevrolet sedan which had to be delivered back to Los Angeles. They even gave me $50 for petrol. The story was that a husband in LA had had a huge row with his wife, took the Chevrolet which belonged to her, drove it to New York then dumped it in a side street. So I set off to take it back.

As I had one month to return it, I thought I would see as much of the US as possible, so I whizzed across to Pittsburgh, then over here to Chicago, down to Kansas City, then Denver, across to Salt Lake City, Las Vegas and finally LA. One thing I do remember vividly. It was hilarious. In the centre of Kansas City I found myself behind a big sedan stopped in the lane I was in. A woman behind the wheel got out as I pulled up and came back to me. 'Can you give me a push?' she said. So I got out and put my hands on the boot to start pushing her, thinking she wanted to just get off the road. She came back and said, 'What the hell are you doing?' Then she explained. She wanted me to run the Chev up to the back of her sedan and get it up to a speed where when she let the clutch out, her motor would kick in. Being young, I was silly enough to agree to do it and got her car up to about 40kms/hour in the middle of the city before her engine started. She roared away without even a wave of thank you. That's America."

Meg: "The main thing I want to see in New York if the Statue of Liberty and I'm told there are fantastic shops along 5th Avenue."

"There are, Meg. And I don't mind if you spend a bit."

"A bit?!"

"Well, a fair bit. Fortunately, big New York shops are quite smart and they nearly all provide soft couches in which husbands can sit and read the paper while wives take ages fondling skirts, blouses, jewellery, shoes and handbags."

"Don't be sarcastic."

"That's not sarcasm. That's realism. Wait and see."

Booked into a hotel on East 33rd Street, David said over breakfast: "Right, Meg. Today I want to give you a fantastic view of the Hudson River, so we'll take a taxi to the High Line."

"What is the High Line, darling?"

"It's an old former rail line running up the East Side that has been turned into a great park, complete with trees, flowers and even seats. There's a walkway runs the full length, so Bruce's pusher will be no problem. They've torn up most of the old train rails but left a few to show where the park once was."

"David, why is it called the High Line?"

"You'll see why, Meg. The rail line was an elevated one, about four metres high."

It was a blue-sky day and the view of the Hudson made Meg gasp. They were able to take a ladder down from the Line and walk along the riverside until at one point they came to a wharf with two huge sailing boats, the 26-metre Adirondack and its identical mate Adirondack 11. The first was about to leave to cruise down the Hudson to the Statue of Liberty and Ellis Island.

"Come on, Meg! Let's get on! You've always wanted to see old Liberty clutching her torch."

The yacht at first chugged out motor-driven, but a strong wind was blowing and the captain shut down and switched to sail. Even the big yacht keeled over, so the tourists clutched at rails, Meg also clutching Bruce tightly.

"Isn't this a barrel of fun!" exclaimed an elderly woman next to them. "I do this every weekend. Have done for years."

David: "Don't you get bored?"

"Young man, if you ever find this boring, you should arrange your funeral details."

The next day it was off to the Rockefeller Centre on 5th Avenue to watch skaters skimming around the famous ice rink. David admired the great golden statue of Prometheus clutching a handful of fire, his genitals covered only by a loose cloth.

"Good job they've got a fountain right under him," remarked David. "I couldn't imagine anything more painful than a burnt dick."

Meg: "David! Don't be so vulgar in public. You'll end up getting us arrested. Let's get out of here and go to the top of the Centre. We should be able to see the whole of New York."

Then it was off to Frank Lloyd Wright's Guggenheim art museum on Fifth Avenue, taking a lift to the top floor then slowly spiralling down pushering Bruce past Picassos, Kandinskys and other great 20th century artists.

As the afternoon headed towards twilight they even made it to the Metropolitan Museum of Art for Rembrandts, Van Goghs, Vermeers and Matisses.

"David, I'm all arts-out. I can't even remember all the great names we've now seen. Can we go home. I have to feed Bruce again soon."

"OK darling. I was hoping to have time to go to the New York Museum of Sex, but we might have to let that wait until next time."

"Yes, David. We will," she said emphatically.

The next day they entered the other great tourist must-see, Central Park and eventually reached John Lennon's memorial, named Strawberry Fields, the title of one of his most famous songs. When Meg saw the large marble disc with the word IMAGINE in the centre, surrounded by flowers she burst into song:

"Imagine there's no heaven

It's easy if you try

No hell below us

Above us only sky ... "

"I had to write a feature about Lennon once," David interrupted. "Richard Nixon tried to have him deported because he wrote *'Give Peace a Chance'* and was anti the Vietnam war.

Meg sang on:

"Nothing to kill or die for

And no religion too"

David broke in again: "It was Lennon's anti-religion view that got him killed if I remember correctly. He was quoted as having said once: 'I'm more popular than Jesus.' When a 25-year-old Hawaiian, Mark Chapman, was offended by that, he waited for Lennon to return one evening to his apartment just over there from the park and slammed five bullets into Lennon's back."

Meg: "Was Chapman executed?"

David: "Oddly, no. He sat down in the street after the killing and just waited for the cops. He got life imprisonment and as far as I know still has not been given parole more than 30 years later."

Meg was determined to have the last word, singing:

"You may say I'm a dreamer

But I'm not the only one
I hope some day you'll join us
And the world will live as one."

"Aah Meg. You're definitely a dreamer, but a lovely one. Next stop Washington?"

"All right Mr Tour Organiser. Next stop Washington it is and of course your lifelong passion ... a visit to the Smithsonian galleries."

"Yes sir!"

"What do you mean Yes sir, you sexist monster."

"Oops ... I mean, Yes Ma'am!"

Down through the park they marched, this time David steering Bruce's pusher and Meg still humming the Lennon tune. They just had time to take a taxi to the site of the Twin Towers blasted by Osama Bin Laden's Al Qaeda flight gang killing 3000. The Memorial Park contains two architecturally splendid pools with the names of the 3000 victims set in gold on the pool edges.

"A permanent reminder of the evil idiocy of many humans," said Meg. David just shook his head sadly. "Evil, but not idiots. It was all carefully planned.

The electric train next morning to Washington gave them a depressing view: whizzing past broken-down factories, huge piles of rubbish in back yards of decrepit homes, stacks of rusting car wrecks.

"Christ, is this the real America now?" David mused aloud. A silver-haired man in a nearby seat glared at him, but said nothing.

The next morning, however, brought another world. They taxied down Independence Avenue to David's mental Everest, the Smithsonian Institute.

"Will we start with the Museum of African Art, David?"

"Ah, no, Meg. I think the Air and Space Museum."

"Of course. I should have realised that."

David took the entire morning, revelling in gazing up at, dangling from the ceiling, the first plane to cross the United States from east to west, then the first plane to cross the Atlantic Ocean, then at the end of the same gallery, a large, black sinister drone. He did then accept Meg's insistence that the next stop was the National Gallery of Art.

After that it was a taxi to the White House, then to the Lincoln Memorial and across the Potomac River to Arlington National Cemetery.

"I've read, Meg, that there are about 300,000 military graves here, but interestingly the authorities also allow relatives of the slain troops to be buried here, too, to be next to loved ones."

As they walked around the forest of graves, David noticed that officers had a select area apart from ordinary GIs. "That's the military, Meg. Know your place – even when you're dead."

On a high section of the cemetery, on Sheridan Drive, they saw the grave of President John F. Kennedy, lit by a permanent flame. But to Meg, the most touching moment was when they came across a memorial garden with lifelike statues of GIs killed in the Vietnam war – the graves and statues all paid for by relatives of the dead men.

Late in the afternoon they had time for one last experience, a haunting two hours in the US Holocaust Museum on 14th Street confronted by scores of photos of parents and children being led off by Nazi troops to go to concentration camps and eventual execution, photos of children behind the wire and a sight that

Meg said would stay with her forever: the whole floor of a long gallery covered with hundreds of stone grimacing images – each representing a murdered Jew. On leaving, Meg and David were given a card which identified a Hungarian Jewish woman, Ilona Geroe, and her husband, who were bashed, had their grain business confiscated and were sent to a labour camp near Vienna. They were rescued by the Red Army in 1945.

As Meg emerged onto 14th Street she held her head in her hands. "Oh God, David. I never want to see anything like that again."

"I understand, Meg. But it's important that millions of people see that sort of thing so we can try to ensure such insane racism never happens again. Come on. Let's get to the pub for a good dinner with a fine bottle of red. After that, it's bed, a bit of fun, a tomorrow morning the airport for home. Taxi!"

As their plane dropped down towards Apollo City 12 hours later, Meg looked out at the spires lining the central river and began to clap.

"What's with the applause, darling?"

"I'm just so glad to be home to get back into a simple routine."

"Hmmn. Yeah. It has been a bit of a slog for you with Bruce and all that travel."

"David, you don't know the half of it."

"What do you mean?"

"What I mean is that every night you were asleep and snoring, sometimes after having some very energetic sex, there I was waking up every four hours to breastfeed his nibs."

"Oh, sorry. Isn't it time you put him onto just the bottle, then?"

"No. Not yet. I do still like the feeling."

"I can understand that. Amen!"

An uneventful month followed at the *Gazette* office, with David writing opinion articles on issues that took his fancy – and also editorials, which were again opinion articles, but written under the title of the *Gazette* and seen by the public as the newspaper's opinion. The broad outline of the latter were dictated to him by editor- in-chief Darryl Sheridan and often he did not agree with parts of them, but typed them in nevertheless. Occasionally he pointed out to Sheridan arguments that he considered mistaken and even won deletions, but not often.

Typing away at his desk one afternoon he looked across the newsroom and noticed reporter Salley Shirham appeared to be sobbing. He went over.

"Salley, are you all right?" She shook her head, her long hair flying.

"Can I help you?" Another shake of the head.

"Obviously something is very upsetting. Would you like to go out to a café where we can talk?" She nodded, got up and they left for the street. With a long macchiato and a weak latte on the table, Salley opened up. "David, I'm pregnant and I don't know what to do."

"Well, I know you're not married, but have you spoken to the father-to-be about what to do?"

"I can't do that."

"Why not, Salley?"

"He doesn't know I'm pregnant."

"Well, just tell him. He'll get used to the idea."

"No. I can't."

"Oh?"

"You don't understand, David. You see, it was a matter of ..." she paused and looked around to check nobody was listening ... "he raped me."

"Hell. Have you thought of going to the police?"

"I don't think I can do that. It would mean my job."

"What! How could it?"

"It was John Ryling."

"Ryling! Our sports writer?"

"Yes."

"How did he come to rape you?"

"He invited me to a cricket club dinner, then instead of driving me home, pulled up in a dark street near a park and suggested sex. He had been drinking a lot. When I refused to be in it, he dragged me into the back seat, pulled up my clothes and had his way. Then he drove me home, said nobody would believe me if I told anyone about it, and dumped me at the gate."

"Salley, you have to go to the police. You can't let him get away with that. It will be unpleasant in court I know, but as a victim, the media cannot identify you. That's the law."

"But it would be the end of my job. The *Gazette* wouldn't want to keep me if I turned him in."

"Well, Sheridan and the board wouldn't like the publicity. But the paper is not to blame for the crime of one individual employee. Look, I'll have a talk with Darryl Sheridan and, without identifying you, I'll tell him about the crime and get his reaction. All right?" She nodded agreement.

The next morning Reed knocked on Sheridan's door. The secretary asked him what he wanted to see the editor-in-chief about.

"It's a private matter, I'm afraid."

"Very well. Please wait."

Sheridan emerged. "Come on in, David. What's the private matter?"

Reed gave him the news, referring to Shirman as just "a staff member".

"Hell, David. Do you think she's telling the truth?"

"Yes, Darryl. I'm sure of it."

Sheridan cogitated, frowning and rubbing his chin. "David. We have to be careful here. We can't jump to conclusions. Let's say we call Ryling in. Confront him with the accusation. If he admits it, we sack him and offer to get the woman an abortion and pay her a substantial sum as a form of recompense if she leaves it at that?"

Reed paused, reflecting. "I don't think we could do that, Darryl. It's kind of you to offer to pay for an abortion, but I don't think we can hush up a crime. It might save the paper some nasty publicity, but it would be a legal offence to let Ryling off the hook with just a sacking.

"The alternative for your woman friend, David, is that she either pays for her abortion, or her parents do, and she forgets the issue. Or she goes to the cops and has to prove she didn't want to be laid. Or indeed, even prove that Ryling was the father. Very difficult."

"Not so difficult, Darryl, if she goes ahead and has the baby, or even if she has it aborted and requests a small sample. Then DNA could prove he was the father. And if he lied about fathering, a judge or jury would probably decide that if he lied about that, he probably also lied about not having raped her."

"All right, David. I can see you are on a determined path here, so, go ahead, persuade her, if you can, to go to the cops. I'm prepared to offer one guarantee. If it all comes out that two *Gazette* staff were involved, I promise you that this woman, whoever she is, will not suffer any penalty by the company. Of course she wouldn't. A sacking? –*That,* mate, *would* be bad publicity for the paper.

Over dinner that night, David related the whole saga to Meg. "Darling, if she decides to have an abortion, would you mind if I helped her to arrange it and helped pay for it? She is in a terrible state of mind."

"Darling, you seem to be very involved in this. You are telling me all the truth are you?"

"What do you mean?"

"Well, you haven't been involved with this girl yourself, have you?"

"Meg! How could you think that. All I did was see her sobbing at her desk."

"Yes, darling. All right. All right. Go ahead and help her."

He did. After a fortnight of indecision, Salley approached him and said she would be glad of his help. A week after the abortion, Reed again approached Sheridan and told him the woman concerned had decided not to take action against Ryling.

"I'm going to," Sheridan responded.

"Beg pardon?" said a puzzled Reed.

Sheridan: "We are off the record here, right?"

"Yes, sir."

"I told him I was moving him off sport and into the finance department."

"How did he take that?"

"He reacted the way I know he would and wanted him to. He said he was quitting. I knew he would hate finance. Sport is his big love. I said OK it was his decision. He leaves at the end of this month. You should be pretty happy with that, Mr Prosecutor Reed."

Sheridan laughed at the label and Reed smiled, shaking his head in amused resignation. It was justice of a sort – rough justice. But if Salley wasn't prepared to give evidence for a prosecution, rough justice it had to be. The whole issue reminded him of the saga of Minister Williamson sleeping with an underage girl. But this time there was not quite the same conclusive ending.

Two days later, Butler called him in. "David, as we reported today there has been another brutal killing in Granitara. The sixth this year. I'd like you to go there and give us a colour piece on the mess. OK?"

"OK, Graham. The town has been a hell-hole for years, hasn't it."

Meg curled her lips when he came home and told her of the project. "Here we go again. Off into a snake pit." She pointed at Bruce. "Just remember that he still needs a father will you."

"Yes, Meg. I will. And he needs a great mother, too."

The general election was due in three weeks, but David had deliberately avoided any direct political comment in feature articles as, while he had caused the Whitaker Government considerable grief over the Williamson affair and a nuclear weapons plant hidden in the desert, he had not wanted to be labelled a media stooge for the Opposition.

Over dinner he and Meg had yet another discussion about how the Government was travelling and whom they would vote for. Previously they both had tended to support the Whitaker Government, but this time, David said, he was changing his mind.

Meg: "Are you really? I know they have had some troubles, but they are still the party that supports business enterprise, sound economic management and strong defence measures. The other outfit under nutty Borley would spend zillions on do-good ventures such as foreign aid, feeding corruption in about 15 countries, and he plans all sorts of new financial impositions on business here. Why on earth would you switch?"

"One good reason, Meg. After the N-weapons plant row, Whitaker even talked of muzzling the media with licences. Anyone who thinks like that doesn't deserve to lead a democratic nation."

"But David, he didn't go ahead with it."

"He thought of doing it, Meg. That's enough for me to change my mind."

"Oh well. I'm going to stick with Whitaker because soon little Bruce will be going to kindergarten, I'll be free to go back to banking – that's if Borley hasn't nationalised all the banks by then and filled them with socialist supporters – and so I'll be helping pay the bills again and under Whitaker they'll be smaller."

David looked down at Bruce in his highchair. "Who are you going to vote for, mate? Whitaker? Yes, you'd better do what your mum says or you won't get any more mummy milk. Understand?"

Meg: "David, you can be such a clown. I think that's why I still love you. Let's go to bed."

"Amen to that."

Four days later Reed was leaving for Granitara. "Darling, I should be away for just a few days. I'll keep in touch by phone every evening." A long, gentle kiss and he was gone. Granitara, a town of 800 people, buried in the rock and sand of the nation's arid centre, had just one financial prop – a small opal mine. The mine employed only 25 men – no women – so most of the families relied on government welfare cheques to stay alive, the cheques to be cashed at the post office and spent at the one store – and at the one small pub. There was one junior school and after the pupils reached its senior class, Grade 8, they either tried to find work at distant cattle properties or headed for a far-off town to live with relatives, or live on the street. The nearest police station was 110 kilometres away so the cop called by just once a week – or if summoned because of a bashing, rape or killing. Pleas to the government to base an officer in the town were ignored. One theory was that a permanent cop would also be in danger. Reed realised it was not going to be an easy assignment; that he would need to tread very carefully. For the long drive, he also put three large cans of fuel in the car boot, not being sure whether there was a petrol station anywhere near Granitara. He figured the first stop should be the pub to see if the owner was prepared to talk – off the record of course. At mid-afternoon when he arrived, there were just three men in the saloon and a balding, tubby man behind the bar.

"Hi. I'm a visitor from Apollo City. Just having a look around the Outback. I'll have a beer, thanks. Are you the owner?"

The barman paused, looking Reed up and down. "Yes, mate."

"How do you find life in Granitara?"

"It's interesting. How do you find life in Apollo City?"

"Likewise. But I hear you've been having quite a bit of trouble here."

"Yes, mate. A bit."

"Look, I don't want to be too much of a stickybeak, but I read in the papers recently that you have had six killings here in the past 18 months. That's a hell of a lot of murder for a town this size. What's been going on?"

"This town is like any other, mate. Men screw other men's wives. They get caught. Blam. Down they go with a slug in the chest. One of them last year even copped a .22 rifle shot in his doodle. Made a fine mess of it. He survived, but probably now wonders if life is worth living."

"You make it sound like it's all a bit of a laugh."

"Well, it was no laugh for the gunner. He's now in the slammer and most of the people around here reckon that's not fair, that Mr Nodoodle, as he's now known, deserved what he got for being careless."

"Careless?"

"Yeah. Careless. He banged the shooter's wife in her own bedroom and the hubby came home from work early by chance and happened upon them … what's the phrase … in flagrante isn't it? Anyway, at least the guy's lucky. He's still alive."

Reed turned to face another drinker at the bar who had been listening to the whole conversation. "You've been in on our talk haven't you. Not all the six deaths resulted from adultery did they."

"Nah. A couple were just family arguments. One was about drugs. Another one was about a guy who borrowed thousands for a business deal, then shot through to another town, but made the mistake of sneaking back later to see a woman to persuade her to go with him, but got spotted by the guy owed the money and, bingo, down he went. Well that's what the town believes. The cops reckoned they knew who did it of course, but couldn't find any weapon, couldn't find anyone who saw the shooting, so gave up and returned to the big city. That's all I remember. Anyway, mate, why are you so curious about this little town's history?"

"I'm a writer and I find such things fascinating. Is there anyone here who keeps tabs on what goes on whom I could interview?"

The pub owner chewed a thumb, cogitating. "Believe it or not, we have an ex copper who lives here, Barry Smethton. He might be able to give you something to write about. He lives just down the end of the main street here, number 62. But you'd better be careful what you put in your book. News from the big city does get back here sometimes, you know."

Smethton was at home, weeding around lettuces in a side garden. Reed introduced himself, deciding that as Smethton was an ex-cop he had better level with him, told him he was a feature writer at the *Gazette* and was looking to write a piece about crime sweeping a small town. Smethton invited him in for a cup of tea but immediately adopted a common course: "Anything I tell you David is not from me, it's just from a 'police source' OK?"

"OK"

"I can tell you what's wrong with this town. Too many people don't have a job and have nothing to do except cash their dole money and go down to the pub. Any evening by 11pm a third of the town is pissed, including plenty of women. There was a move at one stage to get a local regulation to limit the amount of grog the pub could sell each day. It was realised that would be quite difficult to supervise so then a few people put up the idea that the pub's hours should be set – making it shut at 7pm so people would be forced to go home for dinner instead of pissing on. The leader of the group arguing for that was savagely bashed one night, attacked from behind so he did not see who did it. I think he was lucky to survive. Pub owner Greg Rowlander denied knowing anything about it and his pub stays open all day until 11pm. It's the one business in this town going great guns. I must admit I like a beer myself, but not grogging on until I can't tell which side of the road I'm on."

"What about the six deaths in 18 months, Barry? That's a lot."

"Yes. Though I'm retired, I've been in touch with the force, urging them to set up a permanent police presence here. But the Chief Commissioner said the town is too small to justify that. I said if they didn't do something, eventually there would be hardly anyone left to call it a town. He didn't appreciate the retort."

"How is it that there have been six violent deaths and, as far as I know, only one person charged over them?"

"The one charged, David, was a husband who stabbed his wife to death with a kitchen knife. He admitted it and he'll cop 15 or 20 years. The other cases involved night street bashings or, in one case, a hit-run at night on the edge of the town. Probably a drunk driver."

"So that's it? No more investigations?"

"Not unless something turns up."

Reed decided to quiz pub owner Rowlander again and returned to the bar that evening, nursing three beers over more than an hour, then re-opening the old conversation.

"Greg, doesn't it worry you that there has been so much deadly violence in this small town? Do you really need to stay open so late letting guys booze up so much?"

"What makes you bring up that subject again?"

"Well, as I told you, I'm a writer and I thought the story of the town would make a good feature article for a newspaper."

"Did you now."

"Yes, I did. And I plan to talk to quite a few people here to see that the public feeling is about any link between booze and the violence. I'm afraid I've already had comments suggesting that from people who should know."

"Have you now. That's interesting. From whom for instance?"

"Can't say, Greg. That's confidential."

"I see."

"By the way, Greg. I don't want to have to sleep in my car. Is there somewhere in the town where I can get a bed for the night?"

"There's a small caravan park at the end of this main street. It's for the odd tourist we get here. You can hire a van for the night."

"Thanks."

As Reed left, Rowlander picked up the phone to make a call. Reed found the caravan park and was able to hire a van for the night, settling in to make notes on what he had learned. Still restless at 10.30pm, he decided to go for a walk, particularly past Rowlander's pub to watch the exodus of drinkers. But he did not get there. As he walked up the darkened street, night lights dimmed by huge eucalypt trees, he heard steps behind him, began to turn and saw a large wooden club like a baseball bat descending in the arms of a thug. He threw up his right arm but the club smashed into his shoulder, knocking him to the ground.

Christ, he thought. This guy is out to kill me. His mind flew to Meg and Bruce. How on earth would they manage without him?

"No. No. Don't do it!" he cried as the club came down again.

All went black.

www.ingramcontent.com/pod-product-compliance
Lightning Source LLC
Chambersburg PA
CBHW070219030726
47505CB00006B/1732